Hillary Waugh was born in 1920 in New Haven, Connecticut. During World War II he served as a pilot in the United States Navy Air Corps, and has also worked as a cartoonist, songwriter and teacher.

Last Seen Wearing . . ., published in 1952 and only his fourth novel, is considered by many to be a masterpiece of tightly plotted suspense fiction and a pioneer of the police procedural, where dogged police work and attention to detail is as important as the intuition of the series detective. In his study of crime fiction, *Bloody Murder*, Julian Symons stated: 'If a single book had to be chosen to show the possibilities in the police novel which are outside most crime fiction, no better example could be found than *Last Seen Wearing . . .*'

During his career Waugh has written over forty detective novels, mostly featuring tobacco-chewing Police Chief Fred Fellows or, more recently, Detective Second Grade Frank Sessions. He has also published novels under the names Elissa Grandower and H. Baldwin Taylor.

He still lives in Connecticut.

Reginald Hill is best known as the author of the hugely popular Dalziel and Pascoe series of crime novels, which have now been adapted with great success by BBC Television. In 1995 he was awarded the CWA Cartier Diamond Dagger for outstanding services to crime literature.

By the same author

Madam Will Not Dine
Hope to Die
The Odds Run Out
A Rag and a Bone
The Case of the Missing
  Gardener
Rich Man, Murder
The Eighth Mrs
  Bluebeard
The Girl Who Cried Wolf
Sleep Long, My Love
Road Block
That Night It Rained
Murder on the Terrace
The Late Mrs D.
Born Victim
Death and Circumstance
Prisoner's Plea
The Missing Man
End of a Party
Girl on the Run

Pure Poison
The Con Game
'30' Manhattan East
Run When I Say Go
The Young Prey
Finish Me Off
The Shadow Guest
Parrish for the Defense
A Bride for Hampton
  House
Madman at My Door
The Glenna Powers Case
The Doria Rafe Case
The Billy Cantrell Case
The Nerissa Claire Case
The Veronica Dean
  Case
The Priscilla
  Copperwaite Case
Murder on Safari
A Death in a Town

Hillary Waugh

Last Seen Wearing . . .

with an introduction by
Reginald Hill

PAN BOOKS

First published in the United Kingdom 1953 by Victor Gollancz Ltd

This edition published 1999 by Pan Books
an imprint of Macmillan Publishers Ltd
25 Eccleston Place, London SW1W 9NF
Basingstoke and Oxford
Associated companies throughout the world
www.macmillan.co.uk

ISBN 0 330 38989 0

9 8 7 6 5 4 3 2 1

A CIP catalogue record for this book is available from
the British Library.

Phototypeset by Intype London Ltd
Printed and bound in Great Britain by
Mackays of Chatham plc, Chatham, Kent

Introduction
by Reginald Hill

When it came to naming the sub-genres of crime fiction, the copywriters weren't exactly leaping out of their baths crying, EUREKA! *Thriller, Hard-boiled, Noir* and *Gothic* make some attempt to grab the attention; *Great Detective, Psychological Suspense* and *Espionage* give slight pause; *Cosy* is just plain awful; and *Police Procedural* sounds like Mogadon in hard covers.

But this is where real genius comes in. You don't need 20–20 vision to see the imaginative possibilities in the guests at a country-house party being knocked off alphabetically, or in double agents double-crossing their double-dealing spymasters, but to see the real drama behind the unremitting grind of routine police work made up of ninety-nine parts elimination to every one part inspiration is to see a world in a grain of sand.

Hillary Waugh had that vision back in 1952 when he wrote *Last Seen Wearing* . . . . In it he attempted to transplant the flat, detailed, down-to-earth style of the narratives of real-life investigations to be found in factual crime magazines into the world of fiction. A girl goes missing. There is no evidence that a crime has been committed. And even when a body is found, there is still a lot of doubt as to the manner of her death. There is no attempt here to grab our attention with an initial act of violence, an opening *coup de théâtre*. We are a good quarter of the way into the book before we (in the shape of the police investigators into whose consciousness ours has rapidly been subsumed) know for certain we're dealing with a crime. We see clues only as the detectives see them, and we see suspects in exactly the same way – that is, when we see them at all! There is no ludicrously complicated Golden Age puzzle laid out before us, just the kind of crime and motivations which real policemen in real life have to deal with all the time. We are not invited to enter into some sort of competition with a Great Detective, nor are we urged to marvel at his ingenuity of thought when we confess ourselves baffled. This is not crime as intellectual game, crime as metaphysical debate, or crime as gentle titillation. This is crime as it is seen and investigated by the police with all the power and resources at their disposal, and also with all the limitations of time, fatigue, misunderstanding, misinterpretation and misdirection they inevitably suffer from.

The greatest sin anyone introducing a crime novel can commit is to reveal in advance who dunnit either directly or by implication, and I shall go through my text like a military censor to make sure I give no such hint. And yet if I did, in this case it wouldn't make all that much difference. As I reread the book after many years, I gradually began to recall how it all worked out, but this foreknowledge did not slacken the story's grip on me one iota. You see, all the drama is in the detail, and the focus is so intense that not even certainty itself can permit you to leap forward to your inevitable destination. Waugh never takes his eye off the ball. There are no diverting subplots, no godlike authorial meditations on the state of the universe, no human interest glances at the domestic life and personal interests of his characters except insofar as they relate to the investigation. This does not mean there is any lack of characterization. The odd-couple relationship of Sergeant

Cameron and Chief of Police Ford is explored to fine comic effect, but never in a way which distracts from the work in hand. The reactions of the missing girl's father are perceptively and movingly drawn, but never dwelt upon purely for the sake of forcing an empathetic pang. There is no such thing as a minor character in this kind of book, because no one is present who does not have some sort of relationship to the investigation, and that makes everyone important until eliminated from it.

If this is your first encounter with Hillary Waugh and at the end of it you feel, as I guess most readers of this novel do, eager to develop the acquaintance, you may be disappointed to learn that Cameron and Ford and the police department of Bristol, Mass., do not reappear in the oeuvre. But do not despair. In 1959 there appeared *Sleep Long, My Love* (UK title *Jigsaw*), the first of a ten-book series featuring perhaps Waugh's most famous creation, Fred Fellows, Chief of Police in the small town of Stockford, Connecticut. Throughout the sixties, I recall my delight when yet another one appeared on the library shelves (I didn't really come to understand the importance of buying rather than borrowing books till my own first novel came out in 1970!), and when the Fellows books stopped, I was happy to move on to Manhattan North, the stomping ground of Waugh's new series cop, Detective Second Grade Frank Sessions.

Waugh is a multi-talented author, with many kinds of book and a couple of pseudonyms to his credit, but his lasting claim to fame in the annals of crime writing must derive from those of his novels which show the police at their appointed task of saving the sum of things for pay. There were a few precursors, and there have been innumerable successors, but it is hard to think of any book in the *Police Procedural* genre, and not all that many out of it, which can claim to be superior to *Last Seen Wearing*. . . .

I met Hillary Waugh only once, sitting close to him at a conference dinner table many years ago. I wanted to tell him how great I thought he was, but being youngish, shyish, and English, couldn't quite manage it. Well, I hope I have now.

Last Seen
Wearing . . .

To Diana
With a Nod To Ruth, Cornie,
Nora, Joan, and Carter

Friday, 3 March 1950

Marilyn Lowell Mitchell, pretty eighteen-year-old freshman at Parker College in Bristol, Massachusetts, attended her noon history class on Friday, 3 March 1950. At its conclusion she went to the desk to speak to the teacher, Harlan P. Seward. She left the building a few moments later and walked back to her room in Lambert Annex, unaccompanied as far as can be determined.

When her roommate, Peggy Woodling, came up to discard her books, Lowell was lying on her bed. She was wearing the usual blue jeans, white shirt, sneakers, and ankle socks and was flat on her back with an arm across her face. When the chime sounded she made no move to get up. She was not going to lunch, she said. She felt sick, nothing serious, but she wasn't hungry and wanted to rest awhile.

Unable to help her, Peggy went down to the usual Friday lunch of fried fish, boiled potatoes, and cole slaw, ate hurriedly, had a cigarette in the lounge, and read her mail. When she went back for her books Lowell was gone.

This somewhat surprised her but it was not until she came back from her zoology lecture and found the room still empty that she began to wonder. When Lowell did not show up for dinner she was frankly puzzled.

Lambert Annex was one of three Victorian houses that comprised the group known as Lambert Dorm. The other two, Lambert A and Lambert B, were good-sized dwellings housing around twenty-five girls apiece. Ann, as the Annex was called, being smaller, contained six girls, all freshmen, Virginia Grenfell, the faculty resident, and, because the dining hall was in Ann, two cooks and one maid.

Peggy ate with Hilda Gunther and Marlene Beecher, two of the other Ann residents, and they decided that Lowell must have gone to the infirmary. 'Mitch could be dying and she wouldn't let on,' said Marlene.

However, when the three took apples and cookies to the infirmary after dinner they discovered to their real surprise that Lowell was not there and now, for the first time, concern crept into their speculations. They went up to Lowell's room and were somewhat relieved, for Hilda looked in the closet and there were Lowell's things, jeans, shirt, and socks crammed in the top of her laundry bag and her sneakers on the floor. That meant she had changed her clothes, which meant she had got into a skirt and, since girls weren't allowed to leave the campus in jeans, it meant she was going someplace and knew where she was going and didn't expect to be coming back right away. Then they went down and checked the sign-out sheet on which the girls were supposed to note their intention of staying out after ten-thirty up till the midnight curfew. Her name wasn't on it but that didn't mean much at Ann because Ann was small and informal and Miss Grenfell was young and friendly and Mrs Sherwood, the housemother, who lived in A, seldom came around. More times than not, the girls signed the sheet when they came back in and frequently they neglected to do it at all.

Marlene and Peggy were double-dating that night with a couple of boys from Carlton College, which was six miles north of Bristol on Route 19. The boys picked them up in a 1936 Buick about eight o'clock and took them out to the Log Cabin, a plaster and concrete roadhouse halfway between the two colleges where they had an orchestra and soft lights and fancy decorations and where the waiters didn't toss the 'How old are you?' question at the college crowd when they ordered drinks. Patty Short and Sally Anders, the other two girls in Ann, were off at prom week-ends at Yale and Princeton so Hilda, left alone, went over to A and played bridge until ten-thirty. Then she came back to Ann to take over the watch and did homework in the lounge.

At five minutes of twelve there was laughing and talking on the porch outside. At one minute of, Hilda got up and switched the porch light off and on twice and went back to her work. In another moment Peggy and Marlene came in and locked the door. Hilda chucked her books, got up, and said, 'Hi, kids, how was it?'

Peggy made a face and said, 'What a jumping jack.' She took off her coat. 'Mitch back yet?'

Hilda had completely forgotten. 'Good God, no! I don't think so.'

The three girls looked at each other, then ran up the stairs and down the long hall to the large room in back that Peggy and Lowell shared. The room was silent and dark and they knew before they threw on the lights that it was still empty.

'She'll have to report herself to J.B.,' said Marlene, appalled.

'Maybe we ought to call the hospitals,' said Peggy.

'That wouldn't work,' said Hilda. 'They'd have called us if she were there.'

'We've got to do something!'

Hilda's mouth tightened. She turned and went back through the hall and down the stairs, the girls following.

She went on to the porch, opened the storm door, and looked out. The concrete walk curved emptily out between the hedge to Maple Street. Around it, the crusty granular snow stuck like a thin raw waffle to the ground. Taylor House next door was dark and so was the Bristol Inn across the street. The light of the street lamp winked through the branches of the big oak on the lawn and sparkled on the snow. A cab went by fast and, overhead, the stars looked cold.

Hilda breathed vapour clouds into the frigid air for half a minute, looking up and down the silent street. Then she came in and relocked the front door. She was shivering. 'I'm going to tell Miss Grenfell,' she said, and the others nodded agreement.

Miss Grenfell responded sleepily to the second knock on her cream-coloured door. 'What is it?'

Hilda put her cheek to the panel. 'Miss Grenfell, Lowell Mitchell hasn't come in yet and nobody's seen her since noon.'

'What time is it?'

'Quarter past twelve.'

Old bedsprings creaked, a slot of light appeared in the gap under the door, clothing rustled, and a key turned. A pretty, twenty-six-year-old brunette stood in the doorway tying the sash of a rose dressing gown and blinking the sleep from her green eyes. 'Lowell's missing, you say? What happened?'

Peggy told her. Lowell was sick, she had gone away during lunch, she had not come back. 'I don't know how sick she was,' she concluded. 'Mitch doesn't let on very much how she feels about things.'

'Maybe she went home. Did she fill out a blue card?'

'Blue cards! Of course.'

Blue cards were Parker's check on the whereabouts of students. They were filled out in the housemother's presence by girls taking overnights and contained such information as where they were going, where they were staying, and when they would be back. It was something that hadn't occurred to the girls since Lowell had said nothing about going away. 'Spur of the moment,' said Hilda. 'She could have just made the one-thirty train.'

'That must be it,' nodded Miss Grenfell.

'I suppose,' Hilda said tentatively, 'we ought to find out – just to make sure.'

Miss Grenfell compressed her lips. 'I don't like to wake up Mrs Sherwood. Probably Lowell wasn't feeling well and went home for the weekend.'

'Mitch wouldn't leave without filling out a blue card,' affirmed Peggy.

'I know she wouldn't.' Miss Grenfell paused. 'I suppose we *should* check, though.'

'We'd better,' decided Hilda.

Miss Grenfell nodded. 'Wait a couple of minutes,' she said and closed the door to dress.

Saturday, 4 March

But Lowell had not filled out a blue card. Mrs Sherwood said so quite definitely when the four girls roused her from sleep and brought her to the door. She stood there, tall, grey, and big-boned under a sagging plumpness that filled the blue, figured robe she wore over a cotton nightgown. 'Why do you ask?' she said. 'What is the trouble?'

Miss Grenfell explained.

The housemother's brow clouded and she grew less certain. 'I might be wrong. I'd better check, maybe I've forgotten. Come in.' She led the way into a large combination study and parlour, illuminated by the overhead light and lined with a neutral shade of wallpaper on which clipper ships sat at various angles. She sat down in a fragile chair in front of the secretary and pulled out a drawer. 'A lot more girls than usual signed out this weekend. I may have forgotten.' She withdrew a pack of about twenty cards which she flipped through slowly without removing the elastic.

'No.' She shook her head slowly and put the cards away. 'She didn't sign out. I can't understand it.' She stared absently at the desktop for a moment, then withdrew a mimeographed sheet from another drawer, ran a finger down it, held it near the middle, and moved the phone into her lap with the other hand. She dialled O and waited.

Miss Grenfell fitted a cigarette into a holder and lighted it. Hilda lighted one of her own and chopped ashes into the tray on the coffee table in front of her. Mrs Sherwood said, 'Operator? I'd like to put through a person-to-person call to Mr Carl Bemis Mitchell at' – she leaned over the sheet – '560 Evergreen Avenue in Philadelphia. The number is WH-1711.' She drummed on the desk with her fingers.

Hilda took quick, jerky puffs on her cigarette. Peggy twisted a honey-coloured curl and Marlene fidgeted with her hands in her lap. Miss Grenfell relaxed against the couch and let the smoke trickle through her nose, watching it rise and fan out over the ceiling.

'Mr Mitchell?' The housemother's voice came up almost harshly. 'This is Mrs Sherwood, the housemother at Lambert Dorm, up at Parker. Is Lowell with you? . . . I see . . . No, that's the trouble. She was here at noon and then she left while the other girls were eating lunch . . . Oh, I'm sure she's all right. She was probably unavoidably delayed . . . No, we don't have any idea at all . . . Yes, we'll start an investigation right away . . . Yes. I'll get in touch with you just as soon as we hear anything . . . Yes? All right, Mr Mitchell. That will be fine . . . I don't think there's any cause for alarm. It's probably nothing serious at all . . . All right. I'm sure we'll have good news for you then . . . Goodbye, Mr Mitchell. Yes, that's right. Goodbye.'

Mrs Sherwood put the phone on her desk and stared at it. 'She didn't go home,' she said, and the fright in her voice gave it an edge. 'Mr Mitchell is coming up tomorrow.' She pulled a Kleenex from her bathrobe pocket to pat a brow that was beaded with moisture.

Marlene said violently, 'Oh, God! What are we going to do?'

Mrs Sherwood dialled another number with a stubby finger and the phone in her hand quivered against her ear. 'Mrs Kenyon? This is Mrs Sherwood at Lambert. Something extremely serious has come up. One of our girls is missing.' She nodded vaguely while she listened and her normally white complexion was grey in the unflattering light. 'Her name is Lowell Mitchell,' she went on suddenly. 'She lives in the Annex and has been gone since noon . . . No, she isn't there. I just called . . . Mr Mitchell is coming up tomorrow and I think you'd better come over here right away and take charge, unless you think I should call the police.' She stared at the rug and her fingers picked up their drumming once more. She said, 'All right. We'll wait for you there,' and hung up.

After a moment she rose unsteadily, clutching the chair, and said, 'You'd better all go back to the Annex. The Warden is going to want to talk to you. I'll be over as soon as I get dressed.'

They went out quietly and Peggy said to a questioning girl in the hall, 'Mitch is missing. Nobody knows where she is.' Then they went back and sat around the Annex lounge with their coats on until Mrs Sherwood arrived. She left the door unlocked and perched on the edge of a sagging chair staring at nothing.

Mrs Kenyon, the Warden, let the door slam loudly. She kicked off overshoes in the hall and came in, shedding a heavy cloth coat, retrieving a notebook from one of the pockets. She was a gruff, masculine woman, tall and commanding, with short-bobbed grey hair, and her first words were directed at the coat she draped over a chair. 'She hasn't come back yet, I presume. What was her name again?'

'Lowell Mitchell,' said Mrs Sherwood.

'Marilyn Lowell Mitchell,' corrected Hilda.

Mrs Kenyon turned around and sat down and jotted

that at the top of a page. 'Now tell me everything she did today. What time did she get up?'

'Quarter past seven,' Peggy said. 'We got up together and had breakfast.'

'Anything unusual about her behaviour?'

All the girls shook their heads.

'She was exactly normal?'

Peggy said tentatively, 'I think she was a little on the quiet side.'

'She had something on her mind?'

'Possibly.'

'Come, come. She walks out of here and doesn't come back. Certainly she must have been thinking about that at breakfast. Wouldn't you say that was what she was thinking about?'

'Yes, I guess so.'

'All right. Now, you ate breakfast. Then what?'

'I came back to the room and studied for my ten o'clock.'

'I'm not interested in what you did. What did this Marilyn do?'

'She went out. I don't know where.'

'At what time?'

'A little after eight. She got her books and went out and I didn't see her again—'

'What time was her first class?'

'Nine o'clock. She had a biology lecture.'

'In Hancock Hall at nine o'clock.' Mrs Kenyon scowled and made some notes. 'Where did she go in the meantime?'

'I don't know.'

'She left at eight for a nine o'clock class and you didn't ask her about it?'

'No. I thought she was probably going over to A to study or see somebody or something.'

'Don't you get along with each other?'

Peggy nodded emphatically. 'We get along beautifully but Lowell is sort of quiet and doesn't tell us everything she does or thinks about.'

'I don't expect her to,' the Warden said primly, 'but on the other hand, I do expect a little feminine curiosity among you girls. I don't expect you to be nosy, but I can't dismiss it when you say you don't pay any attention when someone you know as well as I presume you know this girl behaves oddly.'

There was silence and she looked sharply around from face to face without result. She shifted her position, wrote something else on her pad, then said in ill-concealed irritation, 'All right. Who saw her next?'

That was Peggy again. She described the meeting at noon, Lowell's illness and sudden departure.

Mrs Kenyon looked at the others. 'None of the rest of you saw her at all?'

They shook their heads and Hilda said, 'We went in to see her after lunch, but she wasn't there.'

The Warden turned back to Peggy. 'What was the matter with her?'

'I don't know.'

'You didn't ask her?'

'No.'

Mrs Kenyon compressed her lips into a thin white line. 'You certainly are the most uncurious bunch of females I ever saw. What did you think was the matter with her?'

'The – uh – time of the month.'

'Did it usually affect her that way?'

'No.'

She sniffed. 'It's never made her sick before so when she gets sick you immediately think that's the cause. Is that it?'

Peggy flushed. 'I didn't know and, if it wasn't that, then I don't think Lowell knew. She said she felt "poohed out".'

'In your opinion, then, it wasn't serious?'

'I didn't think so.'

She wrote that down, leaning forward like a door on a hinge. Then she asked about reasons for Lowell's departure. No one could give any. 'How did she get along with you girls?'

'Very well,' said Hilda. 'We all liked her very much.'

'Let's see. How many girls live here?'

'Six.'

'Where are the others?'

'Away for the weekend,' said Hilda.

'I see. You all get along together well?'

'Very well. There have been occasional arguments, of course, but nothing serious and I don't ever remember Mitch having harsh words with anyone.'

Mrs Kenyon turned to the faculty resident. 'What do you say to that, Miss Grenfell?'

Miss Grenfell seemed to take note of the proceedings for the first time. 'Hilda's right,' she said calmly. 'However, Lowell is a reserved girl. She keeps things pretty much to herself. I don't mean she isn't friendly and well liked, she certainly seems to be. It's only that she keeps a check on her emotions.'

'That's very interesting. It could very well be, then, that she built up resentment against the other girls inside until it reaches the point where she can't stand it any longer and runs away.'

'That's not true,' Peggy insisted. 'I've lived with her and

I know her better than anyone else here and if she felt that way she couldn't possibly hide it from me. She likes us all and she loves the life here and we all like her. She'd never get up and leave.'

'She wouldn't leave, but she did,' Mrs Kenyon reminded her.

'There's some other reason. I'm sure of it.'

'Maybe she met with foul play,' said Marlene. 'She might have been kidnapped.'

'Don't be ridiculous,' snapped Mrs Kenyon. 'The girl left the house of her own accord. She knew what she was doing. There's a reason behind all this and I'm here to find out what it is. If, as you say, there was no bitterness among you, then she had some other reason. Did she ever – think closely now – did she ever indicate a desire to make her own way in the world?'

Shaking heads were her answer.

The Warden took that and swung back to the attack. 'What were her ambitions? What did she want out of life?'

Peggy's eyes clouded and she chewed a lip. 'Marriage, I guess, and a home.'

'Perhaps she eloped.'

'Oh no. I don't mean she was crazy to get married. She wanted a normal life, go through college, work for a year or two, maybe, and then get married.'

'Did she ever have a job of any kind?'

Peggy shrugged. 'She did waitress work last summer.'

'That won't do,' said Mrs Kenyon. 'That leaves only one alternative. She was more interested in getting married than she let on. Mrs Sherwood, after you found Marilyn had not gone home, did you telephone her boyfriend?'

'Why, I – no.'

'Who is he, girls?'

Peggy said, 'She doesn't have a boyfriend.'

'Ridiculous. You mean she never has a date?'

'She has quite a few dates, but not with any special boy.'

'She certainly must favour someone.'

Marlene said, 'She's had a couple of dates with a sopho-more at Yale. He didn't invite her to the prom though, and that might have something to do with it.'

'Quite likely. What's this boy's name and where does he live at Yale?'

'Roger. That's all I know about him.'

Peggy said, 'I think it's Hadley. I'm not sure. But she only dated him twice that I know of and I know she wasn't expecting him to invite her to the prom.'

'What boy did she date the most?'

'Golly, I don't know. There's a Jack Curtis up at Harvard she's gone out with a few times and she goes out quite a lot with a couple of boys from Carlton, a Bob and a Warren. I forget their last names. Of course she's had a few blind dates around.'

'But she didn't confide in you which one she liked the most?'

'No. I don't mean she wouldn't discuss them. I think she just didn't consider them worth talking about.'

Mrs Kenyon rapped her eraser against her teeth. 'Is there any way to get in touch with those boys? Does she have an address book?'

'Yes, I think so. In her bureau drawer.'

The Warden stood up. 'Good, we're wasting time down here. I want to see her room anyway.'

The group shifted their base of activities to the bedroom. It was the largest in the house, with a three-view exposure, two beds, a pair of desks and bureaus, a large worn rug on the floor, two overstuffed chairs and a wicker one by Lowell's bed. There was a table with a record player beside a window, a laundry rack by the door, and a large closet on the other side of the bureaus. Peggy sat down on her bed and the others took chairs, except for Mrs Kenyon, who went to Lowell's bureau and pulled out the top drawer.

A light came into her eye. The shoe box she withdrew held gold. 'A diary,' she breathed. 'Well, well, well, well.'

Mrs Sherwood coughed apologetically. 'I – uh – don't think we have any right to invade her privacy, Mrs Kenyon.'

The Warden smoothed the red leather cover affectionately and laid it down on the dresser top like a baby in a cradle. 'I respect a girl's privacy,' she said to it, 'just as much as anyone else.' She left it in plain sight and dragged herself away like a small child from a cookie jar, turning at last to go through the other contents of the box, holding it against her stomach with one hand. The address book was a small black imitation leather affair from a Woolworth counter and it lay on top of a stack of letters from home and two or three loose ones penned by other hands. The return addresses identified them as being from J. Curtis of Harvard, postmarked February twenty-eighth, R. Hadley of Yale, dated February seventh, and H. Walton of Lehigh, mailed February twenty-third.

Mrs Kenyon held them up and fanned them out. 'Only three boys? Doesn't she write any others?'

'Several,' said Peggy, 'but I think she throws letters away when she answers them.'

The Warden sat at Lowell's desk and thumbed through the address book. It contained about twenty-five names, ten of them boys, the rest girls and relatives. She returned the black book to the shoe box, looked at her watch, muttered, 'Five after two,' and said aloud, 'She hasn't called in, she didn't go home, and she didn't sign out.' She sorted the envelopes as though she wanted to read their contents and the whole effect was one of their sticking to her fingers. Then she exhaled and stood up. 'I'll take the responsibility, but the answer to Lowell's whereabouts lies in that diary and I'm going to read it.' No one objected and she tried the lock on it. It snapped open without a key and Mrs Kenyon folded the book open. It was a five-year diary for the years 1947–51. 'She certainly is a trusting soul,' the Warden said. 'Doesn't lock her diary and leaves it right where anyone can get at it.' She looked around sharply as if she expected everyone to confess to the sin of having gone through it but the same dead, slightly disapproving silence greeted her. The Warden leaned back against Lowell's dresser and read through the last week silently and in full view.

Monday, 27 February – Miss Merrimam says my golf is improving but I'd like to know where. How anyone can play the game, I don't know! Have another English paper to write for Monday. 'The Timeless Elements in Abraham Lincoln's character and Words', using Sherwood's play for source. That will be a lot more interesting than this Feverel paper. Letter from home. Melissa got 4 A's and a B for mid-term. Wish I could say the same. She had a Princeton date last weekend, no less!!! Went for a walk in the evening. Should have finished up Wednesday's paper but can do that tomorrow.

Tuesday, 28 February – Could get an A in Bio. Science, I know, if it weren't for this lab. I guess I don't have a practical mind. I know I don't. Spanish and

English are easy, but you won't get me near a math course. Finally finished my English paper. Recopied most of it tonight until I was persuaded into a bridge game with Hilda, Patty, and Sally. Procrastination, thy name is woman. Now I'll have to try to finish it tomorrow and the History lecture knocks out one period. I'm late again. Something drastic will have to be done.

Wednesday, 1 March – Letter from Jack today when I got back from Spanish. Who cares? Honestly, college boys seem so adolescent these days. All about his exams and how much beer he can drink without getting sick. Seems funny it used to impress me. Nothing's happened. Maybe it's for the best. Imagine marrying someone like Jack! I'd rather have someone older, thank you. None of these boys you'd have to mother. Got the Feverel paper done just in time, thank goodness, and spent the evening in the library doing research until I couldn't stand it. Hilda almost fell over when I came back and coaxed her into a bridge game.

Thursday, 2 March – Bio. Science lecture, Spanish, and History today. Sometimes you wonder why you study. You're not going to use what you learn. At least I'm not. That I now know for sure. Wrote a letter home in the afternoon and got into a gab fest with Peggy and Sally and Marlene on sex relations before marriage, of all things. Marlene thinks it's a good idea. Says your first night with your husband would be more successful – purely an academic opinion. Sally said, 'And that would make him suspicious.' Marlene said, 'If boys do it, why not girls?' but I know she'd never try it. Then we talked about with your fiancé – trial marriage. Peggy says absolutely not. Sex is the whip you get the ring with. If they don't have to marry you for it, they won't.

She's being cynical, of course, though I didn't tell her so. I'll bet a majority of couples sleep together before marriage.

That was the last entry and Mrs Kenyon snapped the book shut with obvious disappointment, clicked the lock, and dumped it in the box.

'Did you get any clues?' asked Mrs Sherwood timidly.

'No. She hadn't planned this in advance, that's certain.' She went after the letters from the three boys belligerently and with no attempt at apology. They were as disappointing as the diary. The letters from Hadley and Curtis were casual and friendly, relating activities, making no specific inquiries about date possibilities, and devoid of endearing terms. The writer of the third, H. Walton, was a boy she knew in Philadelphia. That letter contained news of mutual friends and the comment that he thought he could get his father's car the weekend of 17–18–19th March and could he come up? It was signed, *Love, Hank*.

She threw the letters back in the box in disgust. 'Fat lot to go on,' she grumbled. 'Who's this Hank Walton? Anyone know?'

'He's a boy from home,' said Peggy. 'He came up one weekend last fall and she went down one football weekend. She saw him Christmas vacation, I think, but hasn't had a date with him since.'

Mrs Kenyon's slate-grey eyes went opaque and she seemed to stop listening. She plunged her hand into the box again and brought out Lowell's address book. 'I'll take this with me,' she said with decision, and returned the box to the top bureau drawer. 'All right. Who's her roommate? You?' She pointed a long stabbing finger at Peggy, who nodded numbly.

'I don't want you to let anyone touch anything that belongs to this girl. Don't you touch anything either.' She went to the door and swung it wide in a gesture that brought the others to their feet. 'We'll go downstairs now.'

She led the way and motioned the others into the lounge once more. Then she went to the phone and put in calls to the Bristol hospital and morgue regarding any unidentified new arrivals. That produced nothing and she returned to the lounge entrance and looked down at the seated women. 'Regarding her illness,' she said, and pointed that long finger at Peggy. 'It wasn't morning sickness, was it?'

Tired and concerned as she was, Peggy could not suppress a short laugh. 'Mitch? Never.'

'Unless she's with one of the people in this address book, and I'll find that out first thing in the morning, the only reasonable explanation is that she went to some doctor for an abortion.'

Hilda said, 'That is absolutely impossible.'

Mrs Kenyon waggled a finger at her. 'Don't you tell me it's impossible. I know you girls better than you think I do. I tell you, Mrs Sherwood,' she said, shifting her attention, 'I think that girl's got herself in trouble. Unfortunately, that's a police job. I don't want them in this, but they know who those doctors are and I don't.'

'Neither would Mitch,' said Hilda testily.

'If a girl needs one she'll find one. Don't you worry about that.' She drew herself to ramrod posture again and bent like a hinge for her coat. 'In the morning I'll have the campus police search the grounds. If that and her address book don't bring her back, I'm afraid we're in for a mess. We'll have to call in the – police.' She had as much trouble getting that word out as she would an obscenity.

The sound of it sent a shudder through the housemother. 'If you called the local doctors—' she began tentatively.

'That won't do any good. No, it will have to be the police. There'll be unfortunate publicity and scandal and we'll feel it in next year's registration, don't worry about that. As for you girls, you're going to have to bare your souls to them. I don't think you'll like it very much. Now. Is there anything you want to say before I go? Is there anything you haven't told me, anything at all that might have some bearing on this matter?'

The three girls looked at the Warden in silence and the lines around her mouth grew deeper. She turned her back on them with a motion that, in someone else, would be described as petulant and went for her galoshes.

It was twenty minutes of three.

Saturday Morning

The Saturday morning sun struggled up early into a cloudless sky and threw long blue shadows across the thin tired snow that still clung to Parker campus. The air lay still, conserving its nocturnal cold, and the thermometer said forty in the sun, but only twenty in the shade.

As the sun rose higher its angled rays reached over the roof of the Bristol Inn and caught the front of Lambert Annex, giving its dull yellow paint a brighter glow and warming the girls from A and B who came in groups to the front door and breakfast. Inside, there was only one topic of conversation. Where was Lowell Mitchell? The lethargy that usually accompanied the first meal of the day was missing, for the news of their classmate's disappearance had spread like measles through the dorm. The subject of discussion was would she or would she not be expelled from school? The opinion was that only the most excellent of excuses could keep her in.

And, behind the triangle of Lambert Dorm, across Parker Road and down the embankment to Parker Lake, campus police went through the boathouse, opening lockers and storeroom doors and climbing the stairs to the loft. They poked around in the adjoining crew house and probed the water between the polished shells with crew oars. They fanned out along the lake front, working their way through the woods at the north end, up past the mouth of Wheeler River to the edge of the campus grounds. They moved down below the dam, under Higgins Bridge which connected the campus proper to the gym and athletic fields, on down to the Queen Street Bridge.

In Hancock Hall the janitor climbed the third-storey ladder to the skylight and got out on the flat roof. He went down in the basement and looked in all the wooden lavatory stalls. He opened the paper baler, climbed up on a chair, and peered into that. In the library Mrs Sheldon sent her shelf attendants scurrying through the stacks and, across the river, Mrs Gordon, the physical director, opened the equipment lockers, and turned on the lights in the swimming pool of the new million-dollar Higgins Gymnasium.

At quarter past one the Springfield-to-Boston local rumbled into Bristol station, bringing on it the architect, Carl Mitchell, father of the missing girl. His face was white under the grey felt hat, his mouth a thin-set line as he swung down the steps and commandeered a taxi.

At Lambert Dorm he first burst into the Annex lounge where Hilda, in jeans and shirt, was playing bridge with Marlene, Peggy, and a girl from B. He pulled off his hat and said tightly, 'I'm Carl Mitchell. Is there any news of my daughter?'

Hilda scrambled to her feet, told him no, and took him over to Lambert A and Mrs Sherwood. The housemother's reply to the same question was a shake of the head. 'We haven't heard yet, Mr Mitchell, but I'm sure she's all right. Something must have happened to delay her, that's all.'

He brushed her words aside without the courtesy of attention and said, 'What's being done to find her?'

She was pale and trembled as though expecting to be accused. 'We have notified the Warden, Mr Mitchell. She's taken over the investigation.' She added almost eagerly, 'Would you like to speak to her?'

'What about the police? Haven't they been called yet?'

'No, not yet. We've been conducting our own investigation.'

The man's face hardened and his dark eyes grew savage. 'Lowell's been missing twenty-four hours,' he said sarcastically. 'When did you think you'd get around to notifying the police?'

'We were waiting for you to come, Mr Mitchell. Meanwhile, we hoped we could find her without any scandal.'

His mouth curled momentarily, exposing the glint of a tooth. 'I'd like to see her room, please.'

Mrs Sherwood got her coat and took him back to the Annex, almost trotting to keep up with the architect's determined strides. She panted up the stairs and led him down the long hall to the door. Mitchell stepped past her and stared at the deserted room. The fire went out of his eyes and a bleak look came over his face as though he realized for the first time that his daughter was really gone. He looked around and swallowed once or twice and spoke in a gentler tone to the housemother. 'Has anything been touched?'

'Some. Her roommate slept here last night, but her things haven't been moved. The bed is just she left it.'

Mr Mitchell gazed at the wrinkled coverlet and his face softened. He moved into the room to the foot of the bed and swung around slowly. 'Those her books?' he asked, gesturing with his hat at the sliding pile on the desk near the door.

'I believe so, yes.'

He hitched his shoulders slightly inside his grey overcoat

and moved away. 'I'd like to talk to the Warden now,' he said quietly.

Mrs Sherwood took him down to the phone behind the stairs and got Mrs Kenyon on the wire. Mitchell took the receiver and introduced himself, then said, 'Have you found anything?'

The Warden's voice was clear and decisive. 'We've got one clue, Mr Mitchell. The man in charge of the boathouse says he saw a girl dressed like Lowell walking around the north end of the lake a little after eight o'clock yesterday morning. He saw her again, coming back, about ten minutes of nine.'

'What good is that? That was four hours before she disappeared.'

'I know, but don't you see? That accounts for the hour she was missing yesterday morning. We've checked the attendance sheets and she went to all her classes, biological science at nine, rhythmic work at ten, Spanish at eleven, and history at twelve. We've got every minute of her time accounted for now.'

'But you haven't found anybody who saw her after one o'clock, right?'

'No. I'm afraid that's all we've got so far. I called all the names in her address book this morning and they know nothing about her and we've searched the whole campus. There isn't a trace.'

'It's about time you called in the police, I would say.'

'You're quite right, Mr Mitchell. We've done all we can.'

'And if you weren't so damned afraid of scandal you'd have done it last night when you should have!'

Mrs Kenyon fell all over herself explaining. 'Please don't get that impression, Mr Mitchell. I'll admit we'd like to get her back without any publicity, but our first concern is getting her back! There's nothing, so far, the police could have done that we haven't done! No time has been lost, I can assure you. However, from here on, they have the facilities and we don't and I'll call them right away.'

Mitchell ran a hand through his curly salt-and-pepper hair and said into the mouthpiece, 'I'm sorry if I'm rude and unappreciative. I'm very much upset. Thank you. I'm sure you've done everything possible. As for the police, don't bother to call them. I'll do it right here and now.' He nodded, said goodbye, depressed the hook and released it, listened a moment, then dialled the operator.

Frank W. Ford, the grizzled, fifty-eight-year-old Chief of the Bristol Police, took the call and immediately assigned Detective Sergeant Burton K. Cameron and plainclothesman Donald C. Lassiter to the case. Cameron's first move was to get in touch with Mrs Kenyon and with Edward M. Small, the superintendent of grounds at Parker, with whom he would work, and they gathered in Lowell's room along with Mr Mitchell and Mrs Sherwood. There they listened to and made notes of all the information that was to be had regarding Lowell's activities. When the boathouse keeper's story of the girl walking along the lake edge was told Cameron chewed his lip with bared teeth and said, 'Has the lake been examined?'

'Only from shore,' replied Mrs Kenyon. 'I was contemplating sending out canoes this afternoon to see if there's any evidence that she's in it.'

'A good idea,' said Cameron soberly, and glanced furtively at the architect. 'I'll have Lassiter help you.' He scrawled something else on his pad with a barely legible hand.

Mitchell said, 'If you think maybe she drowned herself, you're absolutely crazy!'

Cameron shook his head. 'I'm not thinking anything, Mr Mitchell. We're just checking all possibilities.' He sat up straighter and addressed the group. 'Inasmuch as she wasn't kidnapped but went out of here of her own accord, the best way to find her is to find out why she left. How were her marks? Could she have been despondent over them?'

Mrs Kenyon said, 'I've already checked them, Sergeant. Her marks were all above average. Close to honours, in fact. She had a C in biological science, C in gym, B plus in English, A minus in history, and an A in Spanish. She has no demerits, no black marks against her at all, either scholastically or socially. And as far as I can make out she got on very well with her classmates.'

Cameron shifted his feet and raised his toes off the floor, leaning forward to stare at them. 'How was her home life, Mr Mitchell? Any family trouble that would make her want to run away?'

Mitchell shook his head. 'No. Our home life has been unusually happy. We're a very close family.'

'Um-hmm. Then we'll have to look for another motive.' The shine of his shoes was dazzling and Cameron seemed to find the sight fascinating. 'Is it possible she might have been in trouble? In plain words, could she be pregnant?'

Mr Mitchell straightened in his chair and his face grew harsh. 'Absolutely not.'

'She never had sexual relations with men so far as you know?'

'She never had them, period.'

'Then, if she did get into trouble, it would be for the first time?'

'She is not in that kind of trouble.'

'Do you think she would tell you if something like that happened?'

'I'm sure I don't know. Such a thing simply could not happen.' Mitchell turned sideways in his chair, facing the policeman. 'You're following a wrong trail, Sergeant. I know, in your business, you run across a lot of such girls and you're cynical but, believe me, I know my daughter and you can take my word for it. It's absolutely impossible.'

Cameron nodded and wrote 'Denies' on his pad. Then he said, 'In that case we don't have any known motive, which means there's no first place to look. The best thing we can do then is send out an alarm and try to have her picked up.' He turned to the housemother and said, 'Those girls playing bridge downstairs. They live here?'

'Three of them do.'

'Want to call them up? I'd like to have them inventory her things so we can get an idea of what she was wearing. And, Mrs Kenyon,' he said to the Warden, 'could you get me Lowell's vital statistics from the office file?'

Hilda, Peggy, and Marlene appeared and, at the Sergeant's request, started through the drawers of Lowell's bureau and her rack in the closet, recognizing what they found, trying to remember what they didn't.

'Did she have two grey skirts? There's one here, but I don't remember if she had another.'

'She was wearing a dark green one a couple of days ago. That's not here. It was hers, wasn't it?'

A yellow button-up and a pink angora sweater were missing. So was a navy-blue jacket.

'Her good pair of white saddle shoes is missing.'

'I don't see her purse, the brown one, do you? Here's her black dress one and her everyday one.'

'I know she had another grey skirt.'

'I think she had more blue jeans than this.'

Peggy turned to Cameron. 'Sergeant, she couldn't have walked out with two or three sets of clothes on, could she?'

Cameron half smiled. 'Not when she could just as easily pack a suitcase. Any of those missing?'

Her blue, white-trimmed overnight bag and the larger cow-hide suitcase were in the closet. 'No, Sergeant. She only had two.'

'Then the rest of her clothes are probably at the laundry. Where did she send them, Miss Woodling? The Student Laundry and Cleaners?'

'Yes, sir.'

Cameron got up and went to the bureau, saying, 'Okay, Don. Check on it.' He pulled out a freshly starched man's shirt. 'Her laundry mark is P dash LA dash 230.'

When the rummaging was completed Peggy listed as missing one grey wool skirt and one dark green one, possibly a third, the yellow and pink sweaters, navy-blue jacket, brown and white saddle shoes, tan polo coat, brown leather shoulder-strap purse with her initials, probably some blouses and socks.

'Hat?' asked Cameron.

'I don't know. There are three hats in her box but I never saw her wear one so I don't know if she had any others.'

'Stockings?'

'Oh no. Not with saddle shoes. She'd wear ankle socks.'

'What about her taste in undergarments?'

'Half slip, pants, and bra. If she wore the angora, though, she'd wear a full slip.'

By the time Lowell's vital statistics record had arrived Lassiter was back with the laundry information. They had, for the regular wash, two pairs of blue jeans, three half slips, one full slip, and three blouses. For dry-cleaning, one dark green shirt, one navy-blue jacket, and one angora sweater.

The statistics sheet described her appearance, and further information was given by her father, who filled in details and told about her jewellery and her financial condition. Examination of the room yielded no clues other than Lowell's letters and diary. These Cameron appropriated and ended the interview. Mr Mitchell promptly left to telephone his wife from the Bristol Inn and the sergeant took that opportunity to draw Hilda, Peggy, and Marlene aside. Lowell's father was certain that his daughter's morals were above reproach but Cameron was, as the man had said, too cynical to believe that meant it was so.

The three girls upheld Mr Mitchell, however. The idea of pregnancy was absurd. Not only was her moral character very high but the boys' interest in her exceeded hers in them, and even were she the type to indulge in sexual promiscuities, they formed no incentive.

Meanwhile, Mr Mitchell reached his wife. There was no news, he told her, but a call would be put through to the State Police and an eight-state alarm would be spread. 'They don't have anything to work on yet, Verna, and it's going to take a little time, I'm afraid. Perhaps you'd better call John and tell him I won't be in Monday. And will you mail me some pictures of Lowell? Sergeant Cameron wants them for the missing persons circular they're going to send out. A good full-length one and some bust shots. And look around, will you, and see if you can find some samples of her printing. They have her handwriting, but they want the printing, too, if there is any.' He listened for a little, then said, 'Do you really think you'd better? It's not pleasant up here . . . I know it's hell sitting around home, but it's hell here too. Besides, what about Melissa? What about her schooling? It may be several days before Lowell's located . . . Well, all right if you'd rather. I'll arrange for a room at the Bristol Inn for all of us. Now please don't worry, dear. She's perfectly capable of taking care of herself. You see, she left of her own accord and she had that fifty-dollar cheque I mailed her on the first. She could go quite a ways on that. What train will you take? . . . All right. I'll meet you at the station. Be sure to have Grenadine watch the mail in case Lowell writes and have her get in touch with us immediately if she does write or phone. We'll have her back in no time once the alarm is spread.'

So Carl Mitchell hung up, feeling that he had convinced his wife that their daughter was safe and well. In his own mind he wasn't so sure. Still vivid was a picture of the cold lake the canoes were about to cover, the lake by which Lowell had walked the morning of her disappearance.

Saturday Afternoon

Sergeant Cameron, having first personally checked the railroad station and bus terminal, reported in to police headquarters at quarter of five Saturday afternoon. Chief Ford had not gone home, however. He got off the table he had been sitting on in the centre of the long main room and moved to the desk. 'About time you got in,' he grumbled. 'What's the story?'

'Nothing as yet. I'm going to have her description broadcast.'

The Chief stood by, his grey crew-cut hair bristling all over his bullethead, his grim, jut-jawed, seamed face still grimmer as the detective plugged in the direct wire to State Police Headquarters across town and gave them the information. When Cameron was finished Ford jerked his head at his office, off one side of the big room, and went in, taking a seat before his battered rolltop desk, making a half turn to face Cameron, who pulled over a wooden armchair and slumped into it. Ford nodded to him and withdrew a cigar wrapped in cellophane from his vest pocket. He held it so it caught the light from the window behind him and began to twirl it between his fingers.

'Frankly, it's a stumper,' Cameron said, and went on to tell the story of how Lowell Mitchell had taken a walk by the lake before her classes, showed up sick, and disappeared. Questioning of the students that afternoon, by him and Mrs Kenyon, had produced a little further information. Lowell had gone from biological science across Higgins Bridge to the gym in the company of a Virginia Rollins and had returned with the Rollins girl after her rhythmic work class, leaving her to go to Spanish. She left Spanish in the company of several girls and parted from them to go to history. Usually she walked back to Lambert with Sue Chappel, who lived in A, but on this occasion she delayed to speak to the teacher and Sue left before she did.

As far as could be ascertained, she was wearing when she disappeared a tan polo coat, grey skirt, white blouse, and yellow sweater. No motive could be found as a cause of her leaving and a check of the bus terminal and railroad station had been fruitless. However, an unusually large number of girls had gone off for the weekend and it was by no means unlikely that she had been one of them. She had no known motive for suicide but the possibility was not ruled out and Lassiter and the girl's father were among the men paddling canoes looking for traces in the lake which, outside of a twenty-foot channel, was no more than three or four feet deep. Mr Mitchell was planning to offer a reward.

'That's it,' said Cameron in conclusion. 'No reason to leave unless she wants to make her way in the world and all she's ever done is wait on table last summer. No reason to leave, but she leaves. Only thing I can think of is her being sick having something to do with it, but she didn't go any place a sick girl would go. We've tried the infirmary, the city hospital, and all the drugstores in the neighbourhood and they haven't seen her. What do you think of that, Chief?'

Ford finally peeled the wrapper off his cigar and held

the naked cylinder up for examination. 'Cherchez le boy,' he said at last.

'Boy? There isn't any boy.'

'Now don't tell me you're falling for that crap her family and friends are dishing out about how pure she is. It's something to do with a boy, I'm telling you.'

'What are you, clairvoyant? The evidence says no.'

'You college guys with your three-dollar words,' muttered Ford. 'No, I'm not clairvoyant, I'm a policeman and I've been one for thirty-three years. Girls have disappeared from Parker before and from Smith and Bennington and Vassar and Bryn Mawr and every other girls' school you want to name. Know why they disappear?' He put the cigar aside, held up one hand, and started folding down the fingers as he counted. 'Causes. Bad marks. Not getting along with classmates. Trouble at home. Foul play. Wanting to make their own way in the world. Men. Six reasons. There's your answer.'

'Six reasons,' said Cameron. 'No evidence for any of them so you automatically say men.'

A leering grin came over Ford's face. 'What a hell of a detective you are! Sit down and figure it out some night. She left Lambert under her own steam. That rules out foul play. If she had bad marks it would show! If she didn't get along with her classmates it would show! If there was trouble at home her folks would know it. If she wanted to make her way in the world it would show! If it was about a man it *wouldn't* show! *Quod erat demonstrandum*, or don't you get it yet?'

Cameron flicked his ear. 'Was that Latin I heard or are these poor old ears playing tricks?'

Ford looked smug. 'Maybe I never went to college, but that doesn't mean I don't know anything.'

'You know but you just forget. You forget for instance that the Warden's already called every boy she's got an address for and she didn't run off with any of them.'

'Did she happen to ask them how far they went with her? My bet is she's holed up in some shady doctor's office right now.'

'Put money on it, will you? The girl was in the throes.'

'That's what you say. Did they ever knock her out before? I thought not. She wasn't having cramps, all she said was she wasn't hungry.'

'What do you know about it? You're no woman.'

'No, but I've got a sixteen-year-old daughter and they double her up once a month.' He leaned forward and put on his leer again. 'I don't suppose it's occurred to you, Mr Detective, but did you ever think that maybe the Mitchell girl's sick spell was just an act?'

'An act? What gives you that brainstorm?'

Ford sat back, picked up the cigar, wiped it on his shirt, and rammed it in his mouth. 'She was fine all morning up through her history class,' he rumbled. 'All of a sudden she's back at the dorm feeling sick. Pretty fast reverse. Why does she pull the sick act? Because it lets her do what she wants to – sneak out of the place without being questioned. Why would anybody question her? Because she's changing into a skirt. She can't leave the campus grounds in dungarees and the moment she puts on a skirt the girls start asking where she's going. She doesn't want to tell them, she doesn't want to make excuses. So what's she going to do? She fakes illness. Nobody saw her leave, remember, and it's my hunch she didn't want them to.'

Cameron chewed his lip. Then he got out a cigarette and scraped a match up the side of Ford's desk. He said,

'And now some doctor's got her and after a week or so she'll appear again, a little wiser and a little thinner?'

'If he didn't botch the job and kill her.'

He waved out the match and threw it across the room. 'Any doctors in mind?'

'Two. Bergman over on White Street and Hill over in East Bristol. It's more likely Bergman because he's closer. Now you know what you're going to do, don't you?'

'Watch them.'

'That's right. Two men in plain clothes on both houses. Have them try to gain entry if possible but don't, whatever you do, arouse suspicion. Get a report on every move they make. In addition, I want every other doctor in town questioned to see if she approached them. They should have reported it to me and since they didn't, if she did see them, they'll try to deny it. Watch their reactions. You'd better handle that detail yourself. Did the girl smoke?'

'Yeah. There was half a carton of Philip Morris in her bureau.'

'Damn. I was hoping she might pick up a pack on the way. There's a drugstore a block from Bergman's. Check it anyway. She might have bought something there if she was going to spend a week away from everything – magazines or something.'

'Check. Anything else?'

'Yep. You're going to read her diary from the day she hit this town in September up till when she stops. List the names of every man mentioned, no matter what the circumstance. I want to know what she says about them. Read her letters. I'm especially interested in the ones from home. I'm not satisfied about the happy-home angle. See what you can read between the lines.'

'Gotcha.' Cameron got up to go.

'One other thing. What did she talk about to her history prof?'

'I don't know. Her assignment, probably.'

'I don't want any probablys. Find out.'

'My God, how picayune can you get?'

'I'll get just as whatever that three-dollar word means as I want. You might remember that the girl was fine, took gym and everything, right up through her history class. She talks to the teacher and five minutes later she's flat on her back, sick.'

'What do you think he did, exhale cyanide in her face?'

'I don't think he did anything, but get this through your thick skull. That wasn't her usual procedure. If things on that campus were normal it wouldn't matter a damn. But things are not normal. I want it understood that everything that happens on that campus the least little bit out of the ordinary is to be thoroughly investigated. I don't care how small and unimportant you may think it is, investigate it. Is that clear?'

'Indubitably.'

Ford ground his cigar in his teeth. 'Shut up and get out of here. I want to go home and eat. And write up your report. I want to study it in the morning.'

Cameron moved to the door and said sarcastically over his shoulder, 'Is it all right with you if I get a little sleep?'

Sunday, 5 March

The Boston *Post-Traveler* ran it under a two-column head on the front page: EIGHT STATE ALARM OUT FOR MISSING PARKER GIRL. The story, like the stories all over the country, was short owing to lack of details but in it were all the elements an editor looked for: mystery, human interest, and a young college girl. In newspaper offices crack reporters were called in, given instructions, and sent out. The press associations dispatched men on the earliest trains. Charlie Miller came in from Hartford and Len Waltzberger from Springfield. From farther points they came by plane, train, and auto, Ken Rafferty of Providence, Murray Talbot from New York, Pat O'Malley of the Boston *Post-Traveler*, John Innes of the Bridgeport *Post*. The first ones arrived early and a steady stream flowed in until noon, followed by latecomers through the evening and the next day.

Police headquarters was the main target and five were waiting for Ford when he arrived. A sixth, more enterprising than the rest, caught the Chief at breakfast and came with him. Ford waded through the tide, obviously riled at having had his morning coffee disturbed, shed his hat and coat, and did not face the onslaught until he had the main desk for a bulwark. Then he said tersely, 'Nothing yet. We're doing all we can. We hope to have her back soon.'

'Is her father Carl Mitchell, the famous architect? The

one who designed the new Brinn Building in New York that's got all that publicity?'

'Ask him.'

'Any theories, Chief? What do you think happened?'

'Yeah. She hopped the night plane for London.'

'Honest?'

Calvin Leslie, assistant editor and star reporter of the Bristol *Bugle*, the town's weekly and only newspaper, sauntered in. 'The vultures are tearing the corpse already,' he observed. 'Hello, Frank.'

'Hello, Les.'

'What a scoop I could have had if we ran a daily. Any news of her?'

'Not yet.'

Somebody else said, 'How about foul play, Chief?'

'You name it, you can have it.'

'Do you think she's alive or dead?'

'Yes.'

Cameron pushed his way through and slipped behind the Chief. He went into Ford's office and tossed a clipped stack of typewritten pages on the desk. Ford followed him. 'The report?'

'It's all there, up till four o'clock this morning. I told you I was going to get some sleep.'

'What about her diary and letters?'

'I'm halfway through the diary. She thinks President Howland is sweet. Her history teacher looks like Gregory Peck, her English teacher is dynamic and sounds like Winston Churchill, and she thinks W. C. Fields is very funny. Remember. You said you wanted to know every man she mentions.'

'And I meant it,' growled Ford. 'Including her English teacher and history teacher *and* the president of the college, *and* the janitor *and* the taxi drivers *and* the soda jerks in the drugstores. That's exactly what I want even if you have to be cute and bring in W. C. Fields.'

'Good. I'm glad you're satisfied. Howland's probably the father of her unborn child.'

'What do you want, more sleep? You had four hours. Now get out and handle those reporters. I want to see what you've got here.'

So Cameron underwent the grilling and he gave them Lowell's description and told them she had waited on table the preceding summer to earn spending money for college. He said the campus had been thoroughly searched without results. The lake had been covered inch by inch and, unless she were at the bottom of the channel, she wasn't in it. She had not taken a taxi anywhere, but might have left town by train or bus. They hoped to find out more about that angle when all the other students who had departed at that time were back and could be questioned.

'Got any pictures of the girl?'

'We'll have them this afternoon. They're coming up from Philadelphia.'

'The girl's father's in town, isn't he? Where's he staying?'

'Never mind. He doesn't want you hounding him.'

'Hell, we're doing him a favour. We're giving him publicity. Get enough people knowing about this and someone's going to recognize her somewhere.'

'Your altruism touches me.'

At eight-thirty Carl Mitchell came up the steps like an old man and turned the corner where eight reporters blocked him from the desk. They recognized him by instinct and swallowed him into their midst. 'Any statement for the press, Mr Mitchell?' He hunched his shoulders inside the grey coat and let them drop slowly. 'You can say I won't rest until I have her back,' he said dully.

They started the questions then, but not in the snappy, rapid-fire manner they had used with the police. These were tenderly asked and came from sober, sympathetic faces and had an almost apologetic ring to them. Mitchell seemed tired to the point of exhaustion but he stood patiently in the centre of the circle, turning this way and that to face his interrogator. Was he the designer of the Brinn Building in New York? Yes, he was. Had Lowell tried to contact him? No, she had not. What was his view of the matter? He thought she must have run away for some reason. Did he suspect foul play? No. Did Lowell pack a bag when she left? She did not. When they asked where the five-thousand-dollar reward would come from his face grew tight and he snapped, 'None of your business.' When they asked prying questions about his private life he said it had nothing to do with the case. Other than that, he was tolerant, almost appreciative of their attention.

When he was finally turned loose Cameron took him into the Chief's office and pulled the door closed behind them. He introduced the two men and dragged a chair over for the father as though he were a superior court judge. He himself hooked a leg over the table.

'I've been reading over Cameron's report,' said the Chief. 'It doesn't tell us a thing. She walked out of the dorm and that's it. She vanished into thin air.'

'She can't just disappear, Chief. Somebody has to have seen her.'

'Somebody did. Probably a lot of people. Only we haven't found them yet.'

'Have you tried all the houses along the street?

Somebody might have seen which way she went. After all, it was broad daylight.'

'One thing at a time, Mr Mitchell. No, we haven't done that yet, but we're going to.'

'She's been gone a long time. You'd better hurry it up before people forget.'

'It's not long, Mr Mitchell. It only seems long. We aren't expecting to find her in time for tomorrow's class. Police work is efficient and thorough, not lightning. The railroad and bus terminals come first. Then the places she'd be likely to go. Then we start fanning out and asking neighbours and pedestrians. When are those pictures of her coming in? The important thing in cases of this kind is wide circulation. We want as many people keeping an eye out for her as possible. Then the neighbours will come to us if they saw her. Or, if she's still alive and moving about at all, other people will spot her.'

'You think she's dead?'

'Hell, no. She just ducked out somewhere. Might be amnesia as a matter of fact.'

Mitchell said quietly, 'I'm no fool, Chief. You don't have to salve me with oil. If it's bad news I can take it.'

Ford waved a hand. 'It's not bad news. How can I give you bad news? I don't know any more about it than you do.'

'You've had experience in this sort of thing, though. Why do girls usually run away?'

'I'd say the most usual cause is trouble at home.' Ford said it casually, but his grey eyes were sharp under his shaggy brows.

Lowell's father shook his head. 'There must be another reason, then. Our family is an unusually close one.'

The Chief leaned an elbow on the desktop and put his

chin in his hand. 'You wouldn't be kidding me, would you?'

'Kidding you? My God, man, don't you think I'd tell you if I thought there were any chance of that being the cause of her disappearance?'

'Not, perhaps, if you thought she could be found without its being known.'

Mitchell leaned forward, his face flushed. 'Listen, I don't give a damn about reputation, scandal, publicity, or anything else. I want my daughter back! That's the only thing that matters! I want her back. I'll tell you anything, I'll do anything, anything at all. Just find my daughter!'

'Okay,' Ford said. 'Calm down. That's exactly what we're trying to do. You get us her pictures so we can give them out to the newspapers and get that missing persons circular off and we'll have her back in no time.'

'My wife and other daughter are bringing them up on the one-fifteen train.'

'Okay. I'll see you then.' Ford waved him out and, as soon as he was gone, turned to Cameron. 'You got men staked out on those doctors' houses?'

'Yep. Starting at midnight last night. Nothing out of the ordinary so far.'

'Let me know how much food they buy, whether it's more than normal.'

'I will when the stores are open.'

'You do that. Now what's the story on the lake?'

'I don't think she's in it.'

'But you aren't sure?'

Cameron said irritably, 'No, I'm not sure. All I know is Lassiter and the girl's father and Ed Small and all his grounds keepers had every canoe going for two hours yesterday afternoon and they poked their paddles down to the bottom everywhere except in the channel and that's all they hit – bottom. If you want to be any surer than that, drain it!'

'Maybe I will,' said Ford thoughtfully. 'If we don't get a lead in the next couple of days, maybe I'll do just that.'

'Do you think she drowned herself just because she walked around there Friday morning?'

'You already know what I think she did. But I'm not aiming to pass up any other bets. It's barely possible I might be wrong.'

'I don't believe it.'

Ford let that one ride. 'That fifty-dollar cheque her father sent her. That interests me. Maybe she's going to pay the doc with it. Only he'd never take a cheque. He's not going to sign anything. She'd have to cash it first.' He snapped his fingers. 'There's an opening lead. If my hunch is correct I know somebody who's seen her after one o'clock Friday. The bank teller. Call him up.'

Cameron got up. 'I don't go for your abortion idea, you know that. But I'll bet you've got something here. No matter what her plans were, she wouldn't go very far without cashing that cheque.'

'You're a lousy detective but you recognize genius when you see it,' growled Ford. 'You got Lowell's letters from home with you? I want to read them over.'

'High school boy makes good,' said Cameron, pulling the letters and diary from his coat pockets and dropping them on the desk. He walked out to the phone.

Ford swung around at the desk and looked at the heap. He picked up the diary tentatively, felt the texture of the red leather cover, popped the lock apart and looked at it blandly, then folded the book open at random and read an item or two. He exhaled with a deprecatory air, closed the book, pushed it aside, and selected one of the letters. He was more alert now as he turned the envelope over and back and sniffed it. He extracted the letter and read it carefully with no change of expression. It was from her father and gave no indication that he was lying when he said the family was unusually close.

When he was finished Ford stuffed the letter back in the envelope and sorted through the rest for one in different handwriting, from Mrs Mitchell. Again it seemed to uphold Mitchell's statement and Ford discarded that, going once more into the pile for one of the few letters from Melissa, Lowell's younger sister. The sisters seemed to be close also and, whatever the reason for Lowell's departure, her family could pretty safely be said not to be it.

Ford peeled a cigar and lighted it and returned to his pet theory that Lowell Mitchell had walked out of her dorm and into a doctor's office. And, unless the operation failed, she would reappear just as suddenly as she had vanished. If she died on the table, however, a desperate effort would be made to get rid of the body. That was what they had to be careful of.

Cameron came back in as Ford was staring reflectively out the window. 'Several girls cashed cheques Friday,' he said, 'but the teller doesn't remember anyone answering her description. He'll go over the cancelled cheques tomorrow but he's sure none of them are for fifty dollars.'

An oath rumbled up from inside the Chief and escaped around his cigar. He got up and took a turn about the room, ending up at the window staring at the driveway. 'Now that doesn't make sense. No doctor performing an illegal operation is going to sign his name to a cheque for it so it can be traced right back to him. And where else but the bank could she cash a cheque for that much money?'

'Maybe at the bursar's office. Or the College Lunch. That place cashes a lot of cheques for the girls.'

'Not for fifty bucks, I'll bet. That little item bothers me.'

'It's something to work on,' Cameron agreed. 'Look, Chief. You're going to have to assign me more men. I want to cover all the shops in town to see if she made any purchases and maybe used her cheque that way. Also we've got to interview a load of students and everybody in all the houses up and down Maple Street.'

'Take as many as you need. We can use the reserves and get some of the night men in. We're all going to be putting overtime in on this. It's got all the earmarks of a first-class mystery and, judging from the crowd of reporters hanging around, it's going to receive a lot of attention.' He turned back with a wry grin. 'Too bad we aren't better-looking. They might run our picture.'

'Too bad if you don't find her. Bristol might sport a new police chief.'

'You, I suppose. Then no girl will be safe at Parker.'

Mrs Mitchell and Melissa arrived in Bristol on the one-fifteen and were immediately brought to police headquarters by Mr Mitchell. They had with them twenty or thirty pictures of Lowell of all shapes, sizes, and angles and three of these, one full-length and two busts, were sent to the State Police for the missing persons circular along with samples of her handwriting and the printing sample they had found.

The two women were questioned at length by Chief Ford, particularly in relation to any boy trouble Lowell might have had, but could offer nothing that the police did not already know. Lowell's affections were attached to no one in so far as they knew.

Ford himself interviewed the druggist near Dr Berg-

man's home but was told no college girls at all had been
in Friday afternoon. Lassiter checked with the bursar's
office and with the College Lunch and Lowell had not
cashed her cheque in either place. Cameron called up
Harlan P. Seward, history instructor, and asked what
Lowell had stopped at the desk to say to him after his
Friday noon class. Seward could not remember exactly but
believed it was something to do with an assignment.

Reporters were in and out of police headquarters all
day, receiving the same answer, 'Nothing new,' to their
questions. Patrolmen Kennedy and Jarrett phoned in at
four o'clock to report nothing out of the ordinary at Dr
Bergman's house. Stevenson and Womrath said the same
for Dr Hill's. Other phone calls were starting to come in
from people offering assistance in the hunt but no calls
were from anyone who had seen her after 1 p.m. Friday.
The State Police had heard nothing from their eight state
alarm.

When Ford left at six he took Lowell's diary home with
him. The air was crisp and sweet after the stale atmosphere
of the police station and Ford drove slowly, relaxing from
the tension of the day, staring at the signs of normality
that he passed, the people, hidden under their overcoats,
hurrying by in the gathering dusk, the glaring headlights
of the cars, a star or two in the empty sky.

There were signs of abnormality too. Traffic was heavier
than usual on Maple Street, loaded with cars from other
counties that slowed to a crawl as they passed the yellow
front of Lambert Annex and its lighted windows. There
were more pedestrians there, too, forming momentary
groups, breaking and gathering and passing and wondering
what it was like being one of the girls behind those walls
and living with drama.

Inside the quiet, warmly lighted house around which the rumours flew, the subject was not mentioned. The piano in the lounge was silent and there was no bridge game, but nothing was said. Sober girls studied and smoked and asked serious questions about their homework.

Elsewhere in the town people talked. It was the main topic of conversation in the restaurants and taverns and around the supper tables. In the other dorms students spoke of nothing else and it was a shocked and sobered Patty Short and Sally Anders who returned late that evening from their weekends at Yale and Princeton.

Monday, 6 March

Monday's headlines were bolder and blacker on the front page. NO CLUES YET IN PARKER FRESHMAN'S DISAPPEARANCE took up three lines two columns wide and a one-column cut of Lowell Mitchell was underneath with the line, *Missing Since Friday* and *More Pictures on Page 3.* The story not only covered the police angle but showed that both the girl's parents had been subjected to a barrage of questions. Mrs Mitchell had stated that Lowell was emotionally normal and had no steady suitor as far as she knew. Lowell's sister Melissa was described as a very sober, pretty fifteen-year-old brunette. Her father was head of the Mitchell-Modleman Architectural Designing firm. A two-column portrait photo of Lowell was on page three and showed a girl with dark long-bobbed hair held back by a clip, large serious eyes, full unsmiling lips, and a soft fullness in her face. Underneath the picture was the caption, *Parker Student Who Has Vanished*, and under that, *Lowell Mitchell, 18, of Philadelphia, Pa., who is the object of a widespread police search after disappearing from her room in Parker College, Bristol, Mass.*

In addition to the newspaper publicity the missing persons circular was ready for distribution. A reward of $5,000.00 if found alive and $2,500.00 if found dead was noted in the corners. Below were three pictures, a full-length photo surrounded by two bust shots. Under the one on the left were a few written words in an even hand, listed as a specimen of her handwriting, and under that, a sample of her printing. Under the right-hand picture were the vital statistics:

Marilyn Lowell Mitchell, 18 yrs. $5'5\frac{1}{2}''$, 125 lb, dark hair, long bob, hazel eyes, pale complexion, features regular, nose slightly turned up. Whitish jagged scar outside right calf, vaccination mark right thigh, small scar on left temple back of hairline. Walks with long graceful step, has erect carriage. Athletic type.

DENTAL CHART ON BACK OF CIRCULAR.

Below the pictures was the following information:

Marilyn Lowell Mitchell, 450 Evergreen Avenue, Philadelphia, Pa., a student at Parker College, Bristol, Mass., disappeared from college on the afternoon of 3 March 1950. Thought to be wearing a tan polo coat with plain brown buttons, yellow wool sweater, mother-of-pearl buttons, white blouse, grey wool skirt, ankle socks, brown and white saddle shoes, size 7, a gold hair clip with initials MLM inside, a small gold Elgin ladies' wristwatch with narrow gold band, and a brown leather purse with shoulder-strap, brass fastener, and initials MLM on the side. This girl likes dancing, tennis, dramatics, swimming, and playing the piano. She is interested in languages and is moderately fluent in French and Spanish. She has also done waitress work.

REWARD. LIVING OR DEAD. $5,000.00 IF FOUND ALIVE. $2,500.00 IF FOUND DEAD. $5,000.00 reward for information leading to the whereabouts of Marilyn Lowell Mitchell and resulting in her being found alive. $2,500.00 reward for information leading to the whereabouts of Marilyn Lowell Mitchell and resulting in the identification of her body. Reward expires 31 December 1950.

Please forward any information to the girl's father, Carl Bemis Mitchell, 560 Evergreen Avenue, Philadelphia, Pa.

Chief Ford was in Monday morning and the reporters were there to meet him. The number had swelled in twenty-four hours. 'How about a statement, Chief?'

Ford flung his hat on the table and sat down on the stool back of the chest-high main desk. 'No news,' he said in his usual growl.

'What angle are you working on?'

'The girl's diary. No clues in it, but we're going to check on all the boys she mentioned.'

'Any truth in the rumour Mitchell's going to hire a private detective?'

'Ask him.'

'What'll you do if he does?'

Ford said, 'What're you trying to do, make news by working up a feud?'

'Just curious, Chief.'

'Keep your curiosity to yourself or get the hell out of here.' Ford stalked into his office and slammed the door.

Cameron found him there when he came in at eight-thirty. He answered a few questions the reporters put to him, then opened the door and walked in on the Chief.

Ford swung around in his chair. 'Where the hell have you been?' he bellowed. 'You're supposed to be here at eight o'clock. If I hadn't come in and relieved Poreda he'd have been stuck half an hour overtime!'

'What of it? Yesterday was my day off and I worked twelve hours.'

'Now ain't that too bad! Today's my day off and I'm going to work twenty-four hours. What did you join the force for, a goof-off job with a pension at the end?'

'I sure didn't join it to listen to you bellyache.' He flung his sheaf of papers on the desk. 'Here's my report.'

Ford ignored it and waved. 'Shut the door for Christ's sake. Do you want those reporters to think there's dissension on the force?'

Cameron shoved the door to, then sat on the edge of the table and pulled out a cigarette. 'Go on, tell me it's against the rules to smoke on duty.'

Ford shook his head. 'Put a guy in plain clothes and he thinks he's a civilian.' He held out a hand. 'Give me one.'

Cameron tossed the pack in his lap and lighted up. Ford did likewise, scowled at the taste of it, and threw the pack back. 'You know,' he said, 'there's an angle in this case I think maybe we ought to pay more attention to.' He swung around and picked up the studio portrait of Lowell that had run on page three and handed it to the detective. 'Know what I'm thinking about?'

'No.'

'Foul play.'

'What's the picture got to do with it?'

'Look at her face. What does it spell to you? It spells S-E-X to me.'

Cameron studied the picture and shook his head. 'You're batty. This isn't the face of a cheap pickup, this is the face of a respectable girl who'll stay away from strange men.'

'I don't mean obvious sex, or conscious sex. I mean unconscious sex, the kind she doesn't even know she's got, but look at those big sombre eyes and those full lips and the soft roundness of her face.' He grabbed up another picture, a full-length portrait this time, and got up to take it to Cameron. 'Look at her figure,' he said. 'Not trim and slender. Slender, yes, with nice long legs, but it's a soft figure, a voluptuous figure. Look at the way she stands. Sort of proud and erect. There's an air about her. She's got what will drive a guy crazy. Hell, I can feel it myself and I'm fifty-eight years old.'

'And lascivious since you were fifteen,' said Cameron. 'So she's the type guys will mentally undress when they pass her on the street. So what?'

'So a degenerate might not be satisfied with doing it mentally. He might try it physically.'

Cameron stuck his hands on his hips. 'What are you telling me that's new? Sex is an angle any time any girl disappears.'

Ford sat down again and threw away his cigarette. 'I'm telling you it's more than an angle in this case,' he said. 'I don't know if it's foul play, or abortion, or running off with somebody, but it's something to do with sex. I'll lay odds on it. That girl is built for it. Sex might even be an ugly word to her but it's going to haunt her just the same.'

Cameron got up and stretched. 'Well, you go rubber-hose the degenerates. I'm going out and interview the doctors around this town as per your orders.' He flicked his cigarette at the wastebasket and walked out.

Monday noon came and went and still nothing resembling a clue was unearthed. The bank teller confirmed the fact that Lowell had not cashed her cheque there. Drs Bergman and Hill had their every move under surveillance but had done nothing the slightest bit out of the ordinary. Cameron came back from his rounds having found no indication that any other doctor was lying when he said no such girl had visited him. He went out again to look up Lassiter, who had joined forces with the Warden and the superintendent of grounds and the campus police to initiate the mammoth task of questioning hundreds of students and faculty members, everyone who could be found to have had the merest contact whatsoever with the missing girl. It was what is known in the police vocabulary as 'routine' – tedious, dull, weary work with dim prospects for uncovering so much as a single grain of gold.

The Mitchells were in, of course, and had another session with the reporters and one with Ford. Lowell had been gone for three days now and they were showing the strain. Melissa kept in the background, quiet and solemn, and Ford couldn't remember having heard her speak a word except in answer to a direct question. Mrs Mitchell, whose small trim figure, soft dark wavy hair, and alert face belied her forty years and two children, looked pale and drawn and her smiling eyes were pained and tormented. Carl Mitchell was restless and taut. The sitting around, the uselessness that he felt, goaded him. The slowly developing police process frustrated him. He wanted things to happen fast.

'What can I do, Chief?' he said. 'That's what I want to know. I can't just sit around and wait. Give me an assignment!'

Ford shook his head. 'We got plenty of men to take care of all that needs to be done.'

'Yes, but what *is* being done? She's been gone three days.' He looked at his watch. 'In an hour and a half it will be three days since anybody's seen her. Three days, man!'

'Do you want to upset your wife? Three days is nothing.

When she's gone three months, then you can start worrying. It takes three days to get the machinery rolling, to lay the groundwork. Give us a couple more days and things should start breaking.'

'Are you sure you're doing all you can?'

'Of course I'm sure. This isn't anything new. Your daughter isn't the first girl who's ever disappeared from this school.'

Mr Mitchell showed some hopeful interest. 'Has it happened very often?'

Ford pulled out a cigar and twirled it. 'Not every year, no. But over the course of the last thirty-three years there've been three or four instances.'

'Did you find them?'

'One of them we didn't.'

Carl Mitchell sat down and ran his hands back through his hair. 'What happened with her?'

Ford shrugged and Mrs Mitchell and Melissa sat up a little straighter. 'It was back in 1937,' said Ford. 'A girl named Helen Chambers disappeared. We traced her to a doctor in Springfield but that's as far as we got. Never could find out what happened.'

'Don't you have any idea?'

'Sure. We think she went there for an abortion and died on the operating table. If she did, the doc was too slick for us. He got rid of the body some way and we never could prove a thing.'

'What did you do, give up?'

Ford shook his head. 'The books aren't closed on it, but I don't think it'll ever be solved. The doc died six or seven years ago and anything he knew about it he took with him.'

Mrs Mitchell leaned forward and spoke. 'What did he die of?'

'Heart attack,' said Ford. 'He was an old geezer.'

'That's terrible. He got away with it.'

Ford shrugged again. 'We don't know that he got away with anything. We traced her there, but we couldn't prove it. Maybe she didn't go to him, or maybe she did and left again. She might be living someplace right now, married and with kids of her own.'

Mr Mitchell said, 'But that's not what happened to Lowell. She's not that kind of a girl and even if such a thing could happen – it couldn't, but supposing it could – she'd come to us.'

Ford merely nodded and silence fell. Then the man said, 'What about the others?'

'Well, back in '22 there was a girl named Barbara Richley or Ritchie. She was picked up in Olathe, Kansas, six weeks later. She'd run off with a travelling salesman. And there was a girl during the war, back in '43 or '44. That one was easy. We found a Boston phone number in her room. We picked her up there at a wild weekend party.'

'But Lowell's case is different,' said her father. 'There's no one she would elope with, or carry on with, and she certainly wouldn't go off on any wild party like that. She's a responsible girl, Chief.'

'They all are, until something comes along and upsets them, like a man, or a war.'

'Not Lowell,' persisted the architect. 'You didn't know her, Chief. If you did you wouldn't think such things. There's some other reason for her not coming back.'

Ford said, 'All right. If you want it point-blank. If it

isn't that, it's kidnapping or foul play. With what we know about her, there aren't any other reasons.'

'But broad daylight, Chief.'

Ford got up and said, 'There's no use speculating about it. There's a good chance we'll get some news in a day or so now that the story has got wide circulation.'

'But you're afraid it's foul play, aren't you, Chief? Look, if it is, something's got to be done. I know your system will bring her back if she's where she can be seen, but maybe she isn't. Maybe she's being held somewhere. I can't just sit around and do nothing. I want to feel I've done everything I possibly can. Chief, would you mind if I hired a private detective?'

Ford shrugged. 'Go ahead. It's your money.'

'It's no reflection on your work, but it would be an extra pair of hands.'

'Don't apologize, Mr Mitchell. Go right ahead if you want. I'll be glad to co-operate with him.'

'Thank you, Chief.'

Ford shrugged again and went to the doorway to look out. Mrs Mitchell called to him, 'Do you suppose we could broadcast an appeal on the radio? Don't you think that might help?'

'Won't hurt any,' said the Chief.

'But you don't think it will help?'

He turned. 'Me? I don't know. In this business you can never tell what's going to produce and what isn't. That might do the trick. It probably won't but it might, so I wouldn't pass it up.'

'Thank you, Chief.' They all rose to leave and Ford stood aside to let them pass. 'You'll let us know the moment you hear anything,' they said.

'Yep. But don't expect it soon.'

He watched them go, three backs showing in the cut of the shoulders the depression they felt. When they passed from sight he returned to his desk, stared emptily at the accumulated papers for a minute, then exhaled and picked up Lowell's diary once more.

Monday Afternoon

Cameron came in again at two and walked into Ford's office. 'Well,' he said, dropping into the wood armchair, 'we've gone over all the blue cards and got a list of every girl who left town Friday. What a job! Big doings at Yale and Princeton and more girls signed out this weekend than any other weekend this year.'

Ford said, 'And while you've been loafing on that job I've been putting together the complete report on the members of the male sex mentioned in Lowell's diary. Guess how many there are.'

'One for every day in the year.'

'Forty-seven.'

'That include Gregory Peck and Gary Cooper?'

'Yeah. You're very funny. Practically a scream.'

'You said every male mentioned. They were mentioned. So were, as I recall, Kirk Douglas, Jimmy Cagney, and W. C. Fields.'

'Don't forget Alan Ladd. You're a great detective. You got a real head for this work.'

'Just following orders, Chief.'

'Oh well,' growled Ford. 'I can't kick. Better to have them in than to have a lot of the others left out because you thought they were too picayune.'

Cameron brushed his ear. 'What was that word?'

'I looked it up. Now settle down and let's go over this.'

Cameron hitched up his chair and Ford said, 'I've

broken down all the stuff we've copied into groups, most
of which can be eliminated without a second look. The
first group is your smart-aleck list of six movie stars and
Winston Churchill which we can dispense with. Group 2
are casuals: relatives and people mentioned once without
any comment. They include a cop she asked directions
from once, Corvath of the campus police, her father, her
uncle Ted, a guy in the post office she bought a stamp
from, a night-watchman she chatted with, a guy in the
student laundry she argued with about a cleaning job, her
uncle David, cousins Rod and Hargrove, Dr Levine,
her dentist, and Mr Peters, the florist here in town.'

Ford shifted to another sheet of paper. 'Group 3 are
people she mentions once but remarks about. First, the
cab driver who takes her to Lambert the day she hits town,
last September twenty-sixth. She says he's old and nice.
Next is President Howland. She calls him "sweet".'

'Bet he'd love that,' said Cameron.

Ford growled something about paying attention and
went on. 'There's Seward, her history teacher. She says
he's dashing, smooth, and looks like a combination of
Gregory Peck and Gary Cooper. Markle, her English
teacher, she says is dynamic and sounds like Churchill.
Shugrue, her science teacher, has "science on the brain".
Last is a Charles Watson, an "older man" who's dining
near them at the Wagon Wheel when they give one of the
girls a birthday party there. He orders them a bottle of
champagne only the waiters won't serve it because they're
minors but they give him a piece of the cake and he says
any time he can do anything for them to let him know.'

'That's one place we won't have to raid for liquor violations when we've got nothing to do.'

'We aren't looking for liquor violations. Get serious, will you?'

'What the hell for? That happened in my half of the diary. I'm the one who wrote that down for you.'

'And it will do you good to hear it again. Now we come to the boys. Group 4 are ones she has nothing to do with. Chuck Taylor from Carlton. He's a friend of Kincaid, one of her beaux. George Allfielder, her date's roommate at Lehigh; Jim Cartwright, Hadley's roommate at Yale who she meets Dartmouth weekend; and Ted Warner, another of Kincaid's buddies at Carlton. That takes care of them.'

'That takes care of all of them so far. But you're making progress. You're down to the right age level now.'

'Group 5,' said Ford, pointedly ignoring the remarks, 'is boys from home, pals, so to speak. Bill Goodyear, starting Ohio State, Ken Williams, now at Penn, and Dick Bardwell at Wesleyan are fellows she swaps a couple of letters with. She has a couple of unimportant dates with Goodyear over Christmas, his sister's cocktail party and the like. No romance involved with any of them. Other boys are someone named Greg, Ben Tisdale, a Frank, a Chet, and a Phil. No dates or letters, just boys she knows.

'Now we come to boys she has something to say about. First is Bob Chester from Carlton. She has one blind date with him and says he's a show-off and overdrinks. Then there's the soda jerk at Bleeckman's. She says that she and Peggy and Sally stopped for a soda and "to admire the cute boy behind the counter. First decent-looking native I've seen". She has a blind date with a Pete Sheldon from Carlton and that was a flop because he was more interested in some other girl there. The last one is Eaton Trowbridge, also of Carlton, another blind date, and she considers him a dull, gawky character.

'Group 7 is the important one. These are the boys she really has something to do with. First there's Bob Kincaid from Carlton. She meets him September thirtieth at a party and they have several dates and eventually reach the necking stage. She seems to like him but not love him, and in fact, after the Christmas holidays, she cools off towards him, starts making excuses, and doesn't want to park any more. She does go to a couple of parties with him this year, but kind of reluctantly.

'His Carlton rival is a Warren Myers who she meets November sixth. He rushes her hard and fast and tells her he loves her only she doesn't know whether he means it or uses it as an excuse to get her to neck. He tries to overpower her in the clinches to make her fall but it doesn't seem to work and she says that even if it did it would only be physical attraction, not real love. Myers and Kincaid both drop in on her the same night before she leaves for Christmas so they know about each other. Anyway, Myers' technique gets tiresome or something because she makes excuses after vacation and he keeps thinking Kincaid's cutting him out which isn't the case at all.

'Then there's Hank Walton, who's got a crush on her but she thinks of him as a kid brother. They have a few dates. She goes to Lehigh to see him back before she meets all these other boys and after that she's trying to discourage him. He takes her out a few times when they're home for Christmas and tries to come up here, only she keeps turning him down. In his last letter he wants to come up the seventeenth, eighteenth, and nineteenth of this month and she writes in her diary, "Ugh!" According to her, he's too adolescent.'

'Did you say these are the important suspects?'

Ford shrugged. 'She's not sold on any of them

according to her diary. There's this Roger Hadley at Yale. They have a couple of fall dates and a couple of kisses and he tries to soul-kiss her and she won't let him. Not much interest. She says of one letter, "Good heavens, I just wrote him," and of another about his Christmas activities, "I'm afraid I don't care particularly".'

Cameron said with a short laugh, 'And one of the girls at Lambert thought Lowell was upset because he didn't invite her to the prom!'

'She's not pining for him, that's for sure. Then there's a boy at Harvard, Jack Curtis. They have a few fall dates and he has to ask if he can kiss her. She starts discouraging him after a while and calls him the serious type and, after his last letter all about how much beer he can drink, thinks he's pretty adolescent.'

'Scratch Curtis.'

'Scratch Curtis. And now we come to the one boy who does interest her – at least for a little while. That's a Curt Masterson at Dartmouth. He's twenty-six and a veteran and she has a blind date with him the weekend of December second. He's smooth, a little too smooth, she says, but there's nothing adolescent about him. Myers is an amateur in love-making compared to him. She calls him exciting and lets him soul-kiss her, which is more than she lets anyone else do, and she writes him after, but he never writes back. She wonders why a little and then gradually gives up so that her last reference to him, on January fourteenth, is to say he hasn't written but she doesn't care. So there you have it. The whole business. What do you think of it?'

Cameron stretched lazily and said, 'My guess is the old cab driver.'

'Who's done what?'

'Fathered her chee-ild, of course.'

Ford pulled out a cigar and studied it. 'I'm beginning to wonder about that child business. It doesn't fit.' He sighed and sat up in the chair. 'It doesn't look rosy but the only thing I can see is to go ahead with what we planned to do with all these names. Have these guys interviewed, see first if they know where she might be, then how far she'd let them go. She lets Masterson soul-kiss her and I'm doubting anybody got any farther than that, but it's worth a try. That diary of hers might be deliberately misleading and we've got to be sure.'

Cameron said, 'Which ones shall we turn the heat on?'

The Chief scanned a couple of sheets. 'We're going to begin by hitting every boy Lowell had a date with since college opened. There are ten of them. Write them down. At Carlton: Bob Kincaid, eight dates; Warren Myers, six dates; Peter Sheldon, Eaton Trowbridge and Bob Chester, one blind date each. At Lehigh: Hank Walton, six dates. At Harvard: Jack Curtis, five dates. At Yale: Roger Hadley, two dates. At Ohio State, Bill Goodyear, two dates. At Dartmouth, Curt Masterson, one blind date. Got it?'

'I've got it.' Cameron got up and went to the door. He was more serious now. 'Between this and interviewing all the girls on campus, we may come up with a different picture of the kid, one that will give us a clue as to what was on her mind.'

Ford scraped a match across the underside of the desk and applied it to his cigar. 'And if that doesn't get results I'm going to drain that damn lake.'

Tuesday, 7 March

The police routine was thorough and complete. By three o'clock Tuesday afternoon most of the reports were in. Drs Bergman and Hill appeared to be above suspicion. Policemen, in the guise of patients and telephone company employees, had got into their offices and homes and found nothing. People in the houses up and down Maple Street had been questioned but no one had seen a girl walk out of Lambert Annex that Friday noon. Nor had any of the likely stores in town cashed a cheque for fifty dollars. The questioning of Lowell's classmates was still in progress but those first on the list, the ones who took trains and buses out of Bristol sometime after noon on Friday, had nothing to contribute. She had not been noticed at either station.

Cameron and Ford studied the results of their efforts in the Chief's office and, when they had laid aside the last paper, the detective sergeant lighted a cigarette and said, 'Well, if those girls are right and she didn't take any trains or buses, she must still be in town.'

'It looks that way,' Ford grumbled. 'The hell of it is, though, she could have been rubbing shoulders with them all over the station and they'd never notice. A flock of dizzy dames bent on a weekend with some stupid college lout, they don't even know the time of day.

'But we been looking outside and maybe they're right. Maybe she is right here, right under our nose.'

Cameron shook his head and knocked ashes on the

floor. 'What a dead end! A healthy, good-looking young girl walks out of her room and vanishes into thin air. It can't be done, damn it. Somebody has to see her.'

'Somebody has. Our trouble is we're asking the wrong people.'

'We've gone up and down Maple Street. We've even tried the pedestrian angle – who was on that street at that time on Friday?'

'Yeah, but maybe she didn't go out to Maple Street. Maybe she went around back and across campus instead. That's the thing we've been overlooking. She climbs into a skirt, so automatically we start figuring it was to go off the grounds. Maybe she put it on for another reason and didn't leave at all.'

'The hard gemlike flame of genius. You could just possibly have something there, Chief. All the girls are having lunch so they wouldn't be apt to see her.'

Ford tilted back his chair, pulled out a cellophane-wrapped cigar, and studied it. 'And once she gets away from Lambert, nobody'd notice her if they did. Twenty-two hundred girls on campus and she's a freshman. She'd know those in Lambert, a few others, and that's all. She could pass a hundred girls and they wouldn't remember it.'

'And where would she go?'

Ford said, 'I don't know, but I have a hunch.' He tipped the chair forward, pulled over his old-style telephone, and leaned on his elbow with the receiver at his ear. 'Get me the superintendent of grounds at Parker,' he said.

Edward Small answered the phone and Ford asked what was new, got the usual reply, and said, 'Feel like draining the lake?'

'We'll drain it if you like, Frank, but we've been over it pretty thoroughly and I don't think the girl's in it.'

'But we don't know that she isn't! We only did a quick once-over because we had a lot of other irons in the fire. The other irons have burned out and I want to be sure. She could be down at the bottom of the channel or under the dock and it's about time we found out whether she is or not.'

'Okay, Frank. When do you want it? Tomorrow morning?'

'Hell, no. Right now. This afternoon.'

'That's no good, Frank. It takes hours. How far do you want to drain it?'

'Drain it dry, right down to the channel, and then we'll drag the channel.'

'Frank, it'll take hours, and I mean hours! It'll be dark before it's half done.'

'I don't give a damn,' Ford growled. 'The State Police have a generator truck and the Fire Department has one and the college has floodlights. We've been going around in circles long enough. If she's down there I want to know it before I go to bed.'

'Okay. It doesn't matter to me. Come on over.'

Ford and Cameron went out of the office and to the desk. Two reporters were playing gin rummy on a bench by the steps to the front door. When Ford stopped to tell Zileski to take charge and to make arrangements for lights, the reporters picked up their cards and came over. 'Something in the wind, Chief?'

'Maybe. We're going to drain the lake.'

'Got a clue that she's in it?'

'Call it a hunch.' He walked on by and they came along.

'What's the hunch? You're figuring on something, aren't you?'

Ford shook his head. 'It's nothing to go on. The railroad

station was crowded all Friday afternoon but nobody saw
her there. It's starting to look like she didn't leave town. If
she's still around, the reason nobody's seen her might be
because she's down at the bottom of the lake.'

The four of them rode to the superintendent of grounds'
office in the spare police car and Ford told the reporters
of the other blind alleys they had encountered, omitting
the watch they were still keeping on Drs Bergman and
Hill.

'The State Police are interviewing the boys she knew
over at Carlton,' he said. 'The New Haven and Boston
police are co-operating in checking on the guys she knew
at Yale and Harvard. Local police in Philly and Hanover
and everywhere else are going after the other guys. We
haven't got the results yet.'

'What do you think they'll be?'

'Negative.'

'Meaning what?'

'Meaning that, no matter what the guys say, I don't
think it's going to do us any good.'

Ed Small came out and got in the car and the group
drove around on Parker Road to where it overlooked the
dam. Several men were there, down the snowy bank on
the platform where the floodgate wheel was situated.

'I got the grounds keepers here,' said Small. 'You can
station them where you want.'

'Two on the bridge,' said Ford. 'Two on each bank
between the dam and the bridge.'

'What's that for?' asked one of the reporters.

'To spot the body if it washes through the gates,' said
Ford, getting out.

'It's a body now? You think she's dead?'

'If she's been in the lake since Friday she hasn't been holding her breath.'

They skidded gingerly down the steep embankment to the platform and Small gave directions to the men and they took up their stations, two on Higgins Bridge, fifty yards downstream, one on each bank of the river near the dam, another midway between. He unlocked the chain that linked the large steel wheel to the iron railing, signalled his men, and started to turn it. Cameron helped him and the water that tumbled over the dam was thickened by the water that started to gush out from the gates. As the wheel turned, the water through the slots spurted farther and farther out in a yellow, foaming arc. The rapids at the base became more turbulent. They foamed and writhed and the river started coming to life. It picked up its steady crawl to a walk and then a run and the water level crept up higher on the snowy banks.

'I saw something!' came almost at once. It was Small on the platform. He pointed and yelled. 'Something black. Watch for it, Stan!'

The men on the bridge leaned over the high railing intently and peered at the foaming torrent. One of them leaped to the far side where the water below was clearer, then came back, waving his hands and shaking his head in a negative signal.

A car pulled up behind Ford's and Mrs Kenyon came down the bank. Above, on the bare road, girls were beginning to gather, watching and wondering. Cal Leslie appeared and joined the group on the platform. 'Might let a guy know what you're up to,' he said.

'You're supposed to have a nose for news,' retorted Ford. 'What do you want me to do, tell you every time I go to the toilet?'

Someone told the Mitchells. They appeared on the road above, detouring around the growing group of curious students. Melissa and Mrs Mitchell came halfway down the embankment and stopped. Lowell's father came the rest of the way. He was white. 'Is she in the lake?' he asked Ford.

'That's what we're going to find out.'

'You must have a reason. You think she is, don't you? Why?'

Ford didn't take his eyes off the swirling waters. 'You know as much as we do. No reason. We just looked everywhere else so we might as well look here.'

Carl Mitchell bit his lip, then turned and climbed back to his wife and daughter. They said something to him and he answered, then they all turned and looked on in silence as the waters continued to spurt through the gates of the dam.

At four-thirty the lake level was down a foot. A band of cold slimy mud now separated the snowy bank from the water and already the piles that supported the canoe dock in front of the boathouse were coming into view. The men were still watching the swift-running current but three-quarters of an hour was too long to maintain the high pitch of intensity and they had relaxed a little. Chief Ford was no longer on the stone platform. He had long since abandoned that post to roam the area, tramping through the crusty snow up to the bridge, across to the other bank, over again and up to the boathouse, always watching the water.

The girls on the road overlooking the lake had swelled to the hundreds. There was some conversation there, some laughter and joking even, but mostly they just stood and watched.

The Mitchells had not moved. They neither walked nor sat, but watched the roaring water transfixed, praying that Lowell was not in the lake, yet staring as though in hopes of spotting her body when it came through. They alone of the watchers had not relaxed the vigil.

The generator trucks came at six, passing streams of girls hurrying away for dinner. Spotlights had been set up on the roof of the boathouse to light up part of the lake and the trucks jockeyed into position and were tested until their great glare was directed full on the swirling rapids, giving the light of day to the small patch of river that foamed in the gathering darkness. When the lights were set Ford sent Cameron back to headquarters for reliefs and told him to get some food. The watches were staggered so the grounds keepers could have their meals and only the Mitchell family seemed ready to keep their post without eating. They were sitting on the snow now, their coats held close, their collars turned up, their cold hands thrust deep into cold pockets.

The lake was down two and a half feet but the flow of water had not lessened. The thunder of it was distracting in nearby Cornwall House. It was noisy in Maltby House and audible as far away as the dining room of Lambert Annex where Hilda, Marlene, Patty, and Sally toyed with their food and Peggy Woodling frankly said, 'I feel sick.'

At quarter-past seven Ford left and drove home to dinner. Sara had kept it warm in the oven as she and their daughter Mary had already had theirs. He ate quickly and heartily and with a minimum of conversation. Then he went back. The water was pouring through the dam more slowly now. He made the rounds, questioning the watchers and wandering along the muddy bank. Nothing had been seen. The night was dense and black now and only the rapids and the near side of the lake were brightly lighted.

Ed Small approached him, his hands cased in heavy gloves, earmuffs folded down from his cap. Thick clouds swirled out when he spoke. 'What's your plan, Frank, when she's drained?'

'We'll bring the boat down and drag the channel,' replied the Chief, referring to the small outboard kept in the garage in back of the police station. 'If we don't find anything, leave the gates open all night. I want to go over the lake bottom when it's light. The Mitchell girl was walking around there that morning. She might have thrown something in.'

'I don't think we're going to find her.'

'Maybe not, but we're going to be sure. No chance of her floating through the gates without being seen?'

'Not one. Every twig and leaf that's gone through has been spotted.'

They stood together awhile in the bitter cold and watched the garishly lighted water flowing.

Not much studying was being accomplished at Parker that night. The bright lights at the lake and the roar of the water were all too grim a reminder of their macabre purpose, and concentration on the prosaic activities of everyday college life was next to impossible. The girls, kept back on Parker Road by the police, were out in force again, wrapped in their overcoats, the lights of their cigarettes perforating the darkness, and they stood there in silence, fascinated at first, bored later, yet not daring to leave lest they miss the kill.

The Mitchells were still there, chilled and numb, yet bearing the cold with the thought of the much colder water that Lowell might have had to bear. They were no longer on the side of the bank but had moved forward to mingle with the grounds keepers and police, as if the companionship would give them the warmth that the air and Lowell's possible fate had taken away. Mr Mitchell talked to the men from time to time in low tones, mostly as to the likelihood of Lowell's presence in the lake, gaining some solace from the general view that she was not, bolstering his hope with public opinion as though that would be the deciding factor. Mostly the family hovered around Chief Ford, the guiding light, watching his moves and his expressions for clues, but he would not face them. When questioned, he would turn away with a gruff answer that could be interpreted as irritation that she had not been found. A dozen reporters roamed the area like vultures waiting to be fed and there was no doubt as to what their hope was. They only wanted it to be realized before their deadlines. As one of them put it, 'Damn nice of Ford to drain the lake tonight. We can make the morning editions.'

By a little after ten o'clock the lake bottom was bare and only the channel where the river had flowed before the dam was built was still running water through the gates. It was a dozen feet deep there and, fed by the incoming river, would never drain dry. A police car had long since towed up the boat on its two-wheeled trailer rack, and now half a dozen men unhitched it and pulled their weight against it as they guided it carefully down the steep slope to the bared top of the illuminated dam. 'Start from the dam and work upstream,' Ford had ordered and he was one of those to climb aboard in his awkward, flappy overcoat when the boat had been carried over the soggy bottom of the lake to the stream. Two men bent to the oars, for Ford had banned the use of the outboard, and three others, including the Chief, armed themselves with the dragging chains and the grappling poles with their ugly three-pronged hooks. The men bent over the sides and sank their hooks deep and groped along the bottom as the boat moved slowly upstream against the current.

One of the men caught something and was almost pulled overboard. The boat lurched and nearly upset and one of the newsmen on the bank said, 'Ford nearly had himself a swim.' The boat was steadied and the oarsmen let it drift back, catching it with gentle strokes, holding it against the current. The man tugged. Ford dropped his pole and went to help. Dead silence fell over the crowd on the shore. The reporters moved in. The hook came free and Ford and the other man started pulling it up. Melissa Mitchell and her parents turned away. It came out dripping slime.

The oarsmen took up more powerful strokes and the boat moved ahead and the probing continued. The crowd inched slowly along, keeping pace, but the hooks picked up nothing. When the boat passed beyond the glare of the boathouse lights a generator truck rolled forward and picked its way down the narrow path up near the far end of the lake, moving down the steep slope to the shore where it threw its light over the unsearched portion of the channel.

At eleven o'clock the men gave up and rowed back to the dam. It was a silent signal of failure to the watchful student body and the last girl had departed for room and books before they had beached the boat. Eight men set the small craft on the trailer and pushed and pulled it to the top of the embankment. More than that was needed for the generator truck, however, which had got mired on the lake shore. A tow truck with a winch and cable had to be called to pull that out.

Ford did not wait, however. He climbed up the bank and said to Carl Mitchell, 'You can breathe easy. She isn't there,' as he passed.

The reporters caught Ford at the police car when they hitched the boat on back. 'Any statement, Chief?'

'You can say,' said Ford, turning, 'that Lowell Mitchell is not in Parker Lake.'

'Can we quote you?' said a Boston reporter sarcastically.

'What the hell do you want me to say?' said Ford bitterly. 'I don't know anything you don't know. It doesn't mean any more to me than it does to you. We'll keep on looking. That's all I can tell you.'

'You expected to find her there, didn't you?'

'I did and I didn't. I just wanted to know, that's all.'

They left him and he grumbled as he opened the car door. Cameron came up and nodded at the huddled Mitchell family standing alone on the road. 'Those poor people. They've been here seven hours without a let-up, without any food or anything.'

'I don't figure they got much appetite anyhow,' said Ford.

'Okay to invite them to have a cup of coffee with us?'

Ford looked pained for a moment. Then he said tonelessly, 'Yeah. Go ahead.'

They had coffee at a little diner two blocks from headquarters. Ford and Cameron sat on one side of the table in the booth while the three Mitchells crowded in the other. Melissa, quiet and solemn, with her big brown eyes showing the pain that lay behind, nodded at the suggestion of coffee though it was obviously a novelty to her. She had still scarcely spoken in Ford's presence. Mrs Mitchell, on the other side of her husband, was equally quiet and her alert eyes were tired and harassed. Only Mitchell himself seemed to want to talk.

He toyed with his spoon and directed his remarks to the tabletop in front of him. 'You were saying, Chief,' he said in a tired voice, 'that one girl who disappeared from Parker was never found. You traced her to a doctor's office in Springfield, but you couldn't prove anything. Why couldn't you?'

A young waitress in a soiled uniform slapped five mugs of coffee with cream on the table and Ford, without waiting for anyone else, dumped two heaped teaspoons of sugar in his and stirred. 'We couldn't find her there,' he said shortly.

'But you knew she went there.'

'We didn't know it. The ticket agent remembered selling her a train ticket to Springfield and we found a cab driver who remembered taking her to the building this doc has his office in. That's where we stopped. She had signed out for several nights so we lost a few days right there and by the time we got to the doctor, if he'd killed her, he had time to get rid of her. Never got any farther than that, though. He was too slick for us. Her suitcase showed up in the Connecticut River and it even had the clothes she'd been wearing in it. We never did find out what he did with the body.'

'Couldn't you give him the third degree?'

Ford smiled wryly. 'We don't do that sort of thing and if we did we couldn't do it to an old guy like him and even if we could we couldn't even be sure she went to him. We only guessed at that.'

'You were pretty certain, though.'

Mrs Mitchell put her hand on her husband's arm. 'What

difference does it make, Carl? We know that has nothing to do with what happened to Lowell.'

'I know,' said Mitchell, 'but any parent who's lost a daughter like this, I know how they feel. It doesn't help, but I want to know about other people who've been in our circumstances.'

Ford said, 'I might as well tell you; we've been keeping an eye on a couple of doctors here in town whose reputations aren't too good. We thought she might be hiding out but it looks like a blind alley. I don't think that's why she left college.'

There was silence for a while and Ford slurped his coffee a little noisily and unconsciously. Melissa watched him but with neither interest nor distaste. It was a vacant stare unmindful of his manners. She watched him because he was tied up in the fate of her elder sister and there was a bond, therefore, between him and Lowell, more right then than between her parents and Lowell, and if you couldn't see Lowell herself, seeing him was the next best thing.

'I've arranged to broadcast an appeal,' said Mitchell at last. 'You still approve of that?'

Ford nodded vaguely. He wished they'd go home. He was tired and they wouldn't let him relax. He wanted to forget, but they reminded him. Because they were nice people and had pinned their faith on him, he felt keenly the responsibility of restoring their daughter to them.

'It's going to be day after tomorrow,' Mr Mitchell went on when it was apparent a nod was all he was going to get.

'Where and what time?' said Ford.

'Springfield at seven o'clock in the evening. Is that all right?'

'Probably is.'

'And I've hired a private detective.'

Mitchell watched the Chief carefully for his reaction but all he got was another nod.

'It's a man from Philadelphia, a John Monroe.'

'Uh-huh.'

'Ever heard of him?'

'Can't say I have.'

'He's very well known.'

Ford said merely, 'We'll be glad to co-operate with him.'

'You don't think he'll do much good?'

The Chief shrugged. 'I can't see what he can do that we haven't, but he may come up with some angle we've overlooked. It's possible.'

'But you don't think so.'

'No.'

Mitchell nodded and his mouth tightened into a hard line. 'Thank you for the coffee, Chief. I think we'd better be going. We're very tired.'

Cameron said, 'We'll drop you off,' and Ford's mouth twitched.

They drove out on Maple Street to the inn and the Mitchells got out, climbed the steps to the porch, and went into the old Victorian building, up to their suite on the second floor from which they could see the windows of Lowell's room in Lambert Annex.

'That Ford,' said Mitchell bitterly to his wife as they took off their things, 'he's inhuman. This is just a job to him, like finding a pocket-book. He doesn't give a damn about Lowell as a person. He's only looking for her because he's supposed to. I actually believe he was sorry she wasn't in the lake.'

Perhaps Carl Mitchell was right. Perhaps Chief Ford

was lacking in human sympathy. The signs that he wasn't were hard to find. For once he did not chastise his daughter for still being up when he got home at midnight. He stared at her bending over her books a little longer than necessary and kissed her good night a little more tenderly. That was all.

Wednesday, 8 March

Girls walking along Parker Road on their way to class Wednesday morning were treated to an unusual sight. In place of the lake, a small river wound through a vast area of frozen mud and washed through the floodgates of the open dam. Wandering around on the icy basin were half a dozen men including, among them, Chief Ford. They seemed to be looking for something.

Whatever it was Ford thought might be there, they did not find it and if he was disappointed it did not show. He gave the order to close the floodgates and returned to headquarters with Cameron and Lassiter in silence. The two men did not press the matter and conceded that Ford, in his meticulous way, was merely taking advantage of the dry lake bed to make sure, lest the question later arise, that there was nothing there.

It was the start of the fifth barren day of the hunt, the fifth day without a clue, and a day that promised no likelihood of uncovering one. There was a lethargy among the men of the Bristol police force brought about by inaction and the feeling that whatever reports arrived would contribute nothing to the question of Lowell Mitchell's disappearance.

Into that atmosphere came the morning mail and, with it, a change. Activity seemed a little more purposeful, conversation a little more animated, laughter a little louder than a policeman's crack was generally worth. A letter had come.

It was addressed to Mr and Mrs Carl B. Mitchell c/o Bristol Police, Bristol, Mass., and was postmarked 4.30 p.m. 7 Mar 1950, Highland Falls, N.Y.

Mitchell was telephoned at the inn and he was down in fifteen minutes, hatless, breathless, and white. Ford handed him the letter and he stood there at the desk, turning it over and over, looking at the handwriting, the postmark, the stamp, the plain white back, afraid to open it. 'Think it's a ransom note?' he said in a voice that quivered.

'If it is,' said Ford, 'it's the first kidnapper I ever heard of who tried to contact his victim through the police.'

The architect did not even seem to hear. He fondled the letter as though it were Lowell herself. The suspense grew too much for the Chief. He opened his penknife and held it out. 'Stop kidding yourself,' he said. 'Maybe it's from the finance company.'

Mitchell flicked a glance at him then, took the knife, and slit the envelope. His face was a strained mask. Slowly he pulled the folded sheet from inside.

'Go easy handling it,' said the Chief. 'There may be fingerprints.'

Mitchell nodded, opened it by holding the tips of the corners, read it, and exhaled slowly. No change came over his face. He handed the paper over to Ford, who held it just as gingerly. It was a short note, written in shaky longhand.

7 *March* 1950

Dear Mr and Mrs Mitchell,
You can rest easy about your daughter Lowell. She is visiting friends near here and will be back in a few days.

There was no signature.

Ford held it up to the light and looked for a watermark. 'Cheap paper,' he said, laying it carefully on the desk. 'Know anybody from up there?'

'I don't have the faintest idea. No.'

'Does Lowell?'

'I don't know. Not to my knowledge. What do you think it means?'

'I don't know. What's your idea, Burt?' he said to the detective, who was standing behind his shoulder.

'If you still like the abortion theory, it could be that's where she went. Either that or it may be the work of a crank.'

'A crank?' said Mitchell. 'You mean someone would deliberately mislead the police?'

'It often happens in a case like this that gets a lot of publicity,' said Ford. 'A lot of little people want to get in on the show.'

'That doesn't mean that's what it is in this case,' said Cameron. 'She may very well be up there.'

'Having an abortion?' said Mitchell coldly. 'If she ever needed one, and she wouldn't, she'd come to me.'

The three reporters who were staying at the inn arrived just then, obviously hastily dressed and sheepish. 'What's up, Chief?'

Ford said, 'You guys are getting lazy. If I was an editor you'd be driving cabs.' Then he read the note and told them the story.

When he was through Mitchell said, 'Do you think the sender can be traced?'

'I hope he can.' He turned to Cameron and said, 'Here, tack this letter to a board and take it over to the State Police. Have the lab develop whatever fingerprints they can find and send them to Washington and the Highland Falls police. Then send them the letter and see what they can do.' He turned back to the architect and said, 'Give us a few days and we may have something for you on this.'

That was the most satisfaction Mitchell could expect and he nodded and went out, followed by the gentlemen of the press, who headed for the nearest phone. Cameron came back with a piece of board and watched them go. 'You know, Chief,' he said, 'that Mitchell answers his own question. He says Lowell would go to him if she got in trouble, then says she couldn't get in trouble. That's just the attitude that would keep her from going to him.'

'You think she's in trouble, Burt?'

'It's possible, isn't it?'

'Not without a man. Who's your choice, one of the movie stars she lists?'

'Who's yours?'

'I'll tell you after I get the reports on her boyfriends.'

The first reports on the men in Lowell's life came in that afternoon but they did not give Ford his answer. The State Police, in conjunction with the Carlton campus police, had completed their interviews with the five boys she had dated.

Bob Kincaid's was first. He admitted that he had seen her several times and was very fond of her. However, since the Christmas holidays she had seemed to lose interest in him and he felt that a fellow classmate, Warren Myers, was the cause. Yes, they had parked – 'You know. Heck, who doesn't?' But it was certainly nothing serious. He'd kissed her, but as for going any further, definitely not.

Q: 'Did you ever try?'

A: 'No.'

Q: 'Did she ever, at any time, act as though she wanted you to?'

A: 'No.'

Q: 'Would you have if she had wanted you to?'

A: 'Gee, I don't know. That's a hard one. I never thought about it.'

Q: 'That's the truth? Remember, this is confidential. We don't care what you answer as long as it's the truth. We've got to know exactly what her moral character is.'

A: 'It's the honest-to-God truth. I never even thought about it.'

Q: 'Have you ever gone any further with any other girl?'

A: 'I – what's that got to do with it? Don't you believe me?'

Q: 'Just answer the question.'

A: 'I – well, I – just once. Just a little bit.'

Q: 'So it wasn't something new. You'd done it before, but you didn't think of doing it with her? Never?'

A: 'No, never. She's a nice girl. She isn't anybody you'd even dream of trying something like that with.'

Q: 'Do you think it's possible she would let someone else go further?'

A: 'No. Well, heck, I don't think so. I couldn't swear to it. A girl can be cold to one guy and hot to another.'

Q: 'But you doubt it?'

A: 'I doubt it.'

The interview with Warren Myers produced much the same information. He had seen her quite a few times before Christmas and he had tried several times this year, but she was always busy. Did he think she was making excuses, or was she really busy?

A: 'I don't know. She goes around with another guy from here and I think he was giving her pretty much of a rush. She was probably really busy. Hell, we hadn't had any fight or anything. She liked me the last time she saw me so I don't know why she'd suddenly say no every time I asked her out unless she really had another date.'

Warren Myers had apparently had no more experience than the Kincaid boy with regard to Lowell's other charms. He had kissed her and that was all.

Q: 'Soul kiss?'

A: 'No.'

Q: 'She wouldn't let you?'

A: 'No.'

Q: 'How was she in the clinches? Hot, cold, what?'

A: 'Medium, I guess. She liked it all right, but she wasn't mad about it.'

Q: 'You told her you were in love with her. Did you mean it or was it just to make her warm up?'

A: 'Who told you that?'

Q: 'Never mind. We know about it. Was it just a line?'

A: 'I don't know. I think I did love her. I don't mean marriage and all that. I mean, well, I'd like to go steady, give her my pin, things like that. Maybe in a couple of years you might get really serious, marriage and all.'

Q: 'But you stopped loving her?'

A: 'Well, hell, she turned down my dates and she wasn't getting serious about me and, what the hell, there's no percentage in that. I guess I wasn't really very much in love with her. I mean it didn't break me up her not going out with me any more. I mean I was sorry, but hell, I didn't feel like jumping out the window.'

The State Police report also included interviews with Robert Chester, Peter Sheldon, and Eaton Trowbridge, all of whom had seen her just once. They had even less information to transmit than Kincaid and Myers.

'Just about what I thought they'd be,' said Ford to Cameron. 'If she's in trouble, it's a cinch it's not their fault.'

'So where does that leave us, with some guy kidnapping her?'

Ford shook his head. 'I don't think she'd accept a ride with a strange man.'

Cameron put his hands on his hips and said with a leering smile, 'You don't believe she'd ride with strange men and you don't believe she'd shack up with some guy. Where's the hard-boiled policeman who doesn't think any girl retains her virginity beyond puberty? You're going soft over a little eighteen-year-old kid.'

'The hell I am,' growled Ford. 'I'm just facing facts, that's all. There are a few good girls in the world, not many, God knows, but a few and the facts say she's one of them. My convictions about girls in general don't enter into it. I've got to face the facts.

'No, I don't buy that for an answer, Burt. If you want my opinion, we'd be ten miles ahead of where we are if we knew where she was going when she walked out of that dorm.'

Wednesday Night

Douglas MacDonald was the duty sergeant Wednesday night when the phone rang about eight-thirty. A girl was on the wire, tense and nervous. 'This is Barbara Wilfred,' she said. 'I live in Taylor House right next door to Lambert Annex. I just saw a man outdoors. He's peering into the windows of the Annex lounge.'

Peeping Toms or a prowler on campus weren't unheard-of things and normally Sergeant MacDonald would refer the girl to the campus police or, if necessary, dispatch a squad car to frighten the intruder away. But Lowell Mitchell was missing from Lambert Annex and that made it a different matter.

'Can you see him now?' he said, a little thrill of excitement prickling the hairs on his neck.

'No. I'm by the phone.'

'Get another girl by the window to keep him in view,' MacDonald ordered. 'Stay on the line and tell me every move he makes.' He turned to Vernon at the switchboard. 'Get the Chief on the other phone and tell him there's a prowler at Lambert Annex and give me the mike.'

Vernon leaped for the mike and the phone.

'Call the campus police and have them send out the alarm,' MacDonald told him. 'Got another girl?' he asked Barbara Wilfred, and said into the mike, 'Unit 1 and Unit 2, stand by.'

'I've got a girl at the window. She says he's still there. He's looking in the front window now.'

'Unit 1, Petroff reporting.'

'Unit 2. Hanson. Go ahead.'

MacDonald said, 'There's a strange man looking in the front window of Lambert Annex. I want him brought in. Petroff, go up Maple Street. Hanson, come down Maple and turn down Parker Road to cut him off from the rear. Petroff, hold at Maple and Sizer until Hanson makes his turn, then go in the drive between Lambert and Taylor. Keep talking, sister,' he snapped into the phone.

'He's still looking in the front window. He's backed away a little and is kneeling down. He's got a pencil flashlight and seems to be holding it in his teeth, shining it on his hands.'

Vernon was saying, 'Chief? Vernon speaking. Something going on at Lambert Annex. Somebody is spying through the windows.'

'No sirens,' said MacDonald into the mike. 'I don't want him frightened away.'

'Now he's standing up again,' said the girl. 'He's coming this way. No, he's going around to the side windows of the lounge. He's disappeared in the bushes by the window.'

'Petroff and Hanson. He's at the side in the bushes.'

'Petroff reporting. I'm at Maple and Sizer and have the Annex in view. I don't see anyone.'

'Send Maddox on foot to cover the front walk. Keep him low behind the hedge. Don't be seen.'

Vernon was dialling the campus police. 'Ford's on his way,' he said.

'Where's the man?'

'He's still in the bushes, we think. She can't see him.'

'Hanson calling. Am approaching Parker Road. What are my instructions?'

'Turn down Parker with your lights off,' said MacDonald. 'Stop back of Lambert A. Have Wolfe ready to chase on foot if necessary. If he gets in range of your lights, turn them on him. Give me a call when stationed.'

'He's in the bushes. Gloria just saw his flashlight.'

'The campus cops are alerted,' said Vernon. 'They're moving in.'

'Stationed. Lights off,' said Hanson.

'Maddox has the front covered,' reported Petroff. 'Ready to go.'

'Hold one minute. Wait for the campus cops to get in position.'

'He's come out of the bushes,' reported Barbara. 'He's starting to move around towards the back.'

'Go get him, Petroff. He's heading around in back.'

'On my way.'

'He's stopped,' said the girl. 'He's running back to the bushes. A car is turning in the drive.'

'He's in the bushes,' said MacDonald.

'The car's swinging around,' said Barbara over the phone. 'It's stopping with its lights on the bushes. The man is running.'

'Where to?' snapped MacDonald.

'Where, Gloria? Across the front lawn. Towards the street. No. A policeman is there. He's turned. He's running around in back of Ann on the other side.'

'Get ready, Hanson,' said MacDonald. 'He's coming your way. Maddox is chasing him.'

'Don't see him yet,' reported Hanson.

MacDonald turned to Vernon. 'Get me that wall map.'

Vernon leaped to the heavy cloth street map of Bristol

and outlying districts, lifted it off its hook, and flopped it on the desk in front of the sergeant. MacDonald helped him straighten it while barking into the microphone, 'Come on, report! Who's seen him?'

The radio came to life immediately. 'Hanson. Not in sight. A car has just turned down Parker Road.' There was a pause, then a sharp, 'There he is, in the road! Get him, Rod!' There were some jumbled phrases.

MacDonald was fairly screaming. 'What's going on? Keep in touch. Tell me what's going on!'

Hanson was back on again. 'It's the Chief. The guy was sneaking across the road when the Chief turned in and caught him with his lights. Wolfe's chasing him. He's gone down the slope to the lake. I've driven across the street. He fell on the snow but he's up and heading for the woods along the north end. He may come up the hill in the president's yard, or up around there.'

'Petroff, get up to Quadrangle Road. Pick up Maddox if you can, but head that guy off if he climbs up the hill through the woods.'

'Petroff. On my way.'

'Here come the campus cops,' said Hanson. 'On the run. The Chief is getting out of his car. He's pointing to the north end of the lake. They're going down the hill. Wolfe and the guy have disappeared.'

There was silence for a little and MacDonald chewed his fingernails and studied the map. Then came a voice. 'Petroff. Couldn't find Maddox but am touring Quadrangle Road. Nobody in sight.'

'Any students up there? Get them to help.'

'Right.'

Hanson's voice came in once more. 'Three campus cops

have gone into the woods. They're following his tracks. The other two are cutting around the top of the hill.'

'Okay. Keep your eyes open in case he doubles back.'

There was more silence, two minutes of it, before the next report. It was Hanson again, saying, 'Here come the floodlights. The boathouse floodlights are on.'

'Right. Any news?'

'Not yet. Wait a minute. There's splashing in the lake. Someone fell in, I think.' He paused, then went on. 'I can't see who it is, he's out of range of the spots. Here he comes! It's the guy. He's coming through the mud back onto the bank. He's all alone.'

'Get after him, damn it. Go get him.'

'He's heading for the boathouse. Here come some others chasing him. They have him in view. Want me to leave?'

MacDonald said frantically, 'No. Stick to the radio. Give me a running report.'

'Okay. He's out of sight now, under the boathouse, I think, down in the mud. Wolfe and two others are approaching. He's hiding out but they know he's there. They're stopping and talking. Wolfe's telling them something. I still can't see the guy. He's under there somewhere.

'Now Wolfe's moving forward again. The other two are fanning out. They're going to surround the boathouse. One of them's waving at somebody else, I can't see who. They're moving in on him now. Wolfe's getting close.

'There he goes! Out the south side. He's scrambling up the snow out of the mud. He's up and going around the rim of the lake. He's heading towards the dam.'

'Stay with him,' MacDonald urged.

'There goes the Chief. He's driving down to intercept him. I'm following. The others are after him, but he's gaining on them. I'm losing him in the dark, he's out of range of the spots and he's not coming up the bank. Ford's down there. He's driving down the footpath to Higgins Bridge. I can see Ford's headlights but I can't see the guy. Wait a minute. Ford's got him cut off. He's starting to come up the hill towards me. I'll—'

There was a dull explosion over the radio, then Hanson came on again. 'Ford cornered him. He fired a warning shot and the guy's stopped. He's got his hands up. Ford has him in his flashlight. He's going back down to Ford with his hands up. Wolfe's catching up. So are the others. Ford's got him, Mac. It's all over.'

MacDonald wiped a sweaty brow. 'Hear that, Petroff? It's all over.'

'I heard it. I'm heading back to join them.'

They brought the man into the police station and they weren't inclined to be gentle with him. He was a young lad of roughly twenty-three with blond wavy hair and would have been quite good-looking in other circumstances. At that moment, however, he was much too frightened and pale to appear anything but ghastly. Ford had him by one arm and Wolfe, a big man bordering on the fat side, had his other firmly gripped with both hands. Two of the campus policemen were with them as well as Hanson, Petroff, and Maddox and, with that army around, the slim boy looked ridiculously inept and harmless.

The humour of it was lost on Ford, who sat the lad down in a chair without ceremony and, flanked by his men, stood over him.

'Now, sonny. You and I are going to talk.'

The lad said, 'I want a lawyer,' in a way that indicated he had no expectation of getting his request or knowledge of what he would do if it were granted.

'What's your name, sonny?'

'Herbert. Herbert McKay.'

'Let's see your wallet.'

The boy said, 'I haven't done anything,' but he reached in his hip pocket and produced it.

Ford looked it over and examined his driver's licence and seemed satisfied the culprit was telling the truth. 'What were you doing around Lambert Annex tonight, McKay?'

'Nothing.'

'He seemed to be writing something,' MacDonald put in.

'Let's see what you were writing, McKay.'

The boy made a gesture of denial, then thought better of it and pulled a small notebook out of his pocket. Ford read it. 'Four girls playing bridge in far left-hand corner by card table. One girl sitting on couch reading a heavy book. Girl studying in chair by piano, knitting a sweater. Bridge players laugh—'

'What the hell is this?' said Ford.

'Nothing. I wasn't doing anything. I was just watching them.'

'What do you know about the Mitchell girl's disappearance?'

'Nothing.'

'Empty your pockets.'

The boy stood up unhappily and started pulling things from pocket after pocket, a dirty handkerchief, jack-knife, set of keys, pencil, pocket flashlight, change, and some clippings. Ford picked up the clippings. One was head-lined, EIGHT STATE ALARM OUT FOR MISSING PARKER FRESHMAN; another, STILL NO CLUE TO PARKER GIRL'S DISAPPEARANCE. A third read, COPS BALKED SEEKING GIRL.

Ford's mouth was grim. 'We're on to something at last,' he announced.

The boy grew whiter if possible. 'Honest, Captain. I swear it. I don't know anything about her disappearance. I—' He slumped down into the chair in dejection. 'Honest, this is the truth. I work for the Boston *Post-Traveler*. Call them up if you don't believe it.'

Ford was still grim. 'We will, sonny. We will.'

'They – I just got out of journalism school a year ago. I want to be a reporter. They gave me a job a couple of months ago. A copy boy. I've been trying to get ahead. They wouldn't let me report anything. I – I thought maybe, if I did a story that was good, they might give me a break.'

Ford's face was more threatening than ever. 'Keep talking.'

'Well, we've got reporters out here and they're covering the police angle and I decided if I could get a new approach that was good, the paper might run it and I might get a break.' His handkerchief was on the table with the rest of his belongings so he wiped a perspiring brow with his hand. 'I wanted to get a human-interest approach. I wanted to do a story on how Lowell's classmates were reacting to her disappearance. All I was doing was peeking in the window trying to see what they were doing and how they were acting.'

'Your paper tell you to do this?'

'Oh no, sir. This is on my own time. They don't know I'm here. I was just going to write it and hand it in and see if they would run it. I was just trying to make myself a break. I want to be a reporter.'

Ford turned away, swearing obscenely. He growled at MacDonald. 'If this doesn't beat all!'

'What are you going to do?' MacDonald said.

'Do?' roared the Chief. 'I'm going to lock him up!'

The boy said, 'You can't. What for? I haven't done anything.'

'I'm locking you up for vagrancy, trespassing, for resisting arrest, for being a Peeping Tom. I'm going to throw the book at you. I'm going to send you to jail for a hundred years.' He turned to MacDonald. 'Get the Boston *Post-Traveler* on the phone. Check his story, double-check it, and check it again. I want to know everything he's done since he was born. Particularly, I want to know what he did last Friday. Check till it comes out your ears!'

MacDonald said snappily, 'Yes, sir,' and Ford stormed home in disgust.

Thursday, 9 March

The Thursday morning papers gave the anonymous letter nearly as full a treatment as had the evening papers before them. The tenor of the articles gave the impression that the case would break wide open at any moment. The optimistic reader viewed Lowell as virtually back in her parents' arms. The Police Department view was somewhat less hopeful. Thursday was not a day that generated a lot of promise around headquarters. A lot of things were happening but nothing changed. The McKay lad was released with a warning to stay in Boston when a thorough investigation showed not only that he did work for the Boston *Post-Traveler* but that he could never have met Lowell Mitchell, much less have seen her on Friday. The rest of the reports were in on the other boys Lowell had dated and they were all the same. The degree of fondness for Lowell varied but her behaviour with them did not. Some she kissed, some she held at arm's length. None of them, so far as could be determined, had had more intimate relations with her. None of them thought it likely that anyone else had, and none of them had seen her after she left Parker that Friday noon. Ford's particular interest in Curt Masterson bore no fruit. The date had been a substitute for his own girl with whom he had had a fight. He had liked Lowell, yes, but he and his girl had made up and he had carried the affair with the Mitchell girl no further.

This was the day that Carl Mitchell brought in his

hireling, Private Detective John Monroe of Philadelphia, and introduced him to the Chief. The reporters, for lack of anything else, contemplated building up a feud between the two but Ford was as unco-operative as he had been previously. If he didn't greet the man warmly, it was because Ford didn't exude warmth. Suffice it to say he was polite and, as nothing else was pressing at that time, he secluded himself in his office with Monroe and Mr Mitchell and went over everything that had been done since the case opened. Ford wasn't a generous man but he was open to suggestions and, if there were anything he had overlooked, he wanted to know it. In addition, a review of activities might give him a better perspective himself, might suggest an approach he had not considered.

If he had any hopes along that line, however, they came to nothing. Monroe, a thoughtful man with a receding hairline and glasses, could only nod and comment that the investigation had been pretty thorough. The rehashing only further convinced Ford of the same thing. He felt inwardly sorry for both Monroe and Mitchell, the former because there was nothing he could do that hadn't been done, and the latter because he was paying for nothing, unless the expense gave him a satisfaction in a feeling of contribution to the case.

The investigation itself was slowing down. There were no new lines to follow and the old ones were petering out. Drs Bergman and Hill were still under surveillance but the reports continued to be so negative that Ford was tempted to abandon a watch that left his force shorthanded. The only other activity still in operation was the slow canvassing of the student body at Parker and the reports that dribbled in were varied, but again not helpful. Many girls thought Lowell had seemed extremely depressed the whole week preceding her disappearance but whether or not that conclusion was arrived at in view of later incidents was difficult to say. Many other girls and the teachers of Lowell's classes thought she was perfectly normal. In any event, none of the girls could give any plausible theory to account for her departure, though several produced highly implausible ones.

Monroe went out in the afternoon to look around on his own and, when questioned by reporters, stated it was too early yet to advance any theory. Ford spent his afternoon at the station waiting for news that did not come and grumbling about the lack of cleanliness in the place, the sloppy condition of his men, and the deterioration of the force in the years since the war. His subordinates pussyfooted around him with the exception of Cameron, who merely growled back about the deterioration of the Police Chief since the war, but even he began to give Ford a wide berth towards the end of the afternoon and all the men breathed a sigh of relief when Ford stalked off for home at four o'clock.

At home his mood failed to grow better and he paced the floor like a caged animal, making one-syllable answers to remarks by his wife in a way that discouraged conversation and speaking sharply to his daughter when she let the door slam coming in. He sat down with the evening papers when they came, but was up and about again less than fifteen minutes later. Three times he called the station to get the same news. No further reports.

In the middle of his dinner he rose suddenly from the table without a word and returned to the living room, snapping on the radio, ripping the cellophane wrapper off a cigar which he promptly started to chew, and continuing his pacing of the floor.

The seven o'clock station break came and there was a few seconds' pause. Mrs Ford said, 'Whatever are you listening to?' but her husband merely ground his cigar more thoroughly between his teeth.

'We interrupt our regular news programme,' the announcer said, 'to bring you a special appeal by Carl Bemis Mitchell, father of eighteen-year-old Lowell Mitchell, who disappeared from Parker College last Friday. Mr Mitchell.' Then Mitchell's voice came on, shaky and slightly choked. 'Lowell darling, this is your father. If you can hear me, wherever you are, whatever you're doing, please get in touch with us, please spare us the torture and misery and worry of not knowing what's happened to you, not knowing where you are, not knowing—' There was silence for two or three seconds. ' . . . not knowing whether you're alive or dead. Remember, my darling, that we love you, that we want to help you. No matter what the reason is that you went away, no matter what troubles forced you to feel that was the only solution, your father and mother and sister are eager to share your burdens. You don't have to face your problems alone. Bring them to us. We will work them out.'

He paused there, either for breath or to get the tears out of his voice. Then he went on. 'Lowell darling, if you feel you can't come back, if you feel you must solve your problems alone, we will try to understand. Only please get in touch with us. Please let us know that you're alive and well. If you have any love in your heart for us, spare us this agony of not knowing what has become of you.

'Wherever you are, whatever you're doing, may God bless you and keep you and bring you back to us. Good night, darling. Please come home!'

The announcer came on again with his smooth

professional voice. 'Ladies and gentlemen, that was Carl Bemis Mitchell, father of Lowell Mitchell, who's been missing from Parker College since last Friday. If you have seen her or if you have any information about her, please get in touch with Mr Mitchell at 560 Evergreen Avenue in Philadelphia, or with the Police Department in Bristol, Massachusetts, immediately. That's Carl Mitchell, five-six-oh Evergreen Avenue in Philadelphia, or the Bristol Police Department. Mr Mitchell is offering a reward of five thousand dollars to anyone with information leading to Lowell's being found alive and twenty-five hundred dollars for information leading to the identification of her body.

'And now, the news . . .'

Ford snapped the radio off and went to his room. And in Springfield Mr and Mrs Carl Mitchell and their daughter Melissa walked out of the broadcasting studio and took a taxi to the railroad station for a bite of supper and the long wait for the eight-fifty-five train to New York. Everything they could do had been done and the work at the office could not be suspended indefinitely. The Mitchells were going home to wait, and to hope.

Monday, 13 March

The weekend passed with no developments and now the Bristol police were doing nothing about the case. The last of Lowell's acquaintances had been interviewed without result and there was no further line of investigation to follow. Ford even pulled the watch on the two doctors so that, by Monday morning, everyone on the Bristol police force had turned to other duties. Lowell Mitchell had apparently vanished into thin air at noon on 3 March and, while the case was still very much open on the books, until some new lead was turned up, nothing more could be done.

Most of the reporters had gone by now, resorting to the telephone for coverage. Their last articles were headlined, MITCHELL GIRL DISAPPEARANCE STILL A MYSTERY. The stories were shorter and no longer found on page one. The interest was waning but all the while the hordes stood poised, ready to descend again on Bristol should the slightest clue turn up regarding Lowell's whereabouts or her fate.

Nothing had come of the anonymous letter. Finger-prints developed on the sheet were not in the files in Washington or in Highland Falls. A watch on the mail collections for a second such letter had proved fruitless. Postmen still had their eye out but the Highland Falls police had abandoned the hunt so that on Monday morning, 13 March, Private Detective John Monroe was the only person still taking an active interest in the case.

It snowed that day. Two inches fell on Bristol, but Monroe was out in it for hours and when he came in he had reached a conclusion. He gave it out to the two or three reporters representing the news services who were still in town and, later on, he gave it to Ford. It was his theory, he said, that Lowell Mitchell had been abducted or had met with foul play. In either case she was dead and the likelihood of finding her body, other than by accident, was not large. Pressed by the reporters for the basis of his conclusions, he stated that an examination of Lowell's diary and papers indicated no discontentment and no plan for an abrupt departure. His interviews with Lowell's friends further bore this out and showed her to be very much contented with Parker College and college life. He discounted reports that she had been depressed shortly before her disappearance, labelling such reports as second guesses and saying that no one at the time had considered her dispirited. Her failure to pack a suitcase or cash her cheque or make any arrangement for her belongings indicated to him that she planned a quick return. He believed that her illness was real but not serious, and the fact that her departure was unwitnessed was accident rather than design.

Just how she could meet with foul play or abduction in broad daylight in the well-populated, friendly town of Bristol he wasn't ready to say, but he was certain it had been effected. He could supply that answer, he assured reporters, if he knew where she was going when she left Parker. If she had been going any distance she might have willingly accepted a ride from an apparently friendly motorist, but her destination would have had to be a place near the outskirts of town, else her attacker could never have concealed his purpose long enough to carry her beyond earshot of help.

Working on that theory, therefore, he was trying to find out what possible places she could have had in mind. So far nearby Carlton College was the only likelihood but he had no answer to the question as to why she should want to pay anyone there a surprise visit.

To the press he had no answer, but he did advance one to Ford. If the girl were pregnant and one of the Carlton boys the father, she might have been on her way to face him with the fact. Even Ford, however, dubious as he was about any girl's morals, refused to take that idea seriously. Lowell's diary and exhaustive interviews with the boys she knew there had convinced him that if she did have sexual relations with men they weren't Carlton men.

Monroe did not discard his theory though. She might have started there for some other reason, or she might have been going somewhere else near the edge, or out, of town, a store, a night club, a rendezvous of some kind. In any event, she had encountered someone who held her against her will and had probably killed her. So convinced was he of that that he went around the station offering five dollars to three that if she were found she would not be alive.

He had no takers.

Tuesday night, however, a report came in that indicated Monroe was wrong. It changed the complexion of the case so abruptly that MacDonald called up the Chief to relay it. A Mrs Emily Durand boarded a Greyhound bus in Cleveland bound for Chicago and sat next to a young girl about eighteen. This girl had brown hair and brown eyes, was wearing a tan polo coat and a grey skirt. The girl's coat was open and, underneath, she had on a yellow button-up sweater and white blouse. She was carrying a brown leather pocket-book and a twenty-five-cent mystery story. The girl had not been conversational but had admitted she came from the East, though she did not say where she was going.

Mrs Durand had not paid much attention to her seat mate until after she got off the bus at Toledo and happened across the description of Lowell in a newspaper there. Mrs Durand had called the police and they were at that moment waiting to pick up the girl in Chicago.

'Looks like we got something at last, Chief,' said Mac-Donald after dispensing that information.

'If they don't let her get away,' replied Ford over the phone. 'What are they waiting for her in Chicago for? Couldn't they pick her up someplace in between?'

'No. The lady didn't call them until the bus was almost there.'

Ford muttered something that sounded like swearing, then said, 'Call me the minute you hear anything.' He hung up and stared at the phone for a minute. His wife came in and said, 'Have they found her?'

The Chief shrugged. 'Maybe. Maybe not.' His was a gloomy point of view but he slept through that night without once waking, which was the first time that had happened since the night of 3 March.

Wednesday, 15 March

Ford received his first jolt when he got down to the station Wednesday morning. The girl in question had not been on the bus when it pulled into Chicago the night before. Police had boarded it the moment it arrived and gone through it, seat by seat, person by person, but there was no young girl. Somewhere between Toledo and the Windy City she had got off. Attempts were being made to trace her, of course, but what had started out as a routine identification job had developed into something infinitely more complex. Passengers on the bus had been questioned but the results were not yet in.

Meanwhile, the phones were starting to ring. The AP, UP, and INS had sent out the item the night before and now reporters from Boston, Springfield, Providence, and other surrounding cities were calling in for late developments.

Noon brought them. The report was in. Midwest police had narrowed the area of their hunt for the missing girl to South Bend and Michigan City. The girl was definitely established as having been on the bus when it left South Bend but not remembered after Michigan City. Those were the only definite facts obtained and it meant the girl had left at either Rolling Prairie, Springville, or Michigan City itself. If it were either of the first two, there was a good chance of picking her up quickly, for the towns were so small that the arrival of a stranger was sure to be noticed.

Michigan City was another matter, however. With a population of well over twenty thousand, it could make the tracing of the girl much more difficult.

Massachusetts State Police tried to narrow the search by calling Lowell's family but they could not help at all. No friends or relatives lived in that vicinity, nor had Lowell at any time expressed the slightest interest in Michigan City or any other point in the Middle West, including Chicago. It meant the Illinois police were going to have to work on it on their own.

Cameron was moved, therefore, to growl, 'That's the disappearingest girl I ever saw. She walks out of a building in broad daylight and poof, nobody sees her any more. She leaves town, but nobody sees her go. They trap her on a bus and, when the police climb aboard, no girl. Nobody sees her get off but all of a sudden she isn't there.'

Ford said, 'Give them time. Somebody in Michigan City is bound to have taken her somewhere. They'll pick up her trail.'

'I hope so. They sure as hell didn't do it here in Bristol where she's known.'

Ford said, 'I wish I could go out there. I'd find her soon enough.'

'Sure you would. You couldn't even find her in your own precinct.'

'Out there,' stated Ford belligerently, 'I'd have a detective sergeant who knew his onions. Here I've got nothing but a college boy who doesn't know anything that doesn't come out of a book!'

Cameron nodded appreciatively. 'What do you know? The Chief is returning to normal. He's getting ugly again.'

'Sure I'm ugly. I'm a son of a bitch, but I'm going to find that girl.'

'If you have to wait a year for her to show up.'

'Yeah. Wait. That's what we're going to do. We're going to sit tight and wait and, pretty soon, something's going to happen and we'll have her. That's what the police business is all about. A lot of leg work, a lot of disappointments, and a lot of waiting.' He pulled out a cigar and rolled it around between his palms. 'Right now we're going to wait for the Michigan City police to find out where she went after she got off that bus.' He sat back and continued to play with his cigar.

The wait wasn't a very long one. There was no further report from the police out west, but the focal point of the investigation turned east again with a dramatic suddenness. Lieutenant Robert Rumbaugh of the Massachusetts State Police telephoned at quarter of four.

Ford was in his office drinking coffee with Cameron when the call came through and Zileski plugged it in from the switchboard.

'Chief,' said Rumbaugh, 'I think we've got your girl for you.' Then he added casually, 'What's left of her.'

Ford took several breaths very slowly. When he spoke his voice was flat and unmoved. 'Where and how?' He picked up his coffee spoon and toyed with it on the desktop.

'Boston. The Harbour Police fished her out of the bay.'

The Chief watched his spoon, turning it at various angles, twisting it, examining it. 'Clothes fit the description?'

'The body was nude,' said Rumbaugh. 'It's been in the water a week or two and the Mitchell girl is the only one reported missing in this area so they think it's her.'

'Anything left of the face?' asked Ford.

'No. No face. No head even. The body was decapitated,

the wrists and ankles bound with wire. They only just brought it in so they haven't had a chance yet to do a PM.'

Ford nodded. 'Any identifying marks on the body? Scars and the like?'

'I don't know,' said Rumbaugh. 'It's in pretty bad shape as I understand it and maybe they can't tell. Anyway, they didn't say. I'll let you know as soon as I get anything further.'

'Okay.' Ford hung up and stared at the spoon.

Cameron said, 'What's up?' and the Chief told him. Cameron whistled. 'I'll bet that'll make Monroe happy,' he said. 'Shows him up as a pretty good guesser.'

'I'll bet her folks will be tickled to death too,' said Ford.

'Going to tell them?'

'Hell no. Not until we know for sure. Looks like Lowell, but we don't know yet. It could be somebody else. God-damn it, Cameron,' he said with sudden spirit, 'you ought to know better than to jump to conclusions in police work. You gotta keep an open mind.'

'That's right. I forgot. Lowell's supposed to be in Michigan City.'

'Yes, or a thousand and one other places too.'

'Only you hope it's Michigan City.'

'I don't hope a goddamned thing,' growled Ford. 'It's no skin off my teeth whether she's alive in Michigan City or dead in Boston Harbour. All I'm supposed to do is find her. That's all I'm hoping to do.'

'So we sit around and wait some more.'

'Yeah. We wait some more. That's the toughest part, the waiting. I'd go up to Boston if this damn police force could get along without me.'

'Go ahead,' said Cameron. 'You'd be missed like a toothache.'

Ford whirled on him. 'Listen, Cameron, you son of a bitch, I've taken all the crap I'm going to from you. You and your smart-aleck remarks. You think because you went to college you can say what you damn well please around here and get away with it. You've got another think coming. I can break you, brother. I can kick your ass right down to patrolman and out on to the streets walking a beat. You think you're a privileged character around this station. You think you can crack wise and I'll lap it up. I'm telling you, any more funny business out of you and you're through. Just once more and you'll wish like hell you'd kept your big fat slobbering mouth shut. Understand?'

Cameron didn't colour and he didn't wince. He didn't even look taken aback. One corner of his mouth twisted up. He said, almost in awe, 'Well, what do you know? The Chief's really bothered. The Chief is really scared that *is* Lowell's body the Harbour Police picked up!' The twisted mouth broke into a grin. 'You know,' he said, 'there are times when I *almost* think you might be a good egg!'

Ford's face reddened slightly. 'It's four o'clock,' he growled. 'You're through for the day, Cameron. Will you get the hell out of here and go home?'

Cameron sat back against the table with his hands in his pockets. 'I will if you'll come over for a drink.'

'I can't, Burt. I'm going to stick around here and wait for the reports. I want to know if we've got a murder on our hands or just a disappearance.'

'The waiting game. I'll stick too. I've got a stake in this as much as you have.' The detective pulled over a straight-backed chair and sat down. He pulled out a cigarette, scratched a match under the table, lighted up, and threw the match on the floor.

They stayed until eight o'clock but only one more report came in. It was from the Illinois State Police. It had been definitely established that the girl on the bus had not got off at either Rolling Prairie or Springville and the search had been narrowed down to Michigan City itself.

Thursday morning brought in the autopsy protocol on the headless corpse in Boston Harbour. The body was that of a woman about twenty-five years of age, weight, 130–135 pounds, height five feet seven to seven and a half inches, brunette, and she had borne a child. Boston police had a mystery of their own on their hands. The girl was not Lowell Mitchell.

The disappearance of the Parker freshman, then, was still not solved but Ford seemed glad and he was less vexed with the unpromising reports that came in from Michigan City. The police there had so far found no trace of the girl. Taxi and bus drivers had been questioned without results and it was thought that she had either walked to her destination or been met. They were doing all they could, however. Every patrolman on every beat had memorized the features of the Mitchell girl and was keeping his eyes peeled for someone who looked like her.

Thursday passed into Friday and the Bristol police were clinging to their one hope, that Lowell would be picked up in Michigan City. Monroe, however, was still roaming the highways and byways of Bristol, following his own theory that Lowell had been abducted, but he seemingly was getting nowhere either. He was patently disappointed that the body in the harbour wasn't his client's daughter but he still maintained the girl was dead and now had a standing offer in the station house of six dollars to four that Lowell Mitchell would not be found in Michigan City. Again he had no takers.

The newspaper articles had switched their locale and now headlined their stories, SEARCH FOR MISSING GIRL CENTRES IN MIDWEST. In bolder type over longer articles were headlines concerning the developments in the case of the unidentified, headless corpse of Boston who had not been the Parker freshman.

Chief Ford, growing desperate, was going over the Mitchell girl's diary again, word by word, re-reading her letters, trying to find something that he might have overlooked before.

Lowell Mitchell had been missing two weeks that day.

Friday Noon

At twelve-fifty that Friday noon a senior at Parker named Jane Reardon was crossing Higgins Bridge from her gym class when her attention was attracted to an object lying at the bottom of the river, gleaming bright gold in the warm sunshine. She paused for a moment and leaned over the wide railing on the downstream side of the bridge and tried to make out what it was. Two of her friends joined her and she pointed it out to them. One of them said she had noticed it several days ago but had paid it no attention. Now, however, she too tried to guess its identity. Several other girls joined the group and they all speculated on the object. A lipstick? Compact? It had too golden a light, it seemed.

Charles T. Corvath, a campus policeman in the company of Private Detective John Monroe, happened along at that point and the two were attracted by the group on the bridge. The girls, tiring of the guessing after a minute or so and anxious to get to lunch, indicated the gleaming object below in deprecating fashion as though it were unseemly for young ladies to gather on bridges and try to identify objects lying under the water beneath. Corvath and Monroe looked, saw the gleam, and went on. The girls forgot about it, Corvath forgot about it, and Monroe almost forgot about it. He retained it just long enough to twit Ford with it. Ford was sitting at his desk eating his lunch out of a paper bag when Monroe dropped in to rest his weary feet a half-hour later. Ford looked out of his office and came forth with his standard query: 'How're things on campus?'

'Fine,' replied Monroe. 'Nothing from Michigan City, of course?'

'Everything's normal, huh?'

'Do you think I'd be hanging around here if it wasn't? Of course everything's normal.' Then it came to him. 'Except that a lot of the girls will probably cut classes and go wading this afternoon.'

Ford looked at him suspiciously. 'What for?'

'A lipstick or compact somebody lost in the river.'

'Why would they go wading for it?'

Monroe looked exhausted. 'Hell, they wouldn't. I'm only kidding you.'

'You mean nothing was lost?'

'I mean nobody would go wading for it.' He saw the Chief didn't understand, so he said, 'Look. There's nothing wrong on campus. A few girls happened to see something shining down in the river by the bridge and they were wondering what it was. That's all. They've forgotten all about it. Nobody's going wading, nobody's paying any attention to it.'

Ford wasn't mollified in the least. 'What was it?' he said.

'Hell. I don't know. A lipstick or compact somebody dropped or threw off the bridge, that's all. It's nothing to get excited about.'

'I'll get damn good and excited,' said Ford, his voice looming up. 'What do you mean a compact or lipstick somebody threw off the bridge? Do you think girls go around throwing stuff like that away?'

'All right, they lost it then. They dropped it over the side accidentally.'

'They did, huh? Maybe you can tell me how a girl can manage to drop something accidentally over a four-and-a-half-foot railing that's a foot wide! You're as bad as my own men. You'll pass up any clue unless it jumps up and bites your nose.'

Monroe said, 'Now don't tell me you think that's a clue!'

'No, I don't think it's a clue, but I don't know that it's not a clue either. What you people can't get through your heads is that under normal conditions you wouldn't pay any attention to something like that, but normal conditions don't exist on that campus. A girl disappeared from there, which means something is wrong about that campus. Therefore, anything that goes on there the least bit different from the ordinary, I want to know about it. If a girl breathes different from usual even, I want to know why.'

'All right,' said Monroe. 'Fine. But there's nothing out of the ordinary about this.'

'There isn't, huh? Listen, Monroe, that object, whatever it is, doesn't belong there. That means it got put there. On a normal campus there'd be a normal reason for it. Parker is not a normal campus and the reason may not be a normal one. It probably is, but I don't buy probablys.'

'Ten bucks to your one says it has nothing to do with the Mitchell case.'

'Make it a thousand to one and I'll take it. The odds aren't any better than that.'

Cameron came in then and said, 'What's it going to be, swords or pistols?'

Monroe said, 'He's going hog-wild because somebody

lost something down at the bottom of the river at the campus bridge.'

Ford said to Cameron, 'He's as stupid as you are.'

Cameron said, 'So what are you going to do about it?'

'Do? We're going to find out what it is and whose it is. We're going wading.'

'You're kidding, Chief,' said Monroe.

'No, he's not,' said Cameron. 'He's just frustrated from sitting around waiting for reports from Michigan City.'

'I'm just picayune,' said the Chief.

Cameron said, 'If you're so hot for action, why don't you go out and direct traffic this afternoon?'

Ford winked at Monroe and said, 'He's scared I'm going to make him go swim for it. Cheer up, Burt. Lassiter's going to take the swim. You need the bath more than he does but you're too old. Your heart wouldn't stand it.'

So Lassiter was summoned and told to get into a bathing suit and join them at Higgins Bridge. He thought, or at least hoped, for a minute that Chief Ford was kidding but it was a faint hope. Ford didn't kid, at least not with anyone other than Burt Cameron. He started to squeal. 'It's March, Chief. That river will be ice!'

Ford said, 'What do you want us to do, drain the lake and run the river dry again so you can walk out? Get on your horse!'

Lassiter departed mumbling something about how much better off he would have been staying in the Army while Ford informed Ed Small and Mrs Kenyon of their intentions. Then Ford left for the campus with Monroe, who was still inclined to believe the Chief couldn't be serious, and with Cameron, who knew only too well that he was.

Lassiter joined them at the bridge at two o'clock. He

had a heavy sweater, pants, and overcoat on over his bathing suit but he was shivering in spite of the moderate temperature, not because of the cold, but because of the anticipated cold. The sun had shifted its position and it had taken five minutes of manoeuvring before a gleam had been sighted. It was a faint one at best and one that threatened to fade out entirely at any moment and Ford was muttering curses at Lassiter in a more and more audible tone until the man arrived.

'Hurry it up,' called Ford. 'Don't come out here on the bridge, get in the water fast. We'll tell you where to look.'

Had Lassiter wanted to complain about the temperature of the water, he held his peace, not through fear of Ford but because stragglers, coming back from gym, were pausing on both banks and on the bridge itself to watch the strange sight of a man stripping off his clothes in preparation for a dip. He braved the waters stoically for the girls' benefit and waded in with concealed gasps up to his waist.

'A little farther,' Ford directed. 'More to your left, a little more. That's too much. Back just a little.' He jockeyed him into position expertly and, when he had him placed to his satisfaction, told him to go straight down for it. Lassiter closed both eyes, held his nose, and ducked. He came up a moment later, gasping. 'Well?' said Ford.

'Missed the bottom.'

'Exhale, damn it, don't inhale, and open your eyes down there.'

Lassiter went down again and his hand was visible through the water patting the bottom, sending up little muddy clouds. He came up with some small stones.

'Goddamn it,' bellowed Ford. 'I said open your eyes! I'm not building a rock garden. Throw those damn things away and do what I tell you. Now you've got the bottom all stirred up and I can't see where it is. Go down right where you are, but move your hand back a couple of inches.'

Lassiter went under again and came up shivering and empty-handed. The girls tittered.

'I'm freezing,' complained Lassiter. 'My hands are numb.'

'The faster you find it,' said Ford, 'the faster you can come out of there.'

Lassiter went down again and Ford started growling that he should have known better, that he should have gone in himself. Lassiter came up for a breath and immediately ducked under once more as though he were close to pay dirt. He came up holding his hand aloft. 'I've got it.'

'Come on out,' said Ford, and hastened off the bridge. Lassiter waded ashore, gave him the object, and started drying himself feverishly with his towel. His lips were blue and his teeth were chattering violently.

When Cameron and Monroe reached him Ford was turning the object over and over in his hands. It was a gold hair clip and on the inside were engraved the initials MLM.

Friday Afternoon

At three o'clock Ford was down by the bridge again but this time with more men and the boat. Cameron and two men were on the east bank of the river on the campus side while Lassiter and two more patrolmen were on the gymnasium side. Ford was standing in the boat giving instructions before he and his oarsman shoved off. Mrs Kenyon, Mr Small, and the other campus employees were grouped around and it was a grim-faced gathering that heard Ford's orders.

Back on the slope, the students had collected a hundred strong, but they weren't tittering girls any longer. They stood solemn and silent with their numbers swelling by the minute. In less than an hour the news had spread over the campus that the hair clip Lowell Mitchell had been wearing the day she disappeared had been found in the river beside the bridge.

Private Detective John Monroe was there. He was in the boat with Ford and shoved it off into the stream when the Chief gave the signal. Patrolman Womrath, at the oars, steadied the craft and tried to hold it against the current. At the same time the men on both banks began moving downstream along the water-line. Wheeler River was a tortuously winding stream that flowed in a south-westerly direction over twenty miles before it finally emptied into the Connecticut a few miles south of Spring-field. Ford and his men were going to cover only the few miles of it that lay in their jurisdiction. Massachusetts State Police would take it from there to the border and the Connecticut police would cover the river from there to the Sound.

They moved slowly along both banks and the boat in midstream outdistanced the men on foot. The boat slowed to a halt three hundred yards downstream where a large fallen tree lay out into the middle of the river. Womrath rested the boat against its damming branches while Ford and Monroe spent five minutes poking in and around it with grappling poles until they were convinced nothing was caught in it under the water. By that time the men ashore had drawn even. Cameron and his group forded a small stream that fed into Wheeler River and kept on. Womrath freed his boat and started it drifting again, slowing it and holding it on course with the oars. Ford and Monroe kept a sharp eye over the sides of the river bottom.

A quarter of a mile farther downstream the river bent sharply in a hairpin turn and went under the Queen Street Bridge. Ford had Womrath let the boat drift ashore there and waited again for the men to catch up. Cameron was perspiring. He shook his head when he came by and shoved the boat off again. They kept going.

Two miles downstream they came to the filled-in area known as the flats. It had once been a marsh but years of dumping and levelling had turned it into a littered, sparsely grassed, desolate plain stretching out an eighth of a mile behind the row of tenement houses that rimmed Front Street. Necking parties frequently parked on its waste in the spring and fall, and in the summer the tenement children crossed it to swim in the shallow river bed.

It was while following the river's edge at this point that Cameron suddenly stopped, backed off, and waved at Ford up ahead. He yelled and pointed and Ford nodded and motioned at the bank and Womrath rowed him to shore. He clambered on to the thin covering of snow closely followed by Monroe and went over. Cameron led him to the upwind side of a little nook and pointed. Ford's eyes were bleak and opaque. He stepped to the edge of the shallow bank and leaned forward.

Half submerged in the water, mud, and dried grass was the body of a young girl. The face had been eaten away, the hair was silty, and the clothes consisted of a grimy, mud-coloured coat, a washed-out, colourless wool skirt, greyish blouse, and dirty faded sweater, but there wasn't any doubt as to who the girl had been.

There was no expression on Ford's face. After a moment he turned away and crunched back to Cameron. He took a deep breath and said, 'I guess we can tell the Michigan City police to stop looking now.'

Monroe, after one last look, scurried back to join them. 'I knew she was dead,' he said. 'I felt it in my bones.'

Cameron said sarcastically, 'That makes this your lucky day.'

'And how. If I hadn't discovered that hair clip she wouldn't have been found till next summer.'

Ford ignored him. 'Steve,' he called to one of the boot-clad men who had been with Cameron. The man came over.

'Yes, sir,' said Monroe. 'That hair clip led us right to the body. It sure is a good thing I found it.'

Ford and Cameron looked at each other, then looked at Monroe piercingly. Then the Chief turned. 'Steve, get to a phone and call Doc Howe. Then call headquarters and tell MacDonald to send down both radio cars and the trailer. And call up Cal Leslie of the *Bugle*. Tell him I want him to come down here and take a few pictures.'

Cameron said, 'And tell Mac to order some coffee.'

'Yeah, coffee,' said Ford.

Stevenson said, 'Right,' and turned. Monroe said, 'I'll go with you,' and started off.

Ford's voice was a bellow. 'Where do you think you're going?'

It brought Monroe up short. He turned around and said, 'Why, I'm going to call the Mitchells.'

'Like hell you are! Come back here!'

Monroe took a step back reluctantly. 'Why not, Chief? They've got a right to know.'

'You and nobody else is going to tell them their daughter's dead until we know for sure it's their daughter.'

'What the hell, Chief? You know as well as I do that that's Lowell.'

'She hasn't been identified yet. Until she is, you aren't calling anybody.'

Monroe balked. 'You can't order me around. I'm not one of your men and I can do what I please.'

'This is a police case and I'm in charge here and you'll do what I tell you to do or I'll throw you in the can. If you think you're going to hold them up for reward money because of that hair clip, I'm telling you right now it'll be over my dead body.'

'What's the matter? I found it, didn't I? What're you trying to do, hog the reward yourself?'

Ford's tone was menacing. 'You and I have got along okay, so far, Monroe. You better keep on the good side of me or, so help me, you'll be sorry.'

Monroe fumed, but he stayed put.

Dr Robert Howe, the medical examiner, came through

the alley from Front Street between the tenements, and crossed the flats in an ambulance at ten minutes past five. A group of fifteen to twenty people standing back at a respectful distance in the cooling air broke ground to let him through. McNamara and Lascom in one radio car and Cal Leslie in his 1946 Ford arrived simultaneously a couple of minutes later as Howe and Ford were viewing the body. Howe was saying, 'Any valuables on her?'

'Haven't seen any.'

'Better check the water around her.'

'We will as soon as you give the order to move her.'

'You can move her. I'll have her taken to the Gardner-Niles Funeral Home and do the autopsy there. We'll have to notify the DA on this, I'm afraid. He'll probably call an inquest.'

Leslie joined them at this point and said, 'Unusual circumstances, huh?'

Ford said, 'What do you think?'

Leslie took a look. 'Damned unusual. How many pictures do you want?'

'Enough to establish how she's lying.'

Leslie got to work with his camera and flash equipment in the gathering gloom while the others stood around and shivered. When he was through the ambulance attendants laid out a stretcher on the snow at the edge and Ford ordered two of his booted men into the water. They waded in and gathered up the body, lifting it dripping from its cold bed and laying it on to the stretcher. The other men backed off as the body came up and Monroe said audibly, 'Pe-ew.'

The attendants covered it with a sheet and shoved the stretcher into the ambulance. The two men in the water waded around where the body had lain but found nothing belonging to it.

'It's the Mitchell girl, of course,' said the doctor as he prepared to depart.

'Probably,' replied Ford. 'Her identity is one of the things I want established, that and the cause of death and anything else you can find out about her.'

Howe nodded. 'I'll have the information in the morning and I'll call the DA tonight.'

'Check her teeth tonight, will you? The newspapers will be hounding me and I want to call her parents before I break the story and I don't want to call them until we know for sure it's Lowell.'

MacDonald had coffee ready at the station house when the officers returned. Monroe was still with them, not so much because Ford desired his company as because he didn't trust him out of his sight. The boat was put away in the garage, the body had been taken care of, and the reporters had not yet got wind of the new developments, so for a few minutes there was a chance to relax.

Monroe was still bitter about Ford's highhanded tactics and he sulked by himself for the most part. Ford was picayune to an extreme degree to his way of thinking, but he suspected more than that lay behind the Chief's actions.

'You've got no right,' he said, 'to order an autopsy without the parents' consent. They may not want her cut up.'

Ford replied, 'The medical examiner has a right to perform an autopsy on any unidentified bodies and this one is still unidentified.'

'You're stretching your reasoning pretty thin,' complained Monroe but Ford thereafter ignored him.

After the coffee the other men, long since off duty, went

home but Cameron and Lassiter, both of whom had the day off, stayed with the Chief and meals were sent out for.

District Attorney Dave McNarry called up about seven. 'Hear there's been a little trouble,' he said. 'The Mitchell girl's dead? That sure is a shame.' The way he said it showed he didn't think it was a shame at all. He thought it was very exciting.

'Yeah,' said Ford. 'There's some question about how it happened. Seems she jumped, fell, or was pushed off Higgins Bridge and floated downstream to where we found her.'

'Sure she didn't wash through the floodgates when you drained the lake?'

'I'm sure,' said Ford abruptly.

'Eh? Yes. I see. Well, it looks like an inquest then. Judge Lee will conduct it. I've already talked to him. It'll start Monday morning. Meanwhile, will you send over the girl's diary and letters and all your reports on the case?'

Ford said, 'Right,' and hung up.

The call he was waiting for came around eight. 'Tried to get you at your home,' said the medical examiner. 'What do you do, live at the station?'

'Yeah. This is my wife's lover's day to have the house. What did you find out?'

'There's a laundry mark on some of her clothes, the blouse and the skirt. P dash LA dash 230.'

'That's Lowell's,' said Ford.

'I thought so. I checked her teeth with the dental chart on your missing persons circular. I'm afraid there's no question about it. The girl is Lowell Mitchell.'

'Any trace of a scar on her right leg?'

'Traces. There had been one there. I don't think there's much doubt about that.'

'Okay, Doc, thanks.'

'By the way, her neck's broken. It's probably the cause of death.'

'Okay.' Ford hung up and said to Monroe, 'You can call her folks now if you want. The body's been identified.' He held out the phone.

The detective ran a palm over his forehead. 'Think I'll wait a little,' he said.

Ford said, 'Call them now or I'll call them.'

'What's the hurry?'

Ford put the phone on the main desk and took off the receiver himself. 'Long distance.'

'Wait a minute, wait a minute,' said Monroe. 'I'll call them. I'll go outside and call them.'

'You'll call them from here where I can listen to you or you won't call them at all. I told you you aren't putting any bite on them for a reward because of her hair clip.'

Monroe said, 'Look, I'm not out after any reward, honest. I just don't want to break that news to them in front of—' He saw the expressionless faces surrounding him. 'Oh hell. Go ahead. You call them.'

Ford did, while the others sat around. 'I'm afraid I've got bad news,' he said, and he broke it very well if any news like that can be broken well. 'We found her.' There was an empty flat look on his face and an empty flat tone in his voice. 'Yes. It was an accident apparently. She fell off the campus bridge into the river. No, she didn't drown. The water isn't very deep there. It was quick and I doubt that she ever knew what happened.' He listened a little, said, 'All right,' a couple of times, and hung up.

'They're coming up,' he informed the group.

Monroe said, 'That was no accident and you know it.'

'You know something we don't?'

'I know it wasn't an accident. How do you think a girl is going to fall over a four-and-a-half-foot railing?'

Ford looked tired. 'There are four ways of dying,' he told Monroe. 'Natural causes, accident, suicide, murder. The inquest will determine which it was.'

Monroe repeated, 'No girl is going to fall over a four-and-a-half-foot railing.'

'Which means she jumped, except she has no motive for suicide, or she was pushed except that nobody would try that in broad daylight in plain sight.'

Three men came bursting in. They were reporters, eager and breathless. 'You found her, Chief? We've been racing in from Boston. What's the story?'

Ford looked suddenly spent. He sighed deeply and turned to MacDonald. 'Send out for some more coffee, Mac.'

Saturday, 18 March

Dr Howe's autopsy protocol came in on Saturday morning. Death was listed as instantaneous and caused by a broken neck. That was borne out by the fact that there was no water in the lungs. Then, buried in with the other technical discussion of the organs was a little item that dropped like a bombshell amid the speculations regarding Lowell's death. The girl, Howe reported, was six weeks pregnant!

Ford exhaled sharply and the mask that froze his face fractured for a moment. He handed the paper over to Cameron, jabbing a finger at the vital paragraph. The detective whistled and sat down. 'Chief, you were right all along.'

Ford shook his head. 'I wasn't right. I thought the way you did about her. I would have staked my life on her virginity.'

'So would I,' agreed Cameron. 'But it answers a few things, like the idea of her falling off that bridge.'

'Of course she couldn't fall, not unless she got smart and tried to walk the railing, and even so, I can't see her landing on her head.'

'Suicide,' Cameron mused. 'That explains a lot of things. That's why she dressed up and didn't leave the campus. That's why she feigned sickness and sneaked out while everybody was at lunch. That's why she picked the noon hour, when the campus would be deserted.'

Ford said, 'It's not suicide, it's murder. I don't care if

she did kill herself, it's murder.' He clenched his fists on his desk and stared at them. 'A girl doesn't kill herself because she gets pregnant. It happens all the time, in the best of families. It's a disgrace, sure, but it's not something that can't be lived down. If my daughter got pregnant, hell, I'd beat the bejesus out of the guy and make him marry her, but I wouldn't disown her. Neither would Lowell's folks. They're not that kind of people. She killed herself for nothing, Burt, and it was because the guy drove her to it. He refused to stand by her, or got her worked up in some way to the point where she thought that was the only way out.'

'She wouldn't shack up with just anybody,' said Cameron, 'so it's a safe bet she was madly in love with whoever it was. He lets her down and she goes off the deep end.'

'Murder,' said Ford. 'That's what it is, murder.' He opened the drawers of his desk and rummaged around until he found the breakdown of Lowell's diary. 'Six weeks pregnant, Howe says. That takes us back to the middle of January.' He thumbed through the sheets.

'What good will that do? You aren't going to be able to stick anybody for it. The guy probably didn't even know what he was making her do for that matter.'

'I want to know who that bastard is,' said Ford. He paused and read. 'Kincaid saw her on January fourth. Myers saw her on the sixth. That guy Curtis came to see her on the fourteenth. That's seven weeks. That's all. No, wait. Kincaid saw her on the twenty-seventh.' He thrust the papers away from him. I wish to hell I hadn't sent her diary over to McNarry. I want to read what she wrote that week.'

Cameron said, 'Hell, you've read it twice and studied it to boot. You know she doesn't put any clues in it.'

'I know she doesn't talk about sleeping with a guy. I know she doesn't even talk about liking one, but I want to see what names she so much as mentions that week.'

'You copied them down. Where are they?'

'McNarry's got them. I only kept the list of boys she dated.'

'You're probably just as well off without it. That diary's a Jonah. There're more blind alleys in that than there are in Boston.'

'She was too damn cagey for her own good,' growled Ford. 'She's so damned secretive I still can't get it through my head that Howe isn't mistaken.'

'Howe wouldn't be mistaken about something like that.'

'I know it, but it's enough to make me doubt my own senses. I'd even begun thinking maybe the body wasn't Lowell's except that we know it was. She put on the best act I ever saw.'

'And what did it get her?' said Cameron.

The newspapermen arrived then, and there were more of them than ever. Innes was back, and O'Malley, Miller, and the rest of them. There were others, too, from New Haven, Waterbury, and Newark. Ford didn't try to hide the latest development. He let them read the autopsy protocol and it brought forth as much of a reaction from them as it had from the police. 'What's your theory now, Chief? Suicide?'

Ford shook his head. 'I'm not giving out any theories. It's for the inquest to decide. District Attorney McNarry is in charge now. Ask him.'

Lowell's parents arrived on the one-fifteen train again, and this time Melissa wasn't with them. Ford sent a radio car to pick them up and bring them to headquarters. They came in, strained but under control.

'How did it happen?' Mitchell said quietly.

Ford shook his head. 'We don't know yet. The district attorney is calling an inquest for Monday.'

'Tell me how you came to find her.'

'Some of the students,' Ford said, 'spotted her hair clip gleaming in the water. We got wind of it and fished it out and it seemed to indicate that she went over the railing off the bridge so we sent searching parties down the river till we found her.'

Mr Mitchell nodded, tight-lipped, and said, 'Do you have it with you?'

'I turned it over to the medical examiner. He takes charge of valuables.'

'May I see the – her – body?'

Ford looked over the architect's head and out the window. 'I think it's better if you don't. We're taking care of everything.'

'I'd like to see the doctor who examined her. Where would I find him?'

'Either at his office or the Gardner-Niles Funeral Home. I've got his report if you want to see it.'

Carl Mitchell did. He accepted it and he and his wife looked at it together. The three or four reporters loitering around edged in a little, watching and waiting for them to run into the bombshell. Suddenly the paper began to shake and Mitchell's face went white. He looked up and his wife pulled the fluttering sheet from his hands. There was something like fear in his eyes. 'What is this?' he said. 'The girl you found was pregnant!'

Ford nodded. 'That's right.'

It wasn't fear in the man's eyes, it was something else. 'There's a mistake. There's a mistake somewhere.'

'I'm afraid not.'

Mitchell said to his wife, 'Maybe it isn't Lowell. It couldn't be Lowell!' He turned back. 'There's something wrong about this, Chief. It's mistaken identity or the doctor's wrong. I know that my daughter could not possibly be pregnant. Perhaps it's another girl dressed in my daughter's clothes.'

Ford shook his head reluctantly. 'The identity has been positively established. There isn't any mistake.'

Mitchell was having trouble controlling his excitement. 'I'm afraid I must demand to see the body. I'm not convinced that that girl is my daughter!'

'I'm afraid she is. There's absolutely no question about it.'

'I want to make sure.'

'It's not necessary. Take my word for it.'

'I won't take your word. Something's wrong. You don't want me to see her. You're trying to hide something.'

Ford sighed heavily and said, 'All right. We'll take you over if you insist, but Mrs Mitchell stays here. Come on, Burt.' He and Cameron went for their coats and Ford said dully, 'They'll grasp at any straw to avoid the facts.'

The three of them drove over in Ford's car to the funeral home on Pickering Street and went in. It was a large Victorian house with a modest sign in gold letters against a black background out by the sidewalk. There were two well-carpeted, sombre waiting-rooms at the front and another larger room midway to the rear with an entrance on to the driveway. A narrow hall lay back of this room and across from it was the bare mortuary.

Mr Hallock, one of the undertakers, met them and led

them through the waiting-rooms into the large parlour. There was a reporter there, standing at the window, watching a hearse run into the drive and dumping ashes from his cigarette into the ferns that grew from a large hammered brass bowl. He was a brash-looking man of about twenty-five who thought it smart to wear his hat in the house.

Ford ignored him. Reporters were like ants around sugar this day. No matter where you went in connection with the case, a reporter was there waiting. 'Doc Howe around?' Ford said to Hallock.

'I expect him back any minute. Do you want to see him?'

'When he comes in, Mr Mitchell would. What we came for was to view the body.'

'I see. It's in the cold room across the hall.'

'Thanks.' They left the reporter standing there and followed Hallock into the bare, chilly room. It was a large room, spotlessly clean, with white walls, white woodwork, fluorescent lights in the ceiling, locked cupboards around the walls, and three tiers of large bins with windows and nameplates over and under the handles. A sheet-covered form lay on a table in the centre and, everywhere, the odour of formaldehyde was overpowering. Strong as it was, however, it could not quite conceal another, more pungent odour that gagged them as they entered.

Ford, Mitchell, and Cameron moved slowly through the thick air to within a few feet of the table as Hallock skirted it to the other side. He paused, then deftly lifted the sheet and folded it back from the head and shoulders.

Mitchell's hands slowly balled up into hard, white fists and he started to tremble. Then he started to choke. 'No. Oh, God, no.'

Then he started to scream.

He lunged at the body.

Ford and Cameron clutched at him and missed, clutched again and caught him as he reached the table. Hallock's face was white. He pulled at the sheet, wrinkling it, dragging it back. Mitchell tore at it. Ford and Cameron pulled him away. He half freed himself and clutched a corner. Hallock got it away from him. Ford and Cameron got him again. He struck at them. They seized his arms. They got their weight set. They started to move him back from the table, inch by inch, then foot by foot. He kicked and screamed and sobbed until they slammed him up against the wall. Then his knees buckled.

Ford tried to hold him up. Cameron half caught him from behind, but he was too heavy for them. He went down slowly, against the wall, sobbing bitterly, until the floor stopped him. He buried his face in his arm against the white plaster and drove his fist into it until the walls shook. He was crying, 'No, God. Not her. Please, God. Not Lowell.'

Ford's face looked as though it had been hewn from bedrock. There was perspiration on his brow and his breath came in short gasps that were choked by the foul air. He turned away from the man at his feet, towards Hallock, who was frozen behind the narrow table. He turned farther. The door they had come through was open and the reporter was standing in it.

Ford took one look and roared, 'Close that goddamned door!' The reporter looked startled for a moment, then backed out quickly, pulling it shut.

Mitchell was crying with great, heaving sobs and his tie and collar were soaked. Ford watched him dispassionately for a moment, then turned to the still frozen Hallock. 'Get

Doc Howe, will you, for Christ's sake?' Hallock became unstuck and almost ran from the room.

The door slammed. Ford bent and put a hand on Mitchell's shoulder. He shook him.

'She was only eighteen,' Mitchell cried into the wall. 'She hadn't begun to live.' He looked up as though Ford could do something about it. 'Only eighteen, Chief. Just a little girl.'

'Get hold of yourself,' Ford said tersely.

Mitchell twisted himself around. He wiped his nose with the back of his hand and dug the heels of his palms in his eyes. 'She held my hand,' he said, and held it out, staring at it in awe with his streaming eyes. 'She ripped her leg on some barbed wire. She was only ten.' He turned against the wall again and smashed it with his fist. 'The poor kid. It needed stitches and she was scared to death.' He struck the wall again. 'I couldn't bear to see her suffer. She knew it but she didn't want me to leave. She couldn't stand it alone.' He buried his face in his hands and sobbed. 'She said, "Don't go away, Daddy. I'll promise not to cry if you won't go away." Scared to death and she said that!' He pounded the floor. 'She didn't, either. She held my hand and she didn't cry. She was the bravest kid I ever saw. I carried the marks of her fingernails for a week, but she didn't cry.'

Ford seized his coat collar and shook him. 'Stop it,' he said viciously. 'Stop torturing yourself.'

Mitchell said, 'She's dead, you know. That's her over there. She's lying on that table, only she's dead. She can't come home any more.'

The door opened and Dr Howe came in, sized up the situation in a glance, and came quickly.

Ford said woodenly, 'Better take over, Doc. I can't do anything with him.'

Howe nodded silently, set his bag down, and stooped beside the prostrate man. Ford did not look back. He walked quickly out the door, followed by Cameron.

The reporter was still there, sitting on the edge of the sofa, spinning his hat on one finger and softly whistling, 'You Can't Be True, Dear'. Ford didn't even glance at him. He went slowly over to the window and stood with his hands clasped behind him, staring out. Cameron moved over to a table and picked up a magazine.

'Feels good to breathe fresh air again,' said the Chief.

Cameron thumbed through the periodical. 'I hate formaldehyde. It makes me think of museums.'

'Does it?'

After a little Ford said, 'Clouding up. Looks like we'll get more snow.'

Cameron put down the magazine, went over, and peered at the sky. 'Looks like it. I'll never get a chance to improve my golf.'

'Me neither.'

The reporter got up, spinning his hat, and moved over to the window. 'Christ,' he said. 'Did you see him? He was going to kiss that corpse! Me, I couldn't stand to look at it and he was going to kiss it!'

Ford didn't move for a moment. Then he turned slowly until he had the man fixed in a baleful stare. 'Get out of here,' he whispered.

'I – what? What's the matter?'

'Get out of here.' His voice was frightening. 'Don't ever let me see you again.'

The man inched back. 'What? I'm a reporter. You can't order me around! I've got a right to be here.'

Ford started moving towards him slowly. There was no doubt as to what he would do when he got close enough. Cameron began moving around in a wide circle. The man backed away. 'What's the matter with you guys?' he whined, but he kept going. Cameron started closing in. The man saw him and went quickly to the door. 'You can't get away with this,' he said. 'My editor will have your scalp.'

They kept coming.

He opened the side door and went out hastily, slamming it shut. Through the window he could be seen backing out the drive, an angry, perplexed scowl on his face.

Monday, 20 March

The papers on Monday morning, 20 March, started their stories, 'A grief-stricken Mitchell family depart today for Philadelphia bearing with them the body of their daughter Lowell, the Parker freshman who so tragically met her death in Wheeler River two weeks ago . . .' The articles ended with the announcement that the inquest into the circumstances of the death was scheduled to start that morning at ten o'clock.

The inquest was a private one, held in the private chambers of Judge Clifford M. Lee of the County Court in Bristol. The decision to close it to the public was due to the disclosure of pregnancy. That fact was public knowledge but it was a ticklish subject to delve into when the man responsible was not known.

Ford and Cameron along with Lieutenant Stewart of the State Police, who was permanently attached to the DA's office, were the only ones permitted to hear all the testimony. They were invited because of their familiarity with the background and McNarry was wise enough to realize the value of anything they might contribute.

The first witness called was Dr Howe, and he described the position of the body, face up, head pointing downstream, his testimony being backed up by Leslie's pictures, which Ford had brought. There was no water in the lungs, he reiterated, no marks of violence, the body had been in the water about two weeks, and death had been caused by a broken neck. The neck, he said, had been broken not forward but sideways.

'If she dove into the water head first,' said McNarry, 'would that kind of a break be possible?'

Howe nodded. 'Not only possible, but probable. Striking the bottom at a slight sideways angle would do it.'

'Assuming she held her breath, which would be natural, and she died instantly, then there would be no water in the lungs?'

'That's right. The lungs weren't entirely devoid of water, of course. There had been some seepage. However, she never inhaled any.'

'Could she have fallen in any other way than head first and broken her neck like that?'

'No.'

Peggy Woodling was the next witness, and she sat in the chair vacated by the medical examiner at one end of the table facing Judge Lee. There, in a hesitating, faltering voice, she told again the story of Lowell's last morning on earth, her apparent sickness and subsequent disappearance. McNarry, sitting on the judge's right, next to Lieutenant Stewart, kept shifting his eyes from the girl's face to the faces of Ford and Cameron across from him. There was nothing in either of the policemen's manner to indicate the girl's tale was at variance in any point with the story she had told before. Ford sat in apparent deep thought, staring into his lap or at the table in front of him. Occasionally he slumped back and stared at the ceiling. He did not look at McNarry, nor did he look at Peggy. He did not appear to be listening.

After she had finished her story McNarry asked her some questions regarding Lowell in general, her behaviour, her interest in boys. Had she ever, in any way, shown more than passing interest in any one boy? She had not.

'Would you have any idea who could be the father of the child she was bearing?'

'None whatever.'

'Would you have any idea how or when it could have happened?'

Peggy shook her head. 'The papers say she was pregnant, but it doesn't sound at all like Mitch. I've known her for six months and I just can't believe it.'

'Nevertheless,' said McNarry, 'it's true. Now, would you say that Lowell was a party girl?'

Peggy twisted her hands in her lap. 'I don't know just how you mean that. She liked dates and parties, yes, but she didn't live for them. If you mean was she wild, no.'

'Did Lowell drink?'

'Yes. Moderately.'

'What do you term moderate?'

'Two drinks an evening.'

McNarry showed off his even white teeth in a rather prissy smile. 'That I would call very moderate.' Lieutenant Stewart chuckled at the joke. Ford and Cameron remained deadpan.

McNarry glanced around for the reaction, then turned to the girl once more. 'That was when she was out dancing for an evening. Would it not be possible for her to indulge in more than just two drinks if she were at a party, say one of the fraternity parties at Carlton College?'

'I don't know, sir. I was never with her at one.'

'You think it would be possible?'

'Yes.'

'Would it also be possible that she might have too much

to drink at some such party, so much perhaps that some unconscionable boy could take advantage of the fact?'

Peggy's denial was vigorous. 'No, sir. She was too strong-willed and she had too much self-respect. She would never let liquor get the better of her like that. And even if she could, she wouldn't go haywire and kill herself because she became pregnant.'

'Interesting,' McNarry said smoothly, 'but the fact remains that that is exactly what she did do.'

Judge Lee raised a restraining hand. 'You are being presumptuous, Mr McNarry. You forget that the purpose of this inquiry is to determine exactly how Lowell Mitchell did come to meet her end.'

McNarry turned to the judge unruffled. 'I confess to getting ahead of myself, Your Honour, but not to being presumptuous. You see, it is my intention to prove to this court that Lowell Mitchell did wilfully and intentionally take her own life.' He turned to Peggy and dismissed her before going on.

'You see,' he continued when the girl had left the room, 'I have discovered something in Lowell's diary that the police' – and here he gave Ford a condescending look – 'failed to notice.' He produced the diary and thumbed through it. 'Allow me to read you her entry for Tuesday, February twenty-eighth, three days before she died. I quote: "Could get an A in Bio. Science, I know, if it weren't for this lab. I guess I don't have a practical mind. I know I don't. Spanish and English are easy, but you won't get me near a math course. Finally finished my English paper. Recopied most of it tonight until I was persuaded into a bridge game with Hilda, Patty, and Sally. Procrastination, thy name is woman. Now I'll have to try to finish it tomorrow and the History lecture knocks out one period. I'm late again. Something drastic will have to be done."

' "I'm late again," ' he repeated slowly. ' "Something drastic will have to be done." Observe that, gentlemen. How carefully it's made to sound, should anyone read it, like a reference to her English paper. Yet the next day she writes, "Got the Feverel paper done just in time, thank goodness—" You see? Nothing drastic was necessary.

'This is the girl, remember, who so carefully concealed any reference to her sexual activities that her pregnancy came as a shock to everyone. In view of that, the "I'm late again. Something drastic will have to be done" takes on a different meaning. She wasn't referring to her English theme, she was referring to her period. It had failed to materialize the month before and she, uncertain, hoping it was just an irregularity, waited another month and it failed to come again. Gentlemen, it is my contention that at this point she knew she was pregnant. The drastic measures she mentions were planned on that walk she took around the lake the morning of the day she died and were put into effect that noon when the other girls were having their lunch!

'To back up that statement, let me read her entry for Wednesday, March first. "Letter from Jack today when I got back from Spanish. Who cares? Honestly, college boys seem so adolescent these days. All about his exams and how much beer he can drink without getting sick. Seems funny it used to impress me. Nothing's happened. Maybe it's for the best. Imagine marrying someone like Jack", and so forth. I only read the beginning so you can see how the remark, "Nothing's happened. Maybe it's for the best", fails to fit in with what she's talking about. It has no relation whatsoever with this boy Jack. It's again a hidden reference to her condition. Her period has still failed to come and at this point she has given up and, as her remark, "Maybe it's for the best", shows, an air of resignation creeps over her.

'On Thursday, the day before she died, she has decided that death is the only way out. Here's what she says. "Bio. Science lecture, Spanish, and History today. Sometimes you wonder why you study. You're not going to use what you learn. At least I'm not. That I now know for sure." The idea of suicide has taken hold of her. She has now irrevocably chosen her fate.

'So you see, Tuesday she realized drastic measures were called for. Wednesday she resigned herself to them. Thursday she built up her nerve to go through with them, and her walk Friday morning was when she decided the question, how?'

Judge Lee then spoke. 'Your arguments have merit, Mr McNarry. However, it is the duty of this court to reserve an opinion until all the facts of a case have been presented. Shall we proceed?'

Hilda Gunther was the next witness and she was followed in turn by Sally Anders, Patty Short, and Marlene Beecher. Their stories of Lowell varied but little from Peggy's and no new information was turned up that would either support or refute Mr McNarry's hypothesis.

At noon the inquest recessed for two hours and Cameron and Ford went off for lunch together. 'It stinks,' said Ford, climbing into a booth opposite the sergeant at Mickey's Diner. 'It stinks like hell.' He picked up a menu and glowered at it.

Cameron said lightly, 'You picked this place, I didn't.'

'I'm talking about the suicide.'

'I know you are. You're burned because the boy involved isn't legally guilty.'

'Like hell I am. It's no skin off my teeth what messes these kids make of their lives.'

'Isn't it? You're mooning about this case as though Lowell were your own daughter.'

'Shut up. You don't know nothing. You only know books. What I'm talking about is that, from what I know about that girl and from what her classmates say about her, she isn't the type to kill herself.'

'From what you knew about her and from what her classmates said about her, she wasn't the type to go get pregnant either.'

'That's different. Given the right circumstances, the right time, and the right guy, any girl will say yes.'

'The cynic. All right, what do you think she did, accidentally dress up and go down to the bridge and accidentally fall over the railing? Or maybe she had a rendezvous there and whoever it was pitched her over the side, right in broad daylight where anyone within three hundred yards could see?'

A waitress slapped two glasses of water on the composition tabletop and Ford ordered himself two hamburgers with plenty of onion. Cameron took minute steak with French fries and the girl departed. Ford leaned forward and said, 'I'll tell you what I don't think. I don't think she tried to commit suicide by jumping off a ten-foot bridge into four feet of water. Suppose you tell me how any girl could reasonably expect to die that way other than by pneumonia? What's wrong with an overdose of sleeping pills? It's a damn sight more comfortable.'

'Okay,' said Cameron in a low voice, glancing around.

'You've got an angle. Why tell it to me? Why don't you tell it to McNarry?'

'Because McNarry, damn his sleek hide, will say, "All right, what do *you* think happened at Higgins Bridge?" and I've got my foot in my mouth. Suicide stinks, but accident and murder stink worse. She's probably dizzy enough to have done just that and McNarry's showed me up once today already coming up with that stuff in her diary that I didn't notice. Twice and people may start thinking Bristol needs a new police chief.'

Cameron laughed sharply. 'So you're getting an inferiority complex over a law school degree! I wouldn't have believed it. Either of us would have picked out those passages if we'd read her diary after we knew she was pregnant the way he did.'

Ford drank up his water and toyed with the glass. 'I should have picked them out before. Remember. I wasn't sold on her purity at the beginning.'

'Genius goes astray. So what are you going to do, retire and lick your wounds?'

'I'll squawk, but I've got to have a better explanation than I've got right now. That means I'm going to have to think.'

'Which will probably rupture your brain,' said Cameron, and lapsed into silence.

Monday Afternoon

McNarry's first witnesses when the afternoon session got under way at two o'clock were the men who had stood guard on the bridge and banks of the stream while the lake was being drained. They testified as a group and assured the judge that not a branch or stick got through the floodgates unnoticed and certainly no body had.

Mr Small, Mrs Kenyon, and Donald Lassiter were called next and related the recovery of Lowell's gold hair clip. McNarry concentrated on the weight and shape of the ornament and the possibility of its being shifted by the currents of the stream. All insisted that it could not have been and, in that, Cameron and Ford agreed.

Having established Higgins Bridge as the point of entry of the body into the water, McNarry then interviewed three girls from Lambert A who, in turn, testified that Lowell had seemed unusually quiet and retiring during the week preceding her death. While they had not anticipated the events that followed, two of them confessed that, in the light of them, they were not surprised at the idea of suicide.

After the last girl had been dismissed McNarry summed up his case to the judge. He pointed out Lowell's depressed spirits, her walk around Parker Lake, and her obvious knowledge of her own pregnancy. He showed how her claim of sickness let her leave the dorm unseen at a time when the campus was virtually deserted and how her change into good clothes was a natural instinct in a girl about to kill herself but unnatural for any other business she might have had on campus. He reminded the judge that Higgins Bridge was the site of the death and called attention to the implausibility of her going over the railing other than by her own volition. It was his contention that there was no other verdict the court could bring in but suicide.

At this point Chief Ford came out of the brown study he'd been in all afternoon. He sat up and spread both hands out in front of him on the table and studied their warped outlines. 'Your Honour,' he said, 'would it be out of order for me to conduct an experiment?'

Judge Lee leaned forward a little and studied the Chief. 'What sort of an experiment?'

'I'd rather not say.'

The judge smiled slightly. 'You're mysterious, I must say. What do you want to prove?'

Ford looked up. 'I can't tell you that because I'm not exactly sure myself. There are a couple of things that bother me and it might clear them up.'

'What's bothering you?'

'Well,' said the Chief slowly, 'Mr McNarry has done a fine job fitting together the facts of this case but there are two things he hasn't explained. One is why does Lowell Mitchell jump off a bridge when she'd have a better chance of killing herself, if she wants to do it that way, by jumping out the window of her room? The second is, what happened to her purse?'

The judge said, 'Her purse?'

'Yes. She had one. A brown leather saddlebag kind of purse with a shoulder-strap. It wasn't with the body, it wasn't at the bridge, and it isn't in her room.'

McNarry said, 'There are, Chief, several answers to both those questions.'

'Yes. But which is the right one?'

Lee said, 'You think your experiment will tell us?'

'I hope it will.'

'How long will it take?'

'I don't know. A couple of hours all told.'

McNarry said acidly, 'That's a long time,' but Judge Lee raised a hand. 'We're after the facts in this case, Mr McNarry. If this experiment of the Chief's will give us any, we'll witness it. Go ahead, Chief. Two hours is a small price to pay to avoid a mistake.'

'Thank you, Your Honour.' Ford swung around. 'Burt,' he said. 'Go out to the icehouse on Ridge Road and bring back a hundred-and-twenty-five-pound block. Wrap it in tarpaulin or whatever you can find to make it as waterproof as possible. Bring it down to Higgins Bridge and have Lassiter send the boat down with a man to row it. We'll meet you there.'

Down at the bridge, McNarry grumbled to Ford about all this mystery. Any fool could tell what he planned to do and what did he think he was going to prove? Ford, however, stubbornly refused to divulge what was on his mind and paced back and forth impatiently on the tarred path. When the police car with the boat on its trailer pulled up on the road above, he almost ran up the path to meet it. Cameron and three other officers stepped out as he came puffing up. 'I don't know what you're doing,' Cameron said, 'but it better be good.'

Ford opened the back door and saw the large block of ice wrapped and tied with canvas on the floor. 'Get this onto the bridge,' he said, 'and put the boat in the water.'

The men worked quickly, sharing his eagerness and,

when his orders had been carried out, he stepped into the boat with his oarsman and had Lee, McNarry, and Cameron climb aboard too, crowding the small craft.

'If we tip over,' McNarry said anxiously, 'I'll have your scalp.'

'Just sit still,' ordered Ford. He called up to the two men on the bridge: 'Throw over the ice, then take both cars and wait for us down at the flats.'

'Right.' The two men lifted the heavy block in its wrappings and heaved it over the railing. It showered the men in the boat with water as it sank explosively to the bottom, then bobbed up again and started drifting. 'Keep close behind it,' Ford ordered his oarsman, and the boat was shoved into the current and started to follow the nearly submerged, bobbing cake of ice.

'What the hell is he trying to prove?' McNarry growled to Lee.

'I don't know, but he's got something up his sleeve,' replied the judge.

'He'd better have.'

Three hundred yards downstream the ice ran into the fallen tree and got stuck. Womrath, the oarsman, guided the boat against the tree at Ford's request and held it there.

'Now what?' said McNarry.

'Wait five minutes,' said Ford, and pulled out his watch.

For five minutes they sat there watching the canvas-covered block bob against the tree, twisting against its branches. When the time was up Ford, the only man standing, got out a grappling hook and tried to wrestle the ice loose. It was caught in the branches and he almost upset the boat twice before he freed it and guided it around the tree and back into the current. He was red-faced and perspiring in his excitement as they followed it on down-stream.

At the hairpin turn under the Queen Street Bridge they got into more trouble. The ice ran aground. He pulled it free with the pole but it kept running aground again each time he let it go until the turn had been passed. Then it floated out into midstream again and moved fast and free. Womrath kept the boat ten feet behind it as it bobbed merrily along in the current. Ford was up forward watching it and calling instructions when necessary. Cameron had a look that almost amounted to awe on his face as he watched the husky old man with the pole in his hand. McNarry was silent and glum while Judge Lee also watched the Chief with something akin to admiration.

No further incident occurred until they reached the flats. The two cars were already there, drawn close to the water's edge, when they came into view. The ice block was in the middle of the wide stream, where it made the slight turn and started skirting the area. They drifted in silence, then Ford called back, 'Where was the body found, Burt?'

'Right there. We just went past it!'

'Row, Womrath, row. Catch up to this damned ice.'

Womrath bent to the oars and drew up on it until Ford hooked it with his dragging pole. 'Okay,' shouted the Chief. 'Take us ashore.'

Womrath manoeuvred the boat to the slightly over-hanging bank and first Lee, then McNarry climbed out. There was a challenge in Ford's voice. 'How about it, Judge? Want me to row back and let her drift by again?'

Lee shook his head. 'I don't think it's necessary, Chief. You win. It's murder.'

Ford leaped ashore and turned the grappling pole over

to one of his men. He was flushed and eager. 'Her clothes,' he said, 'would have caught on the branches of that tree so she'd never have gotten loose, even in the swollen river when we drained the lake. The same goes for the hairpin curve. She'd never have gotten around that. And you could turn that ice loose a thousand times and it wouldn't go into that nook where we found her. It can't be done!'

McNarry said sourly, 'Okay, okay, but why all the mystery? Why didn't you tell us back there in the courthouse you didn't think she ever went off the bridge at all?'

Ford wiped a face that was beet-red and dripping in spite of the crisp March air. 'I didn't want to stick my neck out. If it was just the body, it would be easy to guess maybe it was dumped here, but the idea of someone going back and throwing her hair clip off the bridge, that was plain crazy. There isn't a chance in a thousand of anyone ever finding it. That's even crazier than the idea of her jumping off the bridge in the first place and if I told you that's what I thought and it turned out I was wrong, hell, Bristol would have a new police chief sure.'

Judge Lee was listening. 'I guess you'll be around for a while, Chief,' he said, and turned to McNarry. 'Well, Dave, looks like you've got a murder on your hands. That's the verdict. Murder by person or persons unknown.'

Ford clapped Cameron on the back so hard he nearly knocked him down. 'Come on, Burt. You're going to buy me a drink.'

Tuesday, 21 March

PARKER GIRL MURDERED,
INQUEST VERDICT
CHIEF FORD PROVES BODY PLACED IN RIVER

Bristol, Mass. 20 Mar. – With all the dramatic effect of a Sherlock Holmes, Chief of Police Frank W. Ford swept away all doubts surrounding the disappearance and death of pretty Lowell Mitchell, the Parker freshman who vanished mysteriously two weeks ago. Using a 125-lb block of ice as the best approximation of a floating body, Ford threw it into the water at the point where Lowell was supposed to have entered the river and, by following its progress, proved beyond a doubt that the body of the Mitchell girl could not have come ashore at the spot where it was found.

Heightening the dramatic effect of his experiment, Ford waited until the inquest was nearly concluded and a verdict of suicide was all but brought in. Then, refusing to explain his intentions, Chief Ford induced County Court Judge Clifford M. Lee and District Attorney David McNarry to accompany him down to the river and there, at Higgins Bridge, where Lowell Mitchell's hair clip was found, he dropped in his block of ice . . .

Cameron put down the paper when Ford came in. 'Hello, Sherlock.'

Ford grunted.

'That's what it says here. You've got all the dramatic effect of a Sherlock Holmes.'

Ford said, 'That's just a polite way of saying I was scared to tell what I had up my sleeve.'

' "Examination," ' said Cameron, quoting, ' "of the flats for tyre marks or other clues indicating the identity of the car that carried the body down to the river were fruitless due to recent snows. Residents in the vicinity were being questioned but at a late hour last night no new evidence had been uncovered." '

'At eight o'clock this morning,' added Ford, 'no new evidence has been uncovered. Nobody remembers seeing or hearing a thing.'

'What was her parents' reaction? I suppose they know now their daughter was murdered?'

'They should. It's in every paper in the country. No, I talked to them last night. In a way, I think they feel a little better knowing she didn't take her own life.'

'What are they going to do about it? Are they going to hire that private detective again?'

'Not right away. I think he queered his chances the way he tried to muscle a reward out of them.'

'So you're going to have to solve it all by yourself.'

'Not me,' said Ford. 'McNarry's in charge of the investigation as of yesterday.'

Cameron laughed. 'McNarry couldn't find M in the alphabet and he knows it. You're going to do the work, Chief. He'll just sit back and take the glory.'

'Or the bricks. You're going to do the work, Sergeant. I outrank you.'

'That means Lassiter does it. I outrank him.'

Ford said, 'Let's cut out the horseplay. This is no May

Party. Come into the office. We got things to talk about.'
He moved on, shucking his coat, and Cameron followed.

'Now,' said Ford when they had the door shut against
the expected onslaught of reporters, 'who do you think did
it?'

'The father, whoever he is.'

'How do you figure it happened?'

Cameron lighted a cigarette and said thoughtfully,
'Looks to me as though she found out she was pregnant
and went to see him about it. That's why she pretended
she was sick and put on her skirt and sneaked out when
no one was looking. The guy broke her neck for her and
tried to make it look like suicide by driving down to the
flats late Friday night to dump the body, and later on
tossed the hair clip off the bridge.'

'That's the way I look at it.'

'The only trouble is, how could he possibly expect the
clip to be found? And why would he kill her? Paternity
isn't that bad a crime.'

'The father can answer those questions,' said Ford. 'Our
job is to find the father.'

'It's not going to be somebody too far away, Chief. My
bet is one of those boys over at Carlton, Kincaid or Myers.'

'My bet is closer than that, Burt. Someone here in
town.'

'Why? Because she walked? Someone might have come
in to meet her.'

'But not them. According to her diary, she didn't care
that much for either of those guys.'

'That's what she writes, but remember, she was being
cagey. It might have been an act.'

'I don't see it that way. She was cagey all right, but not
about them. It's my hunch the guy is someone here in

town and he's hardly mentioned in her diary. He might not even be in it at all. Now what do you think of that?'

'I think I'm not going to say no. But, if that's it, how the hell are you going to get a line on the guy?'

'You're going to talk to all her classmates and get a list of every last man she's ever been known to talk to.'

'Ugh.'

'You're going to check into their backgrounds and their alibis.' Ford pulled a sheet of paper from the inside pocket of his coat. 'I've already listed everyone in town she mentions in her diary. Here they are. See if you can find any more.'

Cameron reviewed the list. 'A nice old cab driver. That's great! President Howland. I remember. He's the "sweet old guy". A cop. That brings it right close to home. Which cop is that?'

'It was the four-to-twelve shift on September twenty-seventh. Either Sullivan or Weiss would be the one she asked directions of.'

'Fine. We've got a nameless cab driver, the president of the college, Mike Sullivan, and Sam Weiss. Then Seward, her history teacher, Markle, her English teacher, Charlie Corvath of the campus police. Can't you do better than that, Chief? Here's Mr Shugrue, her biological science teacher!'

'Not very fat,' Ford admitted.

'Fat? It's starved to death.' He went on reading. 'Holy cow! A guy in the post office! Which guy?'

'Probably Bill Shindell. He works at the stamp window.'

'Add Shindell – maybe. And Tom Williams, the night campus cop. And a man at the student laundry. Which man?'

'That's for you to find out.'

'Thanks. That's great. And here's another. The cute soda jerk in Bleeckman's.'

'Take a good look at him, Burt. She only mentions him once and that was in October and she calls him the first decent-looking native she's seen.'

'What have you been doing, memorizing her diary?'

'Only the pornographic sections.'

'Yeah.' Cameron checked that name and went on. 'Charles Watson. Which one is he?'

'You know. The elderly man at the Wagon Wheel who ordered champagne for one of the girls' birthday party.'

'Oh – yes.' He checked that name. 'As I recall it, Lowell favoured the older men.'

'Right, but don't overlook the younger ones.'

'Mr Peters, the florist.' Cameron read the last name with distaste. 'That's quite a list you've got here, Chief. It's just great. I'm supposed to check all their backgrounds?'

'Right. You know what to look for. I want to know which of them were in a position to or of a nature to have illicit relations with the Mitchell girl, or any girl for that matter.'

Cameron ran through the list again, scowling. 'An old cab driver, Howland, Sullivan, Weiss, Seward, Markle, Corvath, Shugrue, Shindell, Williams, a man in the student laundry, the soda jerk at Bleeckman's, Charles Watson, and Peters. Well, I'll check Watson and the soda jerk.'

'Check them all.'

'All? You mean Howland and her teachers?'

'Yes, including Sullivan and Weiss. And you talk to her friends and see if they know of anyone not on that list.'

'Oh, brother.'

'I know it. I'm picayune. Damn it, Burt, you know the spot we're in. There weren't any clues down on the flats.

There's no way of tracing the body back to somebody so we've got to trace somebody to the body. I think it's a local person and I think his name may be mentioned once or twice in the diary but that's all. Maybe it's not mentioned once even, which is why you're to try to add more names to that list.'

'But not her teachers, or the campus cops, Chief. If it was one of them, other girls would have had trouble with them before this one.'

'Maybe they have.'

Cameron thrust the paper in his pocket. 'All right. The works. How many cigarettes they smoked in 1946. Everything.'

'You can get the dope on her teachers from the college office.'

'I suppose the office lists whether or not they chase little girls.'

Ford sighed. 'This is a murder investigation. We investigate every possibility no matter how unlikely.'

Cameron groaned, 'Oh, brother,' and went out.

'I'm picayune. I'm damn picayune,' Ford yelled after him.

Kennedy came in then. 'McNarry's on the phone. He wants you to come to his office.'

Ford heaved himself out of the chair. 'I can't imagine what for.'

Tuesday Afternoon

Cameron called in at noon. 'There weren't any cars reported missing on the night of March third, were there?'

'No.'

'Then forget the cute little soda jerk. He's sixteen, doesn't have a licence, there's no family car. He was working in Bleeckman's noon hour on Friday when Lowell was supposed to have her rendezvous.'

'Scratch one,' said Ford.

Cameron called in again at one-thirty. 'Charles Watson isn't in the phone book or City Directory and nobody at the Wagon Wheel knows him.'

'Check with the girls in Lambert Annex. He might have given them his address.'

'Okay. I'm going to the office of college records now. Later on, when the girls are through classes, I'll hit the Annex.'

'If you don't get through by four o'clock, bring the dope to my house.'

'Four? You must think I only work an eight-hour day.' Cameron hung up.

It was close to six o'clock when Cameron went up to Ford's modest two-storey house and was let in by the Chief's daughter. Ford was sitting in his study reading a small book when the detective entered.

'The grapevine has it McNarry's ordered you to solve the case,' he said.

'He dumped it in my lap this morning, which is where it's been right along.'

'Fine. And what have you been doing while I've been chasing myself all over town besides draw down your pay?'

'Reading Lowell's diary.'

'What for, laughs?'

'Clues.'

'What clues? You've been telling me the guy isn't mentioned.'

'McNarry found things in that diary that I didn't find. I'm not forgetting how he showed me up. It's not going to happen again. I'm trying to spot other references to her condition to find out when she first learned about it.'

'Let's trade jobs.'

Ford yelled for his wife and, when she came to the doorway, he said, 'Bring in that bottle of liquor and the makings, will you? The sergeant's in a temper.'

Cameron grinned a little.

Ford grinned back. He said, 'You're a son of a bitch.'

Cameron said, 'Go look in a mirror, you ape. You're the toughest, meanest police chief this side of the Mississippi. But, goddamn your hide, you're a good one.'

'You got something?'

'Not enough to get a haemorrhage over, but you sure don't miss any bets.'

'That's why I'm Chief instead of you.'

'Sure. Your thirty-three years in the department to my eighteen wouldn't have a thing to do with it.'

Mrs Ford brought in a tray with the liquor bottle and appurtenances on it and left it on the desk beside the Chief. He poured two stiff drinks and handed one to the sergeant. He pulled out a cigar and rolled it between his palms. 'All right, Burt. Let's hear what you've got.'

Cameron took a slug of his drink and leaned forward in his chair, his elbows on his knees. 'Okay. First, this guy Watson. The girls think he gave them a calling card. They forget who kept it and don't know what happened to it. None of them could find it.'

'I like the sound of that.'

'You'll like it better yet. They described him to me. Somewhere in his late forties or early fifties with grey hair and a lot of charm. Sort of the Ezio Pinza type, I gather. He was dining alone and seemed to get a big kick out of watching their party. The waiter wouldn't serve them the champagne he ordered, but they gave him a piece of the cake. He was friendly, but not fresh.'

'And he said any time he could do anything for them,' said Ford, 'let him know. That means he must live somewhere around here. It's going to be a town not too far away.'

'We'll turn him up,' said Cameron. 'Starting tomorrow, I'll turn Massachusetts inside out.'

'Yeah, but let's not neglect the others. What else did you find?'

Cameron shrugged and took another drink. 'Not much,' he said. 'No names to add to your list. I talked to all the girls and they didn't know some of the ones who were on, like Peters for instance, let alone add more to them. They said she maybe spoke to a waiter at the Wagon Wheel when ordering dinner or something but, other than that, she didn't know anyone to talk to outside of her teachers and some of the campus employees. It's possible she may have chatted with some of Small's men from time to time. We can expand the list that way.'

'What did you find on background?'

Cameron pulled out some sheets of paper from his

pocket and smoothed them across his knee. 'This is what I got from the records office. Mrs Kenyon went with me but I asked her to keep it quiet. I don't want any of the campus cops or anyone else to get any ideas about what we're doing. First, Corvath. He was born in 1900 in Brattle-boro, Vermont, went through high school there, got into the Army just before the end of the First World War, got out and worked as a carpenter's apprentice, bricklayer, and machinist. Married in 1924, has three children, two boys and a girl. The girl and one boy are married and he has one grandson. He joined the Police Department of Mans-field where he was living in 1928 and was on that until 1942 when he got in the Army again for four years, getting out in 1946 and coming here as a campus policeman.

'It's sketchy, but you know college records. Some of that wasn't on the sheet, just stuff I knew about him myself. Hell, you know him. He's not the man for the job. Besides, Parker would look pretty thoroughly into a guy's back-ground before hiring him to protect the girls on a college campus.'

'No,' said Ford. 'I don't think it would be Charlie.'

'Next, there's President Howland. He was born in 1890, BA Yale, 1912, MA Harvard, 1913, PHD Columbia, 1915, in education. Was drafted in the Army and got out in 1919, taught in Chester Academy for three years, at Deering for six more, got married in 1925, has two daughters, one a junior at Parker, the other entering next year, was depart-ment head in Gelsing University, wherever that is, until 1932, when he switched to the University of Chicago and then took over the presidency of Parker in 1943.'

'He doesn't sound good,' said Ford, sipping his drink. 'She wouldn't have enough contact with him. How about her teachers? Was she in any seminars or small classes where she'd be thrown into close contact with a teacher? There has to be a way for them to get chummy. She was good-looking to be sure but there are a lot of good-looking girls at Parker and that alone wouldn't stir up a teacher.'

Cameron shook his head. 'There were about forty girls each in her English and history classes and twenty-five in biological science and the rest of her teachers were women. I just can't see the teachers nohow. Watson's our A number one suspect. In fact he's the only one.'

'But I'm picayune and you're going to check on everybody else just the same. Got any more?'

'Yeah. Markle, her English teacher, is forty-one, married, no children. He was not in the war, but has been teaching here for ten years. I've got where he went to school if you're interested. BA from Rutgers and MA in English from Cornell.'

'That tells a lot.'

'You asked for it. Here's Seward. He's thirty-five, graduated with high honours from Virginia in 1937, took a master's there in 1938, taught for three years in the high school in his home town of Richmond, joined the Marine Corps after Pearl Harbor and came out a captain in 1946. Started teaching here that fall. He was in the Iwo Jima invasion.' Cameron slipped that paper under the others and went on. 'Here's the rest of what I've got. An old cab driver. I haven't tried to look him up yet because I'm trying the better prospects first. Sullivan and Weiss, two of our men and you can rule them out. They're married with families and they don't play around, besides which both of them were on duty March third from four to twelve and neither of them are any Greek gods when it comes to looks. Shugrue, her science teacher. I haven't told you about him. He's forty-three and married with a twelve-year-old son, he's chubby and bald and wears glasses. The soda jerk is eliminated. Peters, the florist, is not the type. I took a look at him when I went by this afternoon. He's mousy and ineffectual. Shindell, I haven't looked up. Corvath is out. I haven't checked on Williams or the guy who works in the student laundry.'

'But you will.'

'Yeah,' growled Cameron. 'I will. But first I want to go after this Charles Watson. He's my bet.'

'Sure. He's mine right now, too, but let's keep an open mind about it.'

Cameron helped himself to some more liquor and put the bottle back on the desk. 'The trouble with the way you're running this is that it's all blind. I'm following a list of names and they run from a taxi driver to the college prexy. What about probabilities?'

'Such as?'

'Well, Lowell says in her diary the boys she dates are kids and she likes older men. That, to me, means the guy she sleeps with is going to be anywhere from twenty-five to fifty-five. What's more, it's not going to be an old cab driver or a campus cop, or Sullivan or Weiss. It's going to be a guy she can fall in love with.'

'And that can be anybody, including an old cab driver or a campus cop. One of the nicest girls I ever knew married a lousy drunk and supported him until he died of the DTs, buried him, and then went home and shot herself.'

Cameron set his empty glass down, put his hands on his knees, and pushed himself to his feet. 'All right,' he said in exasperation. 'You win. You and your fairy tales. I'll check them all, every last one of them.' He stuffed his papers back in his pocket and started glumly towards the door.

'You've got to, Burt,' Ford said, and Cameron paused without turning. 'There's nothing else we can do. Hell, Burt, you know police routine. It's leg work, leg work, leg work. It's covering every angle. It's sifting a ton of sand for a grain of gold. It's talking to a hundred people and getting nowhere and then going out and talking to one hundred more.'

He banged the desk sharply with his palm and bellowed, 'What the hell am I talking for? You know this business as well as I do. Get out of here and go home.'

Wednesday, 22 March

Cameron spent Wednesday continuing his check into the background and activities of the men Lowell had been connected with in Bristol. He came to Ford's house that evening tired and unrewarded. Charles Watson was still undiscovered and nothing had been uncovered that would tie any of the other men to Lowell Mitchell.

'There is a Charles Watson up in North Brookfield, but he's a bald-headed druggist with three grandchildren. The State Police haven't located any others between Springfield and Worcester. Boston's next. It's sixty-six miles away but this is the main route to Springfield and the Wagon Wheel is about the best-known eating place on it so it's a likely spot for some guy who travels a lot. There are several Charles Watsons listed there and one of them is probably the guy we're after. The only trouble is, if he does live in Boston, how did he and Lowell get together?'

'We'll worry about that when we find him,' said Ford. 'What about the rest of the local crew?'

'Shindell is a young guy as you know, and anything but good-looking. I don't have any alibi for March third yet but he's married and has two kids and he doesn't own a car. The lad in the student laundry is another kid. His name is Jack Doheny and if you don't like Kincaid or Myers, you certainly won't like him. He also doesn't have a car.'

'And he doesn't have an alibi, I gather,' said Ford sarcastically.

'What do you want, everything tied up in a pink ribbon in one day? I'm only one man. Give me time. The cab-driver business took hours.'

'Any luck?'

'Inasmuch as there are three cab companies in Bristol and most of the drivers are old, there's a month's work eliminating them alone.'

'How much of the month's work did you do today?'

'I narrowed it down to four possibilities. Joseph Krysoski, fifty-one, married, no children, working for the Bristol Cab Company; Joseph Worley, sixty, twice married, Independent Cab Company; Edwin Zarella, forty-nine, single, Hickey Cab Company; and Charley O'Brien, fifty-eight, bachelor, Bristol Cab Company.

'As for Tom Williams, he's single and not bad-looking, but he was on duty the night of March third.'

'And you don't like any of them?'

'They're all people, Chief, that's all. Not Romeos or murderers. Watson's the best possibility we've got.'

'We'll find out how good he is,' said Ford. 'Meanwhile, I've been wringing information out of the diary and I think I've got an idea what the guy's going to be like. For one thing, he's single.'

'How and why?'

Ford picked up the diary from the desk. 'Because I've just beaten McNarry at his own game.' He opened the book and thumbed through a few pages. 'Remember McNarry's remarks on what she wrote when he thought she was planning suicide? Listen to them again. February twenty-eighth: "I'm late again. Something drastic will have to be done." March first: "Nothing's happened. Maybe it's for the best." Know what that sounds like? At first she's frightened. Then she decides maybe her being pregnant is for the best. Why? Because then the father will have to marry her! She's in love with this man, there's no getting around it. She wants to marry him. No doubt he doesn't want to marry her. He hasn't said a flat no, of course, but he's probably been stalling. Now she thinks maybe she's got the weapon that will force him to.

'Now listen to what she says on March second. "Sometimes you wonder why you study. You're not going to use what you learn. At least I'm not. That I now know for sure." Why isn't she going to use it? Because she's going to get married. She really believes that, for she discusses trial marriage with the girls. She writes, regarding trial marriage: "Peggy says absolutely not. Sex is the whip you get the ring with. If they don't have to marry you for it, they won't. She's being cynical, of course, though I didn't tell her so. I'll bet a majority of couples sleep together before marriage." ' Ford looked up. 'Those are pretty broadminded ideas for an eighteen-year-old girl. Maybe I might believe most couples sleep together before marriage, but she shouldn't.'

'What do you mean maybe you believe? Your definition of a virgin is any girl over six who can run faster than her brother.'

'No wonder you stink as a detective. All you listen to evidence for is to find an opening for a smart crack. Now try to get what I'm driving at.'

'I know what you're driving at. She's trying to excuse her own conduct.'

'More than that,' said Ford. 'She's thinking of marriage. She believes the guy *will* marry her and denies to herself her roommate's claim that men don't marry their mistresses.'

'But he kills her instead.'

'Don't change the subject. The point is the man is going to be a slick character. Lowell was inexperienced but she was no fool. It's going to take a clever line to pull the wool over her eyes.'

'So we're looking for an older man with a way with the women – a smooth operator. In other words, Charles Watson again.'

'Could be,' said Ford.

'If he's single and known to Lowell.'

'Which is what you're going to find out.'

'Tomorrow. And what are you going to do? Sit around reading her diary?'

'I've read better books. Don't think I enjoy it.'

'I'll still swap jobs.'

'Uh-uh. I've been through my walking days on this force. I'm too old for leg work.'

'You're too old, period. What more do you think you're going to get out of that book?'

'How often she meets her lover.'

Cameron blinked. He uncrossed his legs, shifted his position, and put his hands on his knees. 'Now I know you're too old.'

Ford slapped the book with his hand. 'This guy, whoever he is, had her buffaloed. He convinced her she shouldn't mention his name in her diary, shouldn't mention anything about him or what they did, there or to anybody. Okay, but, damn it, no girl who's interested in her activities enough to keep a diary in the first place is going to leave something like that out of it! It's in here, Burt. In code, or with pinpricks, or ink blots, or somehow, she's going to mark the days she saw him!'

Cameron's eyes widened slowly and grew brighter. 'Damn it, Chief, if I don't think you're right. Why the hell couldn't I have thought of that?'

'You could if I let you sit around like I do. But then people might get the idea the department could get along without me. So I keep you chasing your tail.'

'You find that,' Cameron said, 'and we'll start getting a good line on the guy.'

'I'll get at it right after supper,' said the Chief, and he did, using as a starting point the week of fifteenth January through the twenty-first, six weeks before Lowell was killed. He looked first for unusual marks on the pages, either accidental or intentional. Finding none, he then studied what she had written:

Sunday, 15 January – Peggy and I went to church for a change. We thought it might be good for our souls. The dinner was good and I spent the afternoon walking it off by myself and it was so nice out that I didn't even get back in time for supper!!! The result was I ate out and got back just in time to be coerced into a bridge game with Hilda, Sally, and Patty. I didn't need much coercing, I'm ashamed to say. There was homework waiting but I just wasn't in the mood.

Monday, 16 January – Got a letter from home this noon. Guess who's getting married! Nora Cook!! Her engagement was announced in the paper yesterday, Mother said. Had a dull English class in the afternoon and wished I'd cut it and studied instead. Went to the library to do my research until dinner and then got into a discussion with Peggy and Sally and Patty on the value of a college education for a girl. Sally thinks she's wasting her time here since she has no desire to be a career girl. Neither have I, but college is more than just a way of passing one's formative years. It gives a girl independence so she doesn't *have* to marry right away and can choose better. It also makes her a more interesting companion to her husband and a better mother.

Tuesday, 17 January – Lab was good today and I should get an A for a change. All my free time was spent working on the English paper and trying to get my other homework out of the way. College may be good for a girl, but there are times when it makes her feel snowed-under. After dinner I went to the library and did more research for that darn theme!!! It's shaping up at last and I should have it out of the way by Saturday.

Wednesday, 18 January – Golf went well today. I seem at last to be getting the knack of keeping my eye on the ball. Maybe, at long last, I'm improving! Caught up a little on my letter writing this afternoon. Wrote Betty and Isabelle and then wrote Hank that I couldn't see him 28 January and made it sound as though I were sorry. Hilda thinks I'm mean to him but heck, what's a girl supposed to do, say yes when she doesn't want to? Jack drove over from Harvard this evening but I was out and didn't get back until after he gave up and left. Too bad he made the long trip for nothing, but if he isn't going to give a girl warning, it's his own fault!!! Spent the rest of the evening finishing the English theme and went to bed a tired girl, but happy.

Thursday, 19 January – Wrote home after lunch and told Mom and Dad I'd meet them at the train Saturday. Got most of my English paper recopied and had time for bridge before dinner even. Peggy wanted me to go to a show with her tonight, but I said I had too many other things to do. It was a good picture she told me afterwards. Just the same, I'm glad I didn't go. It's going to be fun seeing Mom and Dad again even if I've only been back $2\frac{1}{2}$ weeks! Wish Melissa could come, but she and her dates!!!

Friday, 20 January – Hilda and I went to the movies and saw *Ichabod and Mr Toad*, which Peggy had recommended. It was good! Disney is wonderful! Bob called up after dinner and invited me to a fraternity party next Friday. It should be fun and I said yes. After all, I don't want to be a hermit. Maybe it's not fair of me to accept invitations to parties and not accept the necking invitations, but I just don't want to park with those boys any more. It's kid stuff and not a good idea. Peggy and I got talking about that later. She doesn't see any harm in it as long as both parties know it's not serious. Trouble is, how do you know?

Saturday, 21 January – It was a perfect day today and I bought a corsage from Mr Peters, the florist, and gave it to Mother when she and Dad arrived. She was touched, I think. First I took them to their rooms in the Bristol Inn and then led them all over the campus. Dad had his camera and took quite a few pictures and when they were good and tired I took them to Hamlin, where we had a bite to eat and sat around the lounge. Dad took us to the Wagon Wheel for dinner and cocktails and we spent the latter part of the evening in their room talking about home and I got the details on Nora's engagement. It was quite sudden, Mother said. Some out-of-town fellow, about 28, whom she met only a couple of months ago. He works for IBM.

Sunday, 22 January – Had breakfast at the inn with Mom and Dad and we read the papers in the Ann lounge and I took them to dinner at Ann, which they liked very much, and Sally, Peggy, Hilda, Patty, and Marlene sat with us and made a big hit. They left in the middle of the afternoon, for it's a long trip back and I hated to see them go. They'll come up again in the spring sometime when Melissa doesn't have a date and can come too. The kid sister has sure blossomed out this year! Peggy and I skipped Sunday night supper and ate at Hamlin and I spent the rest of the evening getting my paper finished. Now I can relax for a while.

Cameron's phone rang at eight-thirty. It was Ford and he was jumping. 'I've got it, Burt. I know I've got it. Exclamation points!'

'Exclamation points?'

'Three of them. Listen, she wasn't an emotional girl, was she? No. Well, then why would she write she went for such a nice walk she didn't get back in time for supper, three exclamation points? She is really bowled over when one of her friends gets engaged and that only rates two of them. Missing supper gets three! So does her homework. She says, "After dinner I went to the library and did more research for that darn theme, three exclamation points!"'

'I think you've got something, Chief. How often does she use them and when do they start?'

'I don't know yet. I only just figured it out. What threw me off is that she's got those three exclamation points all through that week! Sunday, Tuesday, Wednesday, and Thursday.'

'Hell, the girl was in love.'

'But what's she in love with, a maniac?'

'The guy isn't as old as you are, Chief. Does everything

else check? I mean, does she go out every one of those days?'

'Sunday it was a walk. Tuesday she goes off to the library, or so she says, Wednesday she was out but doesn't say where, and Thursday she won't go out with her roommate because she has other things to do, but she doesn't say what they are.'

'That sounds like it, Chief.'

'I'll know tomorrow. I'm going through this thing page by page and see how often she uses them and when they began. If it is, they should start sometime after September.'

Thursday, 23 March

Ford found Cameron sitting behind the main desk when he walked in at eight-thirty the next morning. 'I thought you were going to Boston today to find Charles Watson,' he growled, unbuttoning his heavy coat.

'I sent Lassiter up. His legs are better than mine.'

'So is his brain.'

Cameron stretched elaborately and smiled. 'Ford's in form and all's right with the world. How're the exclamation points?'

'Puzzling.' Ford got out of his coat and went towards his office. 'I read that damn diary until I can't see straight.' He threw the coat on the table and plopped into the chair at his desk.

Cameron sidled after him and leaned against the door, his hands in his pockets. 'You've been working too hard. You need a vacation. Ever thought of retiring?'

'Why don't you go soak your head?' Ford pulled Lowell's diary out of his side pocket, spread it open on the desk to a folded paper bookmark, unfolded the paper, and said, 'Here are the dates. See what you can make out of them. I read through the whole year of 1949 and the first time she uses three exclamation points is December sixteenth. Then again on the seventeenth. Then there's a gap until January third. Then the seventh, ninth, twelfth, thirteenth, fifteenth, seventeenth, eighteenth, nineteenth, twenty-fourth, twenty-eighth, February third, fourth, fifth, eighth, tenth, eleventh, fourteenth, seventeenth, eighteenth, twentieth, twenty-fourth, and twenty-seventh. That's the last time.'

'They sure went at it hot and heavy. Is that what's bothering you?'

'What bothers me are the December ones. That's when she went home for vacation.'

'You mean she's in Philadelphia then?'

'No, New York. They start in New York and that's the funny part of it. If they mean what we think they do, why New York?'

'What's her diary say for those days?'

Ford leaned over the book. 'For the sixteenth, which was a Friday, she says: "Had my last class at noon and by skipping lunch was able to make the one-thirty train, leaving a bunch of envious girls with their Saturday classes. Got to New York and decided to stay over rather than go straight home. Tried to get tickets to *South Pacific*, which was a waste of time, of course, so I ended up at *Kiss Me, Kate*. It was a very good play, three exclamation points. Celebrated my release from captivity with a little imbibing and then called it a night."

'For Saturday, the seventeenth, she writes, "What a pleasure not to have to get up in the morning, three exclamation points. Had a leisurely lunch and finally, with reluctance, tore myself away from the big town and headed for Philadelphia – " and so forth.'

'Not too anxious to leave her lover and go home,' said Cameron. 'It makes sense to me.'

'I don't know. It sounds pretty fast to me. Anyway, if that's the key, we can cross-check and find out. Guess I'll have to bother her parents.'

The phone rang and McNarry was on the line. 'My

office is crawling with reporters,' he complained. 'What did you tell them?'

'I told them all statements would come from you.'

'What have you been doing? Do you have anything I can tell them?'

'No, not a thing. You can say the usual. We have leads. We hope to turn up something definite shortly. You know.'

'Have you found anything at all?'

'We've got some ideas.'

'What are they?'

'They aren't for publication, Mr McNarry. I can't even tell them to you over the phone.'

'Then come over here and tell me. I don't like all this secrecy. This case has caught the public fancy and they want to be let in on it. They've got a right to know what we're doing.'

'They don't have any right if it interferes with the conduct of the investigation.'

'I'll decide whether it interferes or not. Get over here sometime this morning. The girl's father called up yesterday and again just now. He's going crazy wanting something done. He'll raise all kinds of hell if we try to hold out on him.'

'Yeah, and he's apt to raise all kinds of hell if he gets wind of something. He can be a one-man lynch mob and go off half cocked.'

'It'll be worse if he thinks we're falling down on the job. Right now he wants to know if he should hire a private detective to help.'

Ford groaned. 'Oh, God. Not Monroe again!'

'I don't know who he has in mind, but we can't stop him and it makes us look bad needing outside help. You tell me where we stand and maybe we can dissuade him.'

'Yeah, okay. I'll be over.' Ford hung up gently, then knocked the phone over pushing it away from him. 'That damned McNarry,' he growled. 'He's so scared of what a failure would do to his career!' He picked up the phone again, swearing under his breath, and put in a call to Lowell's parents in Philadelphia. He got Mrs Mitchell.

'Yes, Mr Ford,' she said when he had identified himself. Her voice sounded taut and drawn.

'Lowell,' said Ford, 'came home for the Christmas holidays on Saturday, December seventeenth, didn't she?'

'It was a Saturday. I guess it was the seventeenth.'

'Was she expected sooner?'

'Yes.'

'Do you know why she stayed over?'

'She was visiting one of her classmates. Is this very important?'

'I think it is. Can you tell me the name of her classmate and was it arranged in advance?'

'It was Patty Short. She lives in New York and Lowell came down with her. She sent a telegram saying she was staying with her. They were going to a play.'

'A last-minute decision, so to speak?'

'Apparently. Please tell me, what does this mean?'

'I don't know yet,' Ford said. 'We're just checking up on all her actions.'

'You think it has something to do with her pregnancy, don't you?'

'I'm not sure yet, Mrs Mitchell. We're just checking. Thank you very much.'

The Chief hung up and turned to Cameron. 'She met somebody in New York that day and I don't think it was the Patty Short she told her mother it was.'

'So she left the straight and narrow all at once.'

'It wasn't planned in advance, apparently.'

'And it's going to be someone she knows from here whom she meets there and that someone is slick enough and attractive enough to do a fast job on breaking her down.'

'Difficult, but not impossible.'

'I wonder where our friend Watson was that day?'

'I'm more interested in where her friend Patty Short was. Want to run up to the Annex and find out?'

'Sure, if you'll give me a couple of men to go on checking the suspect list.'

'Pick a couple. I've got to go face the wrath of McNarry and try to keep him from spilling his soul to the papers. He's not a district attorney, he's a public relations man.'

'Going to tell him about the exclamation points and Watson?'

'Got to. He won't blab about Watson but the exclamation points is too good a story. It'll be hell getting him to keep that out of the papers.'

'He's smarter than that,' said Cameron, and put his hands together in prayer.

Thursday Noon

'For what it's worth, and it's worth plenty,' said Cameron, 'Patty Short did not go to New York with Lowell Christmas vacation. And Lowell did not spend the night with her for the simple reason that Patty was still at Parker.'

Ford got up and walked around the office. 'A break at last,' he breathed. 'It's been a long time coming, but what a hell of a beauty! Three exclamation points!' He stared out the window for a moment, then turned and jammed his fists into his hips. 'God, he must have had her under his thumb! Never a whisper about him anywhere. But she couldn't keep it out of her diary. Not completely! She had to mark the days. She misled us all the rest of the way but she came through for us here. She told us when they met.'

Cameron said, 'Now if we can only get a lead on the father, we can cross-check and sew him up.'

'We've got a starting point. He was in New York last December sixteenth. I guess you know what you're going to do.'

'Check the suspect list again.'

'You're getting brighter every day. And this time you've got something definite to go after so maybe you can get it done before Christmas. I got McNarry to hold up the exclamation-point business for a little while because he could see how the lover, getting wind of that, would go into a shell and, if he's the murderer too, he'd never make the slip we could catch him on.'

'A gold star for McNarry.'

'And he's got the New York police hunting for the hotel she stayed at. He's not too dumb for a college man. He hated to hold out on the papers but he would rather have a solution later than a first-rate story now. But you better make it pay or he's going to change his mind.'

Cameron went out to the main desk and brought back the schedule book, flopped it on the table, and opened it to December sixteenth. 'I'll make it start paying off right now. Sullivan had that day off, but Weiss was on duty. That's one guy for sure who was not in New York.'

'Great. You're terriffic. A born detective. Now suppose you go out and see who else didn't go to New York.'

Cameron closed the book and picked up his coat. 'That's what I like about this job,' he said. 'You get so much appreciation. The hours are so good too!' He started for the door.

Ford yelled after him, 'And call in every chance you get!'

Lassiter was the first one to call. He phoned from Boston about one o'clock. 'Two Charles Watsons aren't in town today. The others are ixnay.'

'Where did they go?'

'I don't know that yet. I'll find out.'

'Find out if one of them is our baby first. That's the most important thing. If you can't get that, see if either of them were in New York last December sixteenth or, if not there, out of town that night.'

'I'll see what I can do.'

'Don't see, do it!'

Cameron reported a few minutes later. 'One of those cab drivers might be a murderer but none of them are lovers.'

'Scratched, huh?'

'Scratched. I haven't got alibis for March third, but they were all working here in Bristol the night of December sixteenth.'

'Okay. We're down to twelve possibilities, including Watson.'

'Twelve impossibilities, you mean.' Cameron hung up.

He called again at two-thirty. 'Ed Polk, the soda jerk, is neither a murderer nor a lover. He took his girl to a high-school dance December sixteenth.'

'Try concentrating on the teachers,' said Ford. 'They're more likely to be leaving town for Christmas.'

'I know it. I'm saving the best for the last.'

'Move it up. This isn't a Junior Prom.'

Lassiter called in at three. 'Charles K. Watson isn't our man, Chief, but I think you're going to like the rest of this. Charles M. Watson is forty-three, grey curly hair, and a nice-looking guy from what his cook says. He's a sales representative which is a polite term for travelling salesman if you get what I mean, and he's on the road most of the time. He's married and lives in a house I couldn't pay the rent for with what I earn. He peddles some kind of new varnish coating for some kind of electrical stuff, that's all the cook knows about it, and he's got the New England territory on that and a couple of other items he sells, some kind of rubber shock absorber for machinery, and decals. He operates out of Boston mostly but every five or six weeks he makes a four- or five-day trip all through his territory and every three months or so he takes an extra three days and goes into Pennsylvania. That's where he is right now.'

'What about December sixteenth?'

'I can't spout dates but he made that Pennsy trip just before Christmas.'

'That's a tidy package,' Ford said.

'Want me to pin it down any closer? His wife won't be home until six, but I could wait around and squeeze a little blood out of her.'

'Don't run it into the ground,' said Ford. 'They might start wondering what's going on. Call it a day and come home.'

Cameron walked in as Ford hung up and said, 'You'll get bed sores sitting around all the time like that.'

Ford said, 'It's better than flat feet and where do you think you're going? Home?'

'I don't know what my home looks like. No, I'm going to visit a woman. Seward's maid to be exact. Seward and Markle had their last classes, according to the schedules, at noon on December sixteenth. Seward comes from Virginia. It's just possible he might have gone home for the holidays. Via New York, that is.'

'What about Markle?'

'Less chance there. He lives here and I can't ask his wife about that now because he'll be home.'

'Okay. See what you get on Seward.'

Cameron went out and Ford wandered around the office. He pulled out a New England road map and studied Route 20 from Boston to Bristol and the Route 9 super-highway from Worcester to Boston and gave that up and sat down with the list of seventeen men that comprised the suspect list. Six had not been in New York December sixteenth and another had an alibi for March third. At four o'clock he went home.

At five Cameron came to the house. 'I've got an interesting bit of news,' he said. 'Seward almost certainly took the one-thirty train to New York last December sixteenth on his way to Richmond. He left just before the maid went home and she knows it must be a weekday because she doesn't work Saturdays.'

'And that's the guy,' said Ford with sudden interest, 'who looks like Gregory Peck and Gary Cooper!'

'According to Lowell, yes. It's enough to make you think twice.'

'And he's single,' said Ford. 'Where does he live?'

'Dorchester Street. It's only about three blocks away from Lambert Annex.'

Ford clamped a cigar between his teeth and started walking around the room. 'And a teacher would throw the hair clip off Higgins Bridge. An outsider would more likely pick the Queen Street Bridge.'

'And what's the motive? Think he'd rather kill her than marry her?'

'The hell with the motive. I'm looking at opportunity. I'm not climbing out on any limb, but this guy can stand looking into.' He went to his study desk and picked up the phone. 'I know one way of doing it,' he said, looking up and dialling a number. It was McNarry's home he got and he started right in. 'It's off the record,' he said, 'but we know of two men who may have been in New York with Lowell. When the police find Lowell's hotel, tell them to look for a Harlan Seward or a Charles Watson registered there. If they can't find Lowell's name, have them look for a Mr and Mrs Seward or Watson.'

McNarry gave his agreement and Ford hung up. 'We're going to start moving in on both these guys,' he told Cameron. 'Watson is Lassiter's baby and you're going after Seward. Kennedy and Jarrett, who you picked to work with you today, will handle the others.'

Cameron put on his coat and went to the door. 'Okay, Chief, but don't expect anything sensational. Most of the other suspects live just about as close to Lambert.'

'Find any who were in New York on the sixteenth and I'll turn the spotlight on them too.'

Ford thought that was the end of Cameron for that day but he had no sooner sat down to dinner than the phone rang and it was the detective sergeant on the wire. His voice was normal in tone, but he was speaking quicker and in little jerks. 'Chief! I keep saying no. It can't be a teacher. But damn it, I'm wondering. Maybe it could. I drove by Seward's house on my way home for the hell of it. If he and Lowell made beautiful music together, he's got the place for it. It's the end house on Dorchester, which is a dead end. There's an empty wooded lot between him and the next house. The nearest house across the street is opposite the lot. A girl could come down Crescent Street, behind Dorchester, and cut through the woods from the rear and never be seen.'

'Has he got a car?' said Ford.

'He's got a garage attached to the house. I don't know about the car.'

'Interesting. Very interesting. You know, Burt, I'm starting to take a liking to that guy.'

'Brother,' said Cameron as he hung up. 'The kiss of death.'

Friday, 24 March

'We're turning the heat on Seward,' said Ford. 'It'll kill him or cure him but he's come into the picture all of a sudden and I'm going to find out if he belongs there or not. I want to know everything about him. He's single. He must take care of his sex urges some way. I want to know how. I want to know his relations with girls in the Marine Corps. I want to know his living habits. I want his movements right down to every time he combed his hair or went to the toilet from the sixteenth of December on. I want to know what other girls took the one-thirty train out of here that day and if they saw him on it and who was he sitting with. I want a watch posted on his house. If Lowell ever sneaked in there through the woods she probably wasn't the first girl to do it and she probably won't be the last. No watch in the daytime because, if he gets wise to the trap, we won't catch anything in it but, starting tonight, there's to be one man at least, more if they're needed, hidden in the woods. They're to let a girl go into the house because we have to be sure that's where she's going. When she comes out I want her picked up and brought down to headquarters.'

Cameron was in Ford's office, sitting at his desk. Lassiter was standing beside the closed door. Sergeant MacDonald, in charge of the four-to-twelve shift, was sitting in the other chair and Sergeant Poreda, in charge from midnight until eight, was sitting on the table. It was half past nine.

'Lassiter,' Ford continued, 'your boy Watson isn't due back for a few days yet so you're going to work with Kennedy and Jarrett tracking down these people: take notes.' He read from the sheet. 'I want to know where they were the evening of March third and if they were in New York December sixteenth. James Howland, president of Parker; Roy Markle, Lowell's English teacher; Charlie Corvath; William Shugrue, her science teacher; Bill Shindell, who works in the post office; Tom Williams, the night-watchman; Jack Doheny, who works in the student laundry; and Laird Peters, who runs Peters' Florist Shop. Also check on Mike Sullivan for December sixteenth. All right, don't everybody look popeyed. He was off duty that day and he was possibly mentioned in Lowell's diary and I'm checking my own men as well as anybody else. Got that, Lassiter?'

He turned to Cameron. 'See what you can dig up on Seward at the college office to start with. Find out everything you can, on and off the record, and I don't mean how many degrees he has. And don't let more people than necessary know what you're doing and tell the ones who do it's a routine check for background data for the investigation.'

'I can't see anyone believing that,' said Cameron.

'You're a college boy. You can think up something smart. Mac, you're to assign men to watch the house from dark until midnight. Burt, how many men will he need?'

'Two,' said Cameron. 'One to watch the front of the house on Dorchester Street and one to watch the woods on Crescent. There aren't any houses on that side of

Crescent and any girl going to see him would be likely to sneak in that way.'

'Two men, Mac,' said Ford. 'We're in for some leg work, but I'm going to clear up the picture on this guy.'

The leg work produced information if nothing else. Cameron dispensed it to the Chief around four o'clock. 'The house he lives in belongs to the college. It's on college property. It was the only one available to him when he came here because the locale isn't supposed to be too good, way at the end of a dead-end street and half in the woods and all. Anyway, he's had chances to move closer to civilization since but he's preferred to stay where he is, which would be likely if he entertains females or if he just doesn't want to bother moving everything, there's that angle, of course. His maid is supplied by the college and she works five mornings a week taking care of things. He can have her in extra for parties and such but that comes out of his pocket. Her name is Mrs Bessie Glover and she lives on Orange Street, about ten blocks from Seward. The college doesn't know anything about his personal life, but they have his Marine Corps record and his scholastic record, both of which are very good. He's eminently qualified for teaching and is well liked by the faculty and students alike as far as I could judge. I felt like asking if he'd made any passes at the women teachers but I guess he hasn't. Something like that would get around and he's supposed to be a model of deportment.' He altered his tone and said, 'This is only a suspicion I picked up around there talking about him, but I get the idea that if Seward made calf eyes at the unmarried women they'd leap in his lap. He doesn't bother with them and his eremitic life vexes them.'

'Eremitic? Cut it down to words of one syllable, will you? God damn it, spend one afternoon at a college and you start talking like a professor. You're working for the Police Department, not a PHD.'

'Pardon me,' said Cameron elaborately. 'Are my brains showing?'

'No. Only your degree. What else did you find out?'

'Nothing about his social and sex life. The college office doesn't explore those fields.'

'We'll send a wire to the Navy Department and find out where Seward served—'

'I've got that.'

'Well, we've got to find out his commanding officer, or someone who knew him and can tell us about him. You didn't find out about any of his friends here in town, did you?'

'Only that they're not faculty. He attends the social functions put on by the faculty as part of his job and he entertains the faculty from time to time, but it's duty stuff. They aren't his pals.'

'We'd better put a tail on him and see what taverns he inhabits, who he goes to see and all.' He got up. 'Meanwhile, let's go out and talk to Mrs Glover. She should be able to tell us more than when he went home for Christmas.'

They did a little exploring on the way. Cameron pointed out Seward's house and then Ford drove back to Lambert Annex and paced off the distance via Crescent Street while Cameron inched along in the car. 'Seven minutes,' said Ford, climbing back behind the wheel. 'Lambert Annex to Seward's back door, give her a minute to get through the woods there. Walking at night on the far side of the street, away from the houses, she'd never be noticed.'

Mrs Glover was a plump, smooth-faced woman of indeterminate age, a widow living alone in a small bungalow. She nodded at Cameron and seemed more puzzled than perturbed when Ford flashed his badge and followed her inside.

'You work for Harlan Seward?' was Ford's first remark when they were seated.

Mrs Glover nodded.

'What can you tell us about him?'

Mrs Glover moved her hands. 'Well, I don't know. What is it you're after? I don't see very much of him, he's teaching nearly every morning and I only work until noon.'

Ford said it was Seward's habits they were interested in. Did she have to clean up after parties often? What kind of parties, apparently, had they been?

She replied in the negative. He seldom had parties and the few he did play host at were apparently sedate affairs for the faculty.

'Do you think he entertains women alone?'

'I'm sure I don't know.'

'It's his moral conduct we're interested in. Haven't you ever come across anything that would indicate a woman had been there the night before? Maybe a long hair on the pillow, a tissue with lipstick on it in the wastebasket?'

Mrs Glover looked thoughtful for a moment, but all she said was, 'I've never found any hairs that I can recall and I just empty the baskets. There could be that in them for all of me, but I don't sort the rubbish.'

'You'd remember it if you found some indication like that?'

'I'm sure I would. I'm not interested in Mr Seward's personal affairs or his moral life if you want to put it like that, and I don't know anything about it. I'm sure if I found something I would remember it.'

'You wash the dishes there?'

'Why, yes.'

'Ever find more dishes than you would expect? Ever notice lipstick traces on glasses, or the silverware, or cigarette butts? Ever notice the odour of perfume around the house, or any other odours?'

'I don't think so.' She hesitated and thought of something. 'I haven't ever seen any lipstick traces such as you mention but, for what it's worth, I do remember something. One time there were two dishes with cake crumbs on them. The other dishes were supper dishes, just his, but there were those two cake plates. I remember noticing that, but I just thought he cut himself an extra piece before he went to bed.'

'How long ago was that?'

'I don't know, a month or two, maybe more.'

'He's either innocent or smart,' said Cameron.

'I don't suppose you want to tell me what this is all about,' said Mrs Glover.

'It depends,' said Ford. 'Would you be willing to help us?'

'If you ask me to, I can't refuse. You're the police.'

'We can't make you, even so. How do you feel about Mr Seward? Like him, hate him, feel neutral about him?'

'He's very nice. I like him. I'm not crazy about him, if that's what you mean. I hardly ever see him.'

'You don't like him well enough to try to protect him? If you help us you may turn up something against him. You wouldn't conceal it?'

Mrs Glover shook her head decisively. 'I like him, but if he's done wrong he should be punished for it. I wouldn't protect him against that.' She leaned forward and said in a lowered voice, 'You think he's behaved immorally with some girl?'

Ford said, 'There isn't any question about that. The question is who has he been immoral with recently?'

'But you don't even know that he has been. You're asking me to help you find out.'

Ford said dryly, 'I doubt that there is a normal unmarried man over twenty who has not been immoral with a woman at some time. Mr Seward is normal and thirty-five. I'm sure he's been immoral countless times. What I want to find out is, do his women come to the house? That's where you can help us.'

'I don't see what difference it makes, really,' said Mrs Glover. 'It's wrong no matter where it happens.'

'Mrs Glover,' said Ford with restraint, 'we are not checking up on Mr Seward because we think he may have been naughty with a woman. We think he may have killed one.'

The woman gasped and her mouth popped open. 'Oh no.' She gathered her breath and her wits after a moment and looked bleakly at the Chief. 'The Mitchell girl?'

Ford nodded. 'Now we aren't saying he did. In fact it's quite probable that he didn't. We want to find out one way or the other and to help us do that we need somebody in his house, somebody who can look around. That's why we want you to help. Understand, we're as much interested in things that will point to his innocence as to his guilt.'

Mrs Glover bit her lip and nodded. 'I'll do what I can. Tell me what you want.'

'Right now, all I can say is keep your eyes open for any indications that he's had a woman here. If there's anything specific I'll want you to look for, I'll let you know.'

'What shall I do if I do find something?'

'Save it and telephone headquarters. Don't call from his house and don't come down to headquarters. It's important that he is not to have the slightest idea of what you're doing. Don't mention this to anyone. If he should be guilty, our only chance of catching him depends on his not knowing we suspect him.'

Mrs Glover was extremely nervous. 'I'll do my best,' she said, but her hands were trembling.

'Just behave normally,' was Ford's parting comment as he walked out to the car shaking his head. 'What an actress she's going to be.'

'What do you expect her to do at the prospect of working for a murderer, sing hymns?'

Friday Night to Monday
Morning, 24–27 March

The watch was set up on Seward's house that night and a man was assigned to trail him during the day. An attempt was initiated next morning to locate others in the Marine Corps division in which Seward had served with an eye to finding out his preoccupation with women. More concrete measures were also being taken in an effort to link or unlink Seward and Lowell Mitchell. Ford ordered two of his men to study the schedules of all the girls in Seward's classes. It was hoped some of them had also left for the Christmas holidays a day early and had seen Lowell and Seward together.

'That's going to be a rough job, Chief,' said Cameron.

'There's a rougher one coming up. We're going to interview all the girls in Lowell's history class. I want to know if they noticed anything about her behaviour or his that would indicate they were any more than pupil and teacher.'

'Seward's going to catch on. I suppose you know that.'

'It can't be helped and it may be a good thing. I'd sort of like to see what he does when he gets the idea he's in the spotlight.'

Ford put two other men to work on that angle and left Lassiter, Kennedy, and Jarrett to cope with the other suspects. Simpson, Houkman, and Jensen were called in for extra duty and the regular police routine was turned over to them. Ford himself spent the weekend studying the reports.

By Monday morning most of them were in. Lassiter and his men had talked with several dozen people regarding the other suspects and had uncovered nothing to place them in New York a week before Christmas. The names of some of Seward's Marine buddies had been obtained and phone calls put in to them. The questioning of the girls on campus was being wound up and New York police reported to McNarry.

McNarry broke the news to Ford. 'No girl named Lowell Mitchell registered at any hotel in New York December sixteenth,' he said. 'Sounds to me like she stayed at a private home somewhere.'

'Seward doesn't have one. Watson may have, though.'

'What about Seward's activities?'

'Nothing. He goes to class and comes back. He's spent his evenings at home alone. He hasn't even gone out to a movie since we started the watch on him and nobody's gone in his house.'

'What'll I tell the papers?'

'Tell them we're at a dead end.'

'Are we?'

'On Seward, yes. The only thing on our side are those reports that came in saying he was the biggest and most successful wolf in his company when he was in the Marines.'

'You're clinging to that still?'

'It's all I've got but even that isn't much. He may have reformed, damn it. He wouldn't get very far as a teacher in a girls' school with a reputation like that.'

'Mitchell's still calling up daily,' said McNarry. 'He's

going crazy and he's driving me crazy. What am I supposed to tell him?'

'Tell him we'll find the guy and will let him know as soon as we do.'

'He wants something he can get his teeth in. That hasn't held him so far and it's not going to now.'

'We can't tell him anything else.'

'He's threatening to go to the Governor and the Lieutenant Governor and everybody else.'

Ford said, 'What the hell does he want? Nobody could do more than we're doing. Any killer who's slick enough to come damn close to getting a suicide verdict out of his murder is going to give us trouble.'

'All right. You and I know what police work is like but he doesn't. It's his daughter and he's a raving maniac wanting that killer. If we ever find him, I'd hate to be in his shoes. This guy will kill him with his bare hands!'

'Which is why you've got to hold him off.'

'All right, I'll try to stall him a little longer, but for God's sake turn up something!'

'I'm not sleeping now trying to turn up something,' growled Ford, and hung up. He yelled, 'Hey, Burt!'

Burt Cameron came in. 'How do we stand?'

'We don't. Lowell didn't register at a hotel.'

'If she was signing in for a shack-up job, she might have used an assumed name.'

Ford looked up in slow surprise. 'By God, the man's a detective.'

'Don't tell me you never thought of that!'

'No, because, damn it, I'm working on the theory that she was seduced, not that she planned the thing.'

Ted Trumbull came bursting into headquarters at that

moment. 'He took that train,' he said. 'He took that train. One of the girls saw him on it.'

'Which train, when?'

'Christmas. December sixteenth. Seward was on the one-thirty train. She saw him.'

'Who's the girl?'

'A Marian Lagroe. She saw him in the station and later on the train.'

'Was he alone?'

'In the station he was and that's the point. He was sitting with some girl later on.'

'What did the girl look like?'

'She doesn't remember. She didn't notice the girl.'

'The girls sure don't have eyes for anyone but Seward,' said Ford. 'But it's ten to one the girl was Lowell Mitchell.'

'For once the leg work produces something,' breathed Trumbull.

'Did you hit them all? All the girls who left on Friday?'

'No. There were about seven left.'

Ford said, 'So you're going to quit, huh?'

'Well, I – we know he took that train and he sat with her. What else is there to find out?'

'We don't know *who* he sat with! Go find out. And find out if there was a club car on the train and if he took the girl in there.' He turned to Cameron. 'He probably got that girl drunk, Burt. Masculine charm and a little hero worship in there aren't going to do it alone. There's got to be liquor. If he had her mellow by the time they got to Grand Central, he'd probably find it easy to persuade her to take a later train to Philly and from there, no train. Trumbull, get moving! I don't know what you'll turn up, probably nothing, but you aren't going to overlook a damn thing.' He turned to Cameron once more. 'Burt, I think this guy's our man.'

Trumbull went out a little less exultant than he had come in but the atmosphere in the station house was one of excitement. Cameron tried to temper it. 'We still haven't figured out where she spent the night.'

'Or,' said Ford, 'if Seward spent the night.' He picked up the phone and called the DA once more. 'A break, Mr McNarry. Seward and Lowell took the same train. I don't know whether they met on the train by accident or whether it was prearranged but they met! I'm certain of it.'

'It looks good,' agreed McNarry.

'One thing I want to know. When did Seward get to Richmond? Can you get in touch with his family and find out? Don't, for God's sake, tell them why you want the information. Don't even tell them you're the district attorney if you can help it. Give them some spiel and see if they remember. If he went right on through, he'd get there late Friday night sometime. If he stayed over but did not seduce Lowell, it would probably be Saturday afternoon. If he's guilty, it would be Saturday night.'

'Going to have his own family convict him, huh?'

Ford said, 'Are you dragging ethics into this? I'm trying to catch a killer and I'm doing it any way I can.'

'Okay. No complaints. I'll let you know what I get.'

'Thanks.' Ford banged down the phone and turned to Cameron. 'That panty-waist! But I have to admit he gets things done.' He got up and went to the window. 'That guy must be hell with women! How can someone like that get them so completely? A nice, decent kid like Lowell, been kissed a few times and that's all. A few hours with him and she's in his bed.'

Cameron went over and sat on Ford's rolltop desk.

'Before you blow your top, you'd better remember we don't even know if he's the guy. Hell, what if his folks do say he didn't get home until late Saturday, what will it prove? Do you think a jury will say he's her lover because Lowell puts three exclamation points in her diary on that day?'

'They will if they can prove they stayed together and I'm going to do it. Got a copy of Seward's schedule?'

'Classes? Yeah, here. I got them of all her teachers.'

'His will do.' Ford took it and looked at his watch. 'He's tied up and Mrs Glover is still at his house. She's going to earn her keep as of now.' He looked up Seward's number and got her on the phone. She said, 'I'm sorry. I haven't been able to find a thing.'

'That's all right. I don't expect him to leave anything around. Here's what I do want, though. Can you pick up a sample of his handwriting? Get as much as you can from the wastebaskets and all and take it home. We'll be around for it this afternoon.'

'Yes, sir. I'll try to.'

'Try hard. This is important.' He hung up.

'Part of your tracking plan, Chief?'

'You bet.'

McNarry called back in half an hour. 'You hit the nail right on the head, Chief. Seward got home Saturday night!'

'That's fast work.'

'What's the next move?'

'A tough one for the New York police. I want you to send them copies of Seward's handwriting. They've got Lowell's on the missing persons circular. They registered at a hotel. They must have! But this guy Seward is a cagey character. He kept his name out of Lowell's diary so he undoubtedly kept it off any hotel register. How they signed

199

it depends on whether this was spur-of-the-moment or planned in advance. If she knew what she was doing, they probably took one room as Mr and Mrs. If she didn't, they might have taken two rooms under separate names. It's probably Seward's handwriting because the girl wasn't a liar and at that stage of the game she wouldn't know what he had up his sleeve.'

'Wait a minute, wait a minute. You're over my head. Wait till I get pencil and paper and write this down.' There was a rustling and a muttered remark, then McNarry said, 'Let's have it over again what they're to look for.'

'They're to look for his handwriting first, either as a single man or Mr and Mrs. I think the best bet is a single man because I don't think Lowell knew in advance what he was up to. If she did, it stands to reason she would have told her folks she'd be home Saturday instead of writing them she was coming home Friday and then sending a telegram changing it. I don't think Seward made his move to seduce her until late that night when they came back from the drinks they had after the play. If that's the case they would have taken single rooms and he would have filled out Lowell's room registration card for her because, if he didn't, she would have used her real name. So I think they'll probably find two cards in his handwriting, one for him and one for her.'

There was a pause before McNarry said, 'I got you so far.'

'If they don't have any luck that way, then it may be that Lowell decided beforehand she'd go to bed with him and she signed her own card with a phony name. It's possible, but I don't think it's likely that she was willing to register as Mr and Mrs. That's moving too fast.

'So have them look first for his handwriting on single-man and single-woman cards, secondly for his on a single man's and hers on a single woman's, and lastly for his on a Mr and Mrs card.'

'Okay. I'm with you. I'll notify them right away, but I suppose you know this will take time. It took them three days to hunt for the names without comparing handwriting, you know. Thousands of people registered in New York hotels that day.'

'I don't think they had reservations in advance. That might help.'

'Probably will. When can you get me a sample of his handwriting?'

'This afternoon, I hope. His maid is looking for it. If she doesn't turn any up I'll have to try the college office but I want to avoid that if possible. They're beginning to wonder what we're doing and we can't kid them along with that "routine investigation" line much longer.'

'Okay. Get it to me this afternoon and I'll put it in the mail so they'll get it tomorrow.'

'New York will love us,' said Ford, 'but if they come up with something I'll love them right back.'

'I'll be loving them right along with you. God, I hope you're on the right track. It seems to me you must be.'

'If I'm not we go back to Watson. He'll be back from his trip by then.' Ford stopped and looked up as a breathless Mrs Glover came in. 'Hold on, McNarry. Hold the wire!'

Mrs Glover hurried right up to the desk. 'I came right away. I didn't dare wait. I was afraid Mr Seward would come home early and find me with these.' She thrust two crumpled sheets and a small slip of paper on the desk. 'They were in his wastebasket and I didn't dare wait. I – are they what you want?'

Ford looked at them quickly and called into the phone, 'A grocery list and two sheets of history notes, Mr McNarry. I've got enough handwriting for the forty-eight states. I'm bringing it over myself, right away!' He looked up and said, 'It's perfect, Mrs Glover, absolutely perfect!'

'Oh, I'm so glad. This will decide whether he's innocent or guilty?'

'It'll go a long way towards it. Now you'd better get back there in a hurry. If he catches you out there'll be hell to pay. Whatever you do, don't let him know where you've been or what you've been doing!'

'Oh no, sir. I wouldn't dare. Why, if he's as bad as you say, he might kill me.'

'I doubt that.' He turned to Burt and said, 'Call the radio car and tell them to come here and take her back out on Maple Street and let her off a couple of blocks from Seward's.'

Monday Night

Frank Ford leaned back in the chair and puffed affectionately on his cigar. The radio, turned down low, gave forth
the growling tones of a mystery drama but Ford wasn't
listening. His tie was loosened and his coat was off,
revealing an unbuttoned vest. His close-cropped grey hair
capped a tired face creased with the lines of fifty-eight
years of hard work. His dinner sat comfortably in his
stomach and a heavy drowsiness was creeping over him.
Through half-closed eyes he viewed his surroundings, the
small living room with the plush chairs and large couch,
the portrait photo of his daughter in her junior high-school
graduation costume on the battered old cabinet radio, the
big old garish lamp on the table, and the half-drawn heavy
curtains through which he could see his daughter studying
in the dining room.

He heard footsteps, the curtains were pushed farther
aside, and his wife came in. 'Phone, Frank,' she said.

Reluctantly he heaved himself out of the chair. 'Business?'

'I think so.'

He drew a long breath, clamped the cigar between his
teeth, and moved towards the bedroom and the disturbing
instrument.

'Chief? Houkman. There's a girl in Seward's house.'

There was no lethargy in Ford now. He was straining
at the leash. 'How long has she been in there?'

'Ten minutes.'

'Where are you?'

'Bristol Drug Store.'

'Get back there fast. I'll be right over.'

The lines in his face were still heavy but there was a spring in his step and his eyes were on fire. He shrugged into his coat without removing the cigar from his mouth and clamped on his old felt hat. His wife came in. 'You have to go out?'

He nodded. 'We've got a break.'

'Be back soon?'

'I don't think so. Don't wait up.'

'I'll leave sandwiches in the icebox and coffee on the stove.'

'Thanks.' He kissed her and went out the back door to the car.

Crescent Street, the dead end behind Dorchester, was empty, with neither car nor person visible. On the left was the locked back gate to the college dorms forming Big Quad and the windows were ablaze with lights. Beyond that, near the end of the street, was a collection of faculty houses set well back behind sweeping, snow-covered lawns, and deep behind them were the lights of Little Quad. On the right, except for two or three houses near the corner, there was nothing but a snow-covered dirt sidewalk bordering the thin wooded land that swept through to the back yards of those houses which fronted on Dorchester Street. Ford drove down beyond the street lights to the dead end and turned around. Under his breath he was cursing Houkman for leaving his post unguarded. Then, from nowhere, a figure appeared at the side window.

'Chief?' It was Houkman.

'Get in. Where the hell have you been?'

'Keeping out of sight.' He opened the door and slid into the seat.

Ford pulled into the kerb and shut off the lights and the engine. 'How long have you been back?'

'Five minutes.'

'The girl still inside?'

'I think so. She hasn't left while I've been here.'

'She'd better be. You know better than to leave your post.'

'I know, but I thought you'd want to be in on it.'

'You could pick her up when she leaves without my help. How long were you gone altogether?'

'About twenty-five minutes.'

'The house could burn down in that time.'

'It's all right. I figure, what with her sneaking in the back way, she's going to stay for a while.'

'You aren't being paid to figure. Oh hell. Where did she come from?'

'She came up the street from Maple. I was back here at the end patrolling around behind the trees and bushes. I almost didn't see her. She came down the left-hand side away from the street lights and I just spotted her across from the last house from that street light up there. She came down pretty close to the end and then cut diagonally into the woods towards where Seward's house would be.'

'You didn't see her go into his house then?'

'No. I didn't dare follow her because she'd hear me in the snow and that would scare her off.'

Ford nodded grimly. 'How was she walking? Slinking? Furtive? Outright?'

'Just walking. Like she knew where she was going. She didn't look like she was trying not to be seen, but she kept to where it was hard to spot her.'

'What time did she come by?'

'About quarter of nine.'

'Okay. We'll wait her out.' He looked at his watch. 'Nine twenty-five. I hope the hell she's still there if that's where she went.'

'She is. She wasn't just out for the air.'

Ford pulled out a fresh cigar and got it lighted. 'You can smoke if you want,' he told Houkman, who looked grateful and immediately popped a cigarette in his mouth. They opened the draught windows, turned on the car radio, and settled down. Soft music drifted out from the dashboard and Ford sighed and shifted his position so that he could keep an eye across the street.

'Aren't you going to tune in the police calls?'

'What for? I listen to them all day.'

'I know, but something might come up.'

'So what? A three-alarm fire isn't pulling me away from here.'

Houkman retired to silence and sat sideways on the seat so he, too, could watch the white path opposite.

Silence sat with them and Houkman shifted around and lighted another cigarette from the butt of his first and looked at the stocky, unmoving shape of his superior. The minutes ticked by and the cold began to creep into the car with them. Houkman snuggled deeper inside his coat and watched the vapour of his breath. Outside, a light breeze was rustling the dry bare branches of the trees and the street lights ahead glistened brightly in the cold air. The nearest one was almost dazzling through the crosshatch of branches from the closer maple tree.

The radio gave the only sound of life to the scene, the muted tones of a symphony floating through the car. The Chief had strange tastes in music – if the Chief were listening. Houkman looked at the motionless figure and wondered if he were asleep. He hoped he was. Ford wouldn't be able to jump all over him any more for little miscues were he to be caught sleeping at the switch. Ford. A good guy and you respected him, but what a stickler for details!

The radio commercial came on, then the ten o'clock station change, and some polka music followed. Ford moved then. He took the dead cigar out of his mouth and threw it out, then, without taking his eyes from across the street, fumbled for the dial and came up with a mystery programme.

'Long wait,' Houkman ventured, but Ford only grunted and resumed his watch.

At ten-thirty Ford did not bother to hunt for another programme but let them follow as they would. The eleven o'clock news roundup came on for fifteen minutes and was succeeded by another fifteen minutes of dance music. Houkman was bitterly cold and he wished he were out patrolling, doing anything but sitting still. Nevertheless, he quivered in silence. Ford had shown not the least response to temperature and a twenty-three-year-old reserve officer could not whine at what a fifty-eight-year-old regular ignored. Thirty-three years with the force, thought Houkman. That was a long time compared to his one. One year as a reserve and it hadn't been bad, except for the past three weeks. He'd been called in for more extra duty since the Mitchell girl disappeared than the whole rest of the year put together.

The fifteen minutes of live music supplied by a band someplace in Boston came to an end and fifteen minutes more by another orchestra somewhere else came on. Ford shifted his position and began to mutter. Houkman forgot the cold momentarily and moved a little farther into the corner of the seat away from the Chief. If the girl had come out and got away while he was telephoning there was going to be hell to pay. The Chief was starting to get impatient and that was a bad sign. Police work was a lousy job. Here it was getting on towards twelve when he should go off duty and there never was a night when he wanted to get off duty more than this one, but he didn't dare mention it. Ford would think him a clock watcher and he was in bad enough now for having left his post. He had thought the Chief would be grateful for the call. Or was it that, deep down inside, he wanted the Chief supporting him when he made his first arrest?

Ford turned around and said, 'You stinking bastard! She probably left long ago.'

'I was only gone twenty-five minutes, Chief. They couldn't do it that fast.'

'It doesn't take three hours, either!'

'Maybe she's spending the night.'

'Use your head, stupid. A girl has a lot of explaining to do when she's away all night.'

Houkman was desperate. 'She might have gone out the front door. Maybe Sam Weiss picked her up.'

'I'll just bet.' Ford tuned in the short wave and got silence. He picked up his mike. 'Sullivan, this is Ford. Over.' He scanned the path and woods some more.

'Go ahead, Chief.'

'Any report from Weiss?'

'Negative.'

'Who relieves you? Parella tonight?'

'Yes, sir. He's just come in.'

'Tell him a girl may be in Seward's house. Tell him I want a twelve-to-eight shift on Crescent and Dorchester streets tonight. Get two men out right away. Weiss may have started in.'

'Yes, sir.'

Ford put the mike away and said to Houkman, 'If you let her get away you know what your name will be, don't you?'

'Yes, sir,' said Houkman miserably. He lighted another cigarette but it tasted flat. He flung it out the window. 'The college girls can take a twelve o'clock,' he said. 'She might be waiting until the last minute.'

Ford's arm reached out and clamped on his wrist like a vice. 'Shut up,' he whispered.

Houkman leaned forward, peering beyond the Chief's head at the dark woods and white flooring. Only the hum of the silent radio broke the silence, that and a slight sound from the darkness. Then into the glow of the street light came a girl. She was walking swiftly and steadily, her coat collar turned up against the cold night air, her hands thrust deep in her pockets.

'That her?' Ford whispered.

'Yes. That's the one.'

She was ahead of the car now, opposite the light. Ford dropped Houkman's wrist and started the engine. The car swung from the kerb without lights and gathered speed. Ford was rolling down his window as he passed her and then he cut the car sharply up over the kerbless sidewalk and crunched across the snow in front of her. The car bounced to a sudden stop and he said, 'Okay, sister, we're the police.'

The girl stopped dead, her face drained white in the dull glow of the street light. She stared at him stunned as Ford opened the door and got out. He unbuttoned his coat to show his badge and said, 'Get in.'

Her eyes were huge and her lips bloodless and she did not move until he seized her roughly by the arm and shoved her towards the open door. She stumbled then, still speechless, in beside Houkman, and Ford followed her, crowding her with his bulk. He slammed the door, picked up the mike, and said, 'Sullivan?'

'Yes, sir.'

'Cancel my last order. I've got her.'

They brought her into headquarters, a terrified creature, staring numbly at the group of large uniformed men coming off and going on duty. The men, in turn, looked at her and looked at Ford, but they said nothing. His expression forbade it.

'Get Lassiter and Cameron out of bed, Parella,' he ordered, 'and send out for a quart of hot coffee. We'll be here for a while.' He sat the girl at the big table in the long room stretching back of the desk and told her to stay put. She tried to ask what they wanted of her and tell him she hadn't done anything but he didn't waste time answering her.

By the time Lassiter, who was assigned to the plain-clothes staff because of his ability to take shorthand, and Cameron arrived, the changing of the guards had finished and the station house was deserted except for Parella at the desk, the girl, and Ford. Houkman, feeling a little happier about his job as a reserve officer, had been sent home with the rest of the four-to-twelve shift.

The girl, meanwhile, had had half an hour to get used to her position and muster up a little bravado. She was on the pretty side with short blonde curls, a full small mouth, small blue eyes, and rather delicately cut features in an oval face. The dress she exposed when she shed her coat was plain and black with a square neckline decorated by lace, cut low enough to reveal the beginning curves of two full breasts. It was belted tightly about a small waist to accentuate her voluptuousness.

'You can't hold me here,' she said when Ford, Cameron, and Lassiter, armed with coffee mugs, descended upon her. They sat on the tabletop, giving them a height advantage over the seated girl, and Ford did not bother to answer that remark either.

'What's your name?' he said.

'What are you arresting me for? I haven't done anything.'

'Answer the question!'

'Mildred Naffzinger.'

'Where do you live, Mildred?'

'One-fourteen Putney Street. Please. You've got to let me go. I haven't done anything. My folks will be worried.'

'The sooner you stop wasting time, the sooner you'll get home. Now answer the question. What have you been doing tonight?'

'Me? Nothing. I went for a walk.'

'Where?'

'Oh, just around.'

'At midnight?'

'I was just coming back.'

'From quarter of nine to quarter of twelve? That's a long walk.'

'No. I wasn't walking all that time. I was visiting.'

'Who?'

'A friend.'

'Harlan Seward, huh? How long have you been a friend of his?'

She looked startled. 'Oh no. No. I don't know any Harlan Seward. I was visiting a girlfriend.'

'Where does she live?'

'Huh?'

'Stop stalling. You went to see Harlan Seward. My man spotted you going in at quarter of nine.'

Mildred looked as though it just came to her. 'Oh yes. Of course. You mean the house at the end of Dorchester Street. Of course. I delivered a package to him.'

Ford got off the table and swigged his coffee. 'Now we're getting somewhere. Now we're starting to understand each other. That's right, the last house on Dorchester Street. Harlan Seward. You delivered a package to him at quarter of nine this evening. Is that straight?'

The girl looked tentative but she nodded.

Ford sat down again. 'Only my man didn't see you carrying any package.'

'Oh, it was a small package. I had it in my pocket.'

'What was in it?'

'Uh – cough drops. See, I work in the Bristol Drug Store and he called up and wanted the box of cough drops delivered. So I delivered them.'

Ford jerked a thumb. 'That the kind of dress you wear when you work?'

She looked down at herself and coloured slightly. 'No,' she said. 'See, I get through work at six o'clock. Mr Gregory, he's the owner, he didn't have anyone to deliver it and 114, where I live, is down in back a block so he called up and asked if I'd take it over to Mr Seward for him.'

'So you put on a dress like that and stay three hours.'

She was almost in tears. 'No. No. I just happened to have this dress on and I didn't stay three hours. I went for a walk afterward, I tell you.'

'And you go in the back door—'

'Of course. I was only delivering something.'

'Yes, a box of cough drops. Seward's so sick he can't go get them himself. You go to the back door, but you cut through the woods to get there.'

'It was shorter.'

'Which you already knew and you knew just how to get through the woods to his house.'

'Please.' She started to cry. 'I'm all upset. I'm tired. I want to go home.'

'You're damn upset and you're tired, but you're not going home.'

She looked up, frightened. 'Please. You've got to let me go home. My parents will be frantic!'

'There's a phone there. You want to call them up and tell them where you are and where you've been?'

She started to weep in earnest.

'Maybe you'd like me to call them up and tell them where we picked you up.' He took two steps towards the main desk.

'No,' she wailed through her sobs. 'Please. Just let me go home.'

Ford came back and sat on the table again. Lassiter got off and moved to a more comfortable spot, a chair against the wall. He was taking notes furiously.

'How long have you known Seward?' Ford shot at the girl.

'I want to go home,' she sobbed.

Ford poured the last of the thermos of coffee into his cup and held the empty bottle up. 'Here, Parella, we'll need this filled again.' The officer came for it from the desk and Ford turned back to the weeping girl. 'Take your time. Stall all you want. When I get tired I'll have somebody else ask you the questions, and when he gets tired somebody else will, and when that man gets tired I'll take over again. We can keep this up all through the night, all day tomorrow, and all tomorrow night. We can go on for weeks.'

The girl kept on sobbing.

'You won't have to worry about your parents. They'll be in sometime tomorrow afternoon wanting us to find you, only we won't have to look. You'll be right here. They won't have to worry at all.'

The sobs turned into wails.

'How old are you, Mildred?'

'Twenty.' The word was muffled.

'How long have you known Seward?'

'I don't know him.'

'You were in his house for three hours tonight.'

'I wasn't,' she wailed. 'I only delivered a package.'

'My man saw you go in the back door. How come he didn't see you come out again?'

She broke up her sobs after a moment and said, 'I went out the front door. I remember now. I went out the front door.'

'Funny thing,' said Ford maliciously, 'but a man was watching the front of the house. You did not go out the front door, Mildred.' He pounded the table sharply and bellowed, 'Now don't try to tell me you climbed out a window!'

She recoiled, stunned and frightened, tried to say, 'I remember, I did—' then broke down completely, burying her head in her arms on the tabletop. Ford got up and stretched, but it was only a gesture. There was no hint of fatigue about him. 'All right, Mildred,' he said pitilessly. 'Have yourself a good cry. When you're all through feeling sorry for yourself we'll start over again.' He left the girl there and walked into his office. From the top right-hand drawer he brought out a battered deck of playing cards held together by a broken and knotted elastic band. He walked back without a word, took a chair across from the girl, slipped off the elastic, and started to shuffle the cards. Cameron sat silently on the table's edge. The girl raised her head and stared at the Chief in fascination, her face wet and stained, a faint glow of pink on her cheeks and around her eyes. He ignored her and proceeded to lay out three cards vertically, then two more, one on each side of the middle card, forming a cross. The sixth card he turned over was a three and he laid that in the lower left-hand corner of the cross. He turned over the next card, looked over at Mildred, and said, 'Through crying?'

She put her head down on her arms again.

Ford stared at her for a moment, then went on with his game, turning over card after card, playing black on red alternately, building down on the five cards of the cross, building up by suits on the threes which he laid in the corners. Mildred remained motionless, not crying, not doing anything, but wishing herself away from that dreaded place, trying to think of a means of escape, permanent if possible, temporary if not.

Without taking his eyes off his solitaire game Ford said conversationally, 'When did you first get laid, Mildred? Seventeen, eighteen, nineteen?' That brought no reaction other than a noticeably heightened tension in her body.

'Was Seward the first or were there others before him?' asked Ford, playing one pile on to another and getting a space. There was no response.

'Did he give you anything to drink tonight?'

No reply.

'Rule 4-G on how to deal with the police,' said Ford to

Cameron without interrupting the game. 'Be stubborn. Don't talk. Maybe they'll go away.' He reached the end of the pack and was stuck. He swept the cards into a pile, shuffled them and began again, lost a second time and started a third game. Mildred came out of her shell a little and was now resting her chin on her arms, watching him, her mouth set. Cameron, too, was watching the cards and Lassiter was leaning back against the wall watching the group. Ford played carefully as though his sole purpose there was to win a game of solitaire.

Mildred waited patiently until he had lost a third time, and since he acted as though he had forgotten she was there she tried to catch his eye. Failing that, she said hesitantly, 'Could I go to the ladies' room?'

The Chief left the cards, leaned back in the chair, and clasped his hands behind his head. 'Maybe we can make a little deal,' he said. 'You answer my questions and I let you go to the john. You got to go bad?'

Mildred's mouth tightened and she sat back in the chair, turning away from the Chief.

'You will,' Ford informed her. Then he said, 'Speaking of the john, that's a good idea. Guess I'll go.' He stretched again, grandiosely, rose, and went away.

When he came back Cameron said to him, 'Mildred will give me three hundred and seventy-five dollars if I'll get her out of this.'

Ford sat on the table again. The cards were forgotten. 'That's interesting,' he said. 'Where would she get three hundred and seventy-five dollars? From Seward?'

'It's her own. All the money she's been saving.'

'Who are you trying to protect, Mildred? Yourself or Seward?'

Mildred wasn't having any. She glared at Cameron with as much hate as she had previously reserved for the Chief.

'Trying to bribe a police officer,' Ford went on. 'That's a pretty serious offence.'

Mildred's lip began to quiver. The hate went away. She was a frightened girl again.

'You can go to jail for a long time for that.'

She buried her face in her hands and started to cry again.

Ford watched her and a note of tenderness crept into his voice. 'Why don't you come clean, Mildred? Are you afraid of what we'd do to you if you told the truth? We aren't going to hurt you. You can sleep with Seward or anybody else you like. We don't mind a bit just so long as you're discreet about it. Hell, we know you do it, but we aren't going to put you in jail. We know all about this Seward. We know he lured you into it. He's got a reputation for that. He had every girl in San Diego before he went out to the Pacific back during the war. He's an old hand at the Casanova stuff, Mildred. He's been at it for years.'

'No, no. We didn't do anything,' she moaned.

'You were in there for three hours.'

'No. No. I want to go home.'

'Did he give you a drink?'

She shook her head.

Cameron looked at Ford and shrugged. The Chief got up and walked around the room again.

At half past two they were still at it. The second thermos bottle of coffee was almost empty and Mildred still had admitted nothing. Most of the time she had been crying and her eyes and whole face were red and swollen from weeping.

'Your parents waiting up for you, Mildred?'

'I don't know,' she sobbed.

'Maybe I should call them up and find out.'

'No. Please. Don't drag them into this.'

'How about Mr Gregory? Should I ask him about that little errand you say he sent you on?'

She shook her head and cried some more.

'When did you meet Seward?'

'I tell you I don't know him.'

'You don't know him, but you go to his house for three hours wearing a dress that just asks a man to put his hands inside of it. You aren't that kind of a girl, Mildred. You aren't promiscuous, are you?'

'I tell you nothing happened,' she said miserably with her face still buried in her hands.

A little after three, when the third jug of coffee was brought in, Cameron took the Chief aside. 'I think you're handling her the wrong way,' he said.

'What other way is there? I've tried to scare her about what her folks will do to her if we tell them, about what we'll do to her if she doesn't talk. If she won't talk she's got to be frightened into it.'

'She's protecting Seward. She's scared, sure, but she's more scared for him than she is for herself.'

'Hell, we haven't said we were going to do anything to him.'

'That's why she's scared. She knows we had men watching his front and back door. She isn't dumb enough to think that was a trap for her. It's a trap for him and she isn't going to do anything to help you spring it. Call it loyalty or love or whatever you want, she's not going to get him in trouble no matter what you do to her, no matter how many lies you catch her in, she won't admit the truth.'

Ford shook his head, almost in awe. 'What that guy does to women is a crime. But, goddamn it, I'm not going to try to turn her against him by letting her know we think he's a killer. You know as well as I do she's going to tell him everything that happened tonight just as soon as she gets the chance! That's one thing he's not to know!'

'You're right there, Chief, but try to convince her you don't mean him any harm.'

'That'll be easy,' growled Ford. 'I mean him all the harm in the world.'

'But not for what he and she did tonight. Maybe you can convince her of that.'

'Maybe. If not, we'll just have to keep her here and hammer away at her until she's so exhausted and confused she doesn't care about anything any more except getting away from this place.'

They went back and began again. Ford said, 'Mildred, you're in love with Seward, aren't you?'

She said dully, 'You want me to say yes so then you'll be sure something happened tonight. I tell you, nothing happened.'

Ford's voice took on a tone of kindness. 'If you say nothing happened we can't prove anything did, Mildred. We think something did, but we don't care whether it did or not. That's not why we brought you down here, to find out what went on in his house those three hours. It's none of our business and if you don't want to admit to anything you don't have to. All we want to do is find out about some of his girl friends, how many of them there are and how they feel about him. You love him, don't you?'

'Yes, I love him,' she shot back fiercely. 'Go ahead, do what you want to me, you can't stop me.'

Ford was soothing. 'Take it easy, Mildred. We don't

want to stop you. We don't blame you for loving him. I guess a lot of girls do. He's a pretty attractive man.'

She was silent about that and Ford poured himself another mug of coffee. 'He's fifteen years older than you, Mildred. Doesn't that make any difference to you?'

'No.'

'Is he in love with you?'

She shook her head.

'He's told you that?'

'No.'

'How do you know then?'

'I can tell.'

'Does he say he loves you?'

She remained silent.

'How long have you known him?'

'About a year and a half.'

'How did you meet him?'

It went on like that, either Ford, through his switch in tactics, drawing her out or she, numb and exhausted, unable to fight him any more. He kept it up, short questions delivered in a monotone, apparently undamaging questions that she answered equally briefly in a beaten-down, dead voice. She admitted that after their meeting she had gone to visit him frequently although she steadfastly denied that anything immoral took place. No, her parents didn't know about him. Nobody did. Their 'dates' were arranged by him coming to the store, but Mr Gregory was totally unaware of it. They never spoke to each other but made their dates by a code he worked up. His asking for a box of cough drops meant he wanted her to come out that night. If she could, she gave him a box of Luden's. If not, she gave him Smith Brothers. If he got the Smith Brothers and wanted to let it go at that, he paid for it with a nickel or a bill. If he wanted to make it the next night he gave her a quarter. The way she made the change gave him the answer. Two dimes in change meant yes for the following night. A dime and two nickels meant no.

'About how often would he come in and buy a box of cough drops?'

'It used to be once or twice a week.'

'How often is it now?'

She shrugged.

'When was the last time he bought a box?'

Her mouth twitched and she looked dully down at her hands in her lap. 'I don't remember.'

'A long time ago, wasn't it?'

Her lip trembled a little but she didn't speak.

'He's told you he loves you, Mildred, but you don't believe him. Why not? Why shouldn't he love you? You're pretty and young.'

She said in dull pain, 'Why should he? He's thirty-five and educated and knows the right things to do and the right things to say and where to go and all the rest of it. Me, I'm nothing.'

'You think there's somebody else?'

'I don't know.'

'Do you think he's in love with this other person?'

'I don't know.'

'When did you first suspect there was someone else?'

She said, 'I didn't say there was.'

'But there is. Somebody recently, right?'

'I don't know.'

'When was the last time he bought cough drops? Before Christmas, wasn't it?'

'I guess so.'

'Three months ago and now, today, he buys another box.'

She nodded, not looking at anything in particular.

'Why the long wait? What was his explanation?'

'I don't know. I didn't ask him.'

'You didn't ask him?'

'It wasn't any of my business.'

It was four-thirty in the morning when Ford sent Mildred home in a squad car. He was haggard and worn but triumph rode in his face, giving it a fresh, alert appearance despite the deepening lines that creased it. He strode around the room on wires and talked as though someone had turned on a faucet. 'He's our man. Seward's the man. And what a man! I never heard of anything like him before! He's incredible. What he can do to a woman I just can't believe. Look at this Mildred, a little tart who knows her way around. He's shacking up with her for the better part of a year and then along comes Lowell and she's a better dish so Mildred goes into the discard until Lowell's through and then he picks her up again, just like that. How the guy could have the nerve I don't know, but what beats all is that she comes back the moment he whistles. She doesn't even ask him for an explanation. She knows he's never going to marry her and she knows he'll throw her over any time someone new comes along and she'll still climb into his bed whenever he feels like asking her.'

Lassiter said, 'She denies that he's her lover, Chief. It's possible she might be telling the truth.'

'Truth, hell! What do you think they did all evening, play canasta? And in that dress? She didn't even have a bra on!'

'How do you know?'

'Because I was sitting on the table looking down the

front of her.' He pulled out a cigar and threw the wrapping on the floor. 'What a man with the women! All kinds! A cheap little girl like Mildred will bribe you with every cent she's got to protect him and a nice little girl like Lowell will throw her morals out the window for him in the time it takes a train to get to New York. And that code he worked out! It's something out of a spy story. All that to keep it quiet and she agrees to it. There wasn't anybody in the world until tonight that had any idea what they were to each other!

'And Lowell. I bet he had a code in his history class with her. Something he said, some phrase or something that's part of the lesson to everybody else but means, "Can you come over?" to Lowell. And she probably had some way of answering yes or no; the way she sat in her seat, adjusted her hair clip, chewed a pencil, or something.' He stopped munching the cigar and put a match to it.

'Only she couldn't wait to be asked that last day,' he said through puffs. 'She had to see him right away and there was no code for a noon get-together so she had to go up to the desk to talk to him. She thought he would marry her but she didn't know her way around like Mildred. Mildred didn't believe his "I love yous" but she was so stuck on the guy she would jump through the hoops for him anyway. Lowell, poor kid, she fell for the line but she wouldn't hoop-jump. She wanted a wedding ring and she wasn't going to be talked out of it. So he had to break her neck.'

'Yeah,' said Cameron dryly. 'I'd rather go to the chair any time than marry somebody like Lowell.'

'It's a spur-of-the-moment deal, Burt. He isn't thinking consequences. All of a sudden his whole system is blowing up in his face. Gone is his position in Parker, his reputation, everything. He's panicked by her threat of exposure.'

'Murder blows up everything too, only more so.'

'Maybe he doesn't stop to think about that. I don't know, Burt, I haven't tried to figure out all the details yet. Give me a good night's sleep and maybe I'll have an answer for you.'

'That's just what I was going to ask you,' said Cameron, rising. 'If you'd let us go home and get some sleep.'

Friday, 31 March

The last day of March was a Friday and little new evidence had been uncovered in the time since Monday night when Mildred Naffzinger had been picked up. Two trips to Boston by Lassiter disclosed that, while Charles M. Watson was the man who had tried to buy the girls champagne in the Wagon Wheel, he had not been in New York December sixteenth and had never seen any of them again. Of the other suspects, all had been in Bristol that December evening and, by process of elimination, only Seward remained as Lowell's lover and probable killer. Trumbull, in his canvassing of the girls in Seward's classes who had left for the holidays early, found one other who had seen him on the sixteenth. It was at the Springfield station between trains and he was talking with some girl.

On Thursday Avery Jarrett, the man assigned to follow Seward, saw him enter the Bristol Drug Store and, as ordered, entered the store himself. He reported that Seward made a small purchase at the counter from the young blonde girl who worked there and was brought into what seemed to be excited conversation by the girl. It was brief and apparently unfinished owing to his own presence as a customer, and late in the afternoon Seward drove to Ross's Bar, well out Maple Street near the edge of town. Jarrett parked across the street, and waited and at six-twenty the same blonde girl appeared, walking up the street. She got into Seward's car and in a few minutes the history teacher came out, got in, and drove off with her. They rode aimlessly for half an hour before the girl was let out on Putney Street, a couple of blocks from her home.

It was plainly evident Seward now knew what had happened after Mildred left him Monday night. Ford, as soon as he learned of this, assigned two additional men to trail the history teacher. His men weren't experienced and, even with three men working together, he couldn't be sure that Seward, looking for such a thing, wouldn't spot them. However, he did what he could with the men he had and his three reserve officers were working full time these days.

Early Friday afternoon McNarry was on the phone. Ford took it in his office.

'I got news for you, Chief,' the district attorney said.

'I hope it's good.'

'You'll love it. The handwriting on the samples we sent the New York police checks with the handwriting on two cards at the Hotel Bentley on West Forty-fifth Street. The cards are for a Norman Carter and an Althea Merkle for rooms 412 and 414.'

'Connecting door between?'

'There is. What does that do for our case?'

'It clinches the paternity part. Seward's the man.'

'Do we tell the papers?'

'Hell, no. Say we've got a lead, that's all. We're looking for a murderer and we haven't got anything on that score. I don't want to frighten this guy by saying we think he's a murderer, not when we don't have any proof.'

'Why don't you drag him in and give him a going over?'

'Because if he doesn't break we're licked. He was a tough Marine captain in the war and he won't crack easy, not yet. I want to let him stew awhile. He knows something's going on, but he doesn't know what. Not knowing is going to worry him a damn sight more than knowing. This way he doesn't know how to defend himself and he's going to start sweating. It's taken a lot of work to get where we are and we can't afford to ruin it. Not a word of this to anybody, not even your wife!'

'If you say so, Chief,' sighed McNarry sadly. 'You're the doctor. I want this solved and you're doing it and I'm not going to rock the boat.'

'Thanks, Mr McNarry.'

'How's Seward acting so far?'

'No report yet. He only just found out we caught his girlfriend yesterday. I'll let you know how he takes it.'

Ford hung up and sat back without too much exultation showing to await the return of Cameron and Lassiter. When they came in half an hour later he gave it to them. 'We know where Seward and Lowell stayed in New York!'

'Where and how?'

He told them about it.

'When do we move in on him?' said Lassiter eagerly.

'We don't. All this does is confirm what we already know – that he made Lowell in New York. Okay. I've pieced together the whole story of what happened to Lowell four weeks ago today. I've pieced together the whole story of what happened the day Lowell left for her Christmas vacation. I can prove that part of it, but I can't prove the March third part and that's the important one.'

Lassiter said, 'How do you figure it, Chief?'

Ford peeled a cigar and lighted it. 'Here's the way it looks to me, based on what we know,' he said. 'Lowell had no Saturday classes so, while the Christmas vacation officially began at noon on the seventeenth of December, she was through at noon on the sixteenth. A number of other girls were too, but she was one of the few that took the one-thirty train to New York. By chance, Seward also took that train and he, being one with an eye for the girls, recognized her as one of his students and sat with her. Lowell was a damned attractive girl and from what we know of Seward, that's all, brother! He turned on the charm. Lowell's inexperienced. She's had dates, sure, but with kids. She's never run into someone as smooth and subtle as Seward. Look what he can do to someone like Mildred, and Mildred knows her way around.

'Seward's the shining knight to Lowell, but he comes off that pedestal. He doesn't talk to her like teacher to pupil, he talks man to woman and Lowell discovers the untouchable Mr Seward is the very touchable Harlan. I thought maybe he lured her into the club car to get her mellow, but we don't have anything that says he did. Maybe the charm was enough. Anyway, they get to New York and they're talking pretty intimately and Lowell is in the process of being swept off her feet. He suggests they have cocktails together before she gets her train and she wants to hold on to him as long as she can and get herself in as solid as she can so she accepts. Trust him to pick a spot with plenty of atmosphere and where the drinks are good, there's probably dancing too, and he pours the drinks down a little fast and she's afraid he'll come out of it and realize she's nothing but a kid if she balks so she keeps pace.'

Cameron said, 'Where did this theory come from, your own personal experience?'

'Hell, no. All I ever did was buy a dame a beer and then tell her if she wanted another one she was going to have to come across.'

'If I was a dame you'd buy more than two beers to make me.'

'I was prettier in those days. Now shut up and let me tell this. After a while she gets fuzzy enough so that grabbing another train seems like an ordeal and then he suggests a big dinner and the theatre. Having him around to lean on in her condition is much better than getting to Philadelphia on her own and he's going to stay over anyway and she doesn't need much persuasion to decide she ought to too. At this point she's trusting him. What he's been thinking about all afternoon hasn't even occurred to her. So they conspire to send a telegram to her folks, which he probably writes, and they go get hotel rooms, only he handles that detail and she doesn't know he uses phoney names.

'So off they go to dinner and the play and they hold hands probably and the whole evening is pretty glamorous to her. They have some more drinks after and probably bring some up to her room and she's fuzzy again and likes the idea because it might make him like her still better. She probably thinks she's capturing him and that's where she's making her big mistake because it's playing right into his hands. They have another drink sitting side by side on the bed and then he kisses her and immediately says he has no right to, that he's too old for her and she could never consider him seriously and that gets her trying to prove she does. Between the too many drinks and her feeling that this is real love, she's weakening and getting less and less aware of what she's doing until, before she knows it, she isn't a virgin any more.

'He probably stays the night with her so he can be right on hand to comfort her when she wakes up in the morning and assure her he still feels the same way and this is the once-in-a-lifetime love and make sure she's hooked good. Then he sells her the idea this has to be kept secret, he'd lose his job if it got around that he was in love with one of the Parker girls, and he convinces her no mention should be made of it anywhere or any place, her diary included. The big deep secret! Of course they can't get married right away, not for a couple of years yet, and she believes that and, of course, since they've gone that far already, it would be sort of silly to quit and she probably is afraid if they did quit he might stop loving her so she's willing to carry on. In fact, after she's gone out to his house a couple of times, she's probably eager to and she thinks this is real love and that men do marry their mistresses and she's out to his house every chance she gets. How does that sound to you?'

Cameron said, 'It's rough in spots, but he's probably better at it than you are.'

'It probably varies in spots but I'll lay you ten to one that's what happened.'

'Of course it did. Hell, we've got the proof – her diary and his handwriting on the cards. The only thing that stumps me is how you can figure out a slick technique like that. That's way over your head.'

Ford said, 'I didn't go to college so I couldn't learn about people in books. I had to learn about people from people. While you were getting yourself educated I was out discovering what made people tick, all kinds. I got an education out of the Police Department.'

'Does that education of yours give you a motive for the murder besides Seward's getting panic-stricken? A guy who went through the Iwo Jima invasion isn't going to run amuck because some girl threatens to tell on him.'

'Yep. The answer is accident.'

'Accident? You mean you can break a girl's neck by accident?'

'That's right. Listen.' Ford relit his cigar stub and

choked a little. 'Somewhere along the line, when Lowell and Seward were going at it hot and heavy, they got a little careless and Lowell finds out she's pregnant. As she says in her diary, "Something drastic will have to be done." She's probably plenty scared and thinks about abortions and what have you. The only real answer a girl like her would come up with, though, is for the guy to marry her. It's bad for his career, of course, but she doesn't have any doubt about his doing the honourable thing. Her diary shows she believes that.

'As I've said, they had no code for the kind of meeting she proposed so she goes up to his desk and says she's got to see him right away, can she come over that noon? No doubt he doesn't like that one bit, what with the maid maybe not gone yet and it being daylight and all, and he probably tries to stall her only she's insistent and agitated and the girls haven't all left his classroom yet and he doesn't want this to look like anything more than a question about an assignment so he has to soothe her and he probably says it's okay if she makes absolutely sure no one sees her. The maid should be gone by that time, but if she isn't he'll signal her some way, meet her outside, or pass her on the street, something like that.

'So she goes back to her room not knowing she's only got an hour more to live and puts on the sick act so she can change her clothes and sneak out without anybody knowing about it. She makes sure no one sees her, she makes too damn sure! We haven't turned up a single person who even thinks they might have! Okay. She gets to his house and she tells him she's pregnant and what he's got to do. He tries to talk her out of that idea but he doesn't have anything to offer her himself, outside of an abortion, and she isn't having any. He puts on all the charm he can but, as I say, Mildred might jump through hoops for him, but Lowell won't. She draws the line right there. He's coming through for her.

'Of course he has no intention of doing anything like that but his charm isn't working now. The more he talks against taking that step, the more Lowell begins to open her eyes. Maybe she starts to see him as he really is, or maybe she's just trying to force him into it or maybe she's just terrified at the idea that she's being left all alone to face the shame and so forth. Seward could, and maybe did, tell her to go to hell, she couldn't prove he even knew her name outside of the classroom. He's seen to it there isn't a shred of evidence around. If Lowell went to the Bentley Hotel to prove they spent the night in adjoining rooms, what a shock she'd get to find neither of them were even registered at the joint!

'Whatever the cause, I figure she got hysterical and started screaming. She might be doing it on purpose, but Seward sees he's got to shut her up before the neighbours hear her. Her story about him wouldn't need so much proof if they found her screaming in his house.

'So he shuts her up. Now, he's not frightened, he's not the kind of guy who scares easy, but he is mad. He's also an ex-Marine who's been well grounded in hand-to-hand combat, judo stuff where you can kill a guy with your bare hands in three seconds. He's not going to kill her. He has no intention of doing that but he wants to shut her up and, at the same time, he's mad and, because he's mad, he wants to hurt her. He probably wraps one arm around her neck and yanks her in close and then locks his other hand around her face and he gives her a wrench that's a little sharper than he means because he feels vicious. Maybe he hears her neck snap or maybe the first indication he gets is when she goes limp against him. Anyway, he lets her down and she flops on to the rug and from the way her head is twisted, he can tell she'll never move again. Hell, he's seen dead people before. He must have known she was dead before he even knelt down beside her but, by God, I'll bet your tough Marine who couldn't be panicked was panic-stricken now. I'll bet he spent a couple of minutes trying to revive her even though he knew she was already starting to cool.

'It's my guess he was the most terrified guy in the state when he stood up and faced the facts. There he was in an empty house and not a sound anywhere. The sun is shining bright outside and everything is peaches and cream except there's a dead girl in his living room. Probably his first impulse was to run to the neighbours for help and secondly to call the police. Then he starts to think a little bit about how it's going to look. He can claim it's an accident, but he doesn't have any witnesses and, when it turns out she's pregnant and he made her that way, who do you think's going to believe it was an accident? Who the hell's going to care whether it was or not? Whatever the verdict, he'll be buried – in the ground or in a cell.

'So, with the cunning borne of desperation – I got that out of a book, Burt – he starts casting around for a way out. She's already told him nobody saw her so nobody knows she's there. That's fine, but she can't stay there. He can't burn her in the furnace or bury her in the cellar or back yard because, if she's ever found, he's dead. Now, a body is just about the hardest thing in the world to get rid of and he's smart enough to know that, no matter what he does with it, it's almost certain to come to light sooner or later. The thing is, therefore, to take it far away and dump it. Then, when it's found, it won't incriminate him. Since nobody had the slightest inkling that he and she even knew each other, there's a good chance that it won't be traced back to him.

'That strikes him as the best thing to do and he probably goes around racking his brains for a place where. Then he thinks of the flats and then maybe he thinks the river's even better. The body will drift down into the Connecticut and maybe all the way into Long Island Sound.

'There's only one thing he's afraid of and that is that he or Lowell may have slipped up somewhere. Maybe the police might be able to find out he's her lover. Nothing points to him, but at the same time nothing's going to point to anybody else either, and in a murder case the police are going to look awful hard for the father. He's scared we might catch and hang him, for he knows that if he gets rid of the body he doesn't have a prayer of convincing anybody he killed her by accident.

'Now, it's somewhere around here that he gets the brainstorm, or what he thinks is a brainstorm. If he can make it look as though Lowell killed herself, then the police wouldn't have any reason to look for the father. If a suicide verdict was turned in at the inquest the case would be dropped. It sounds like a terrific idea to his rattled brain. He could dump her in the river down by the flats where she'll eventually be found and we'll find out she's pregnant and that she died of a broken neck without another mark on her to prove she didn't break it herself. There's Higgins Bridge right there on campus, a perfect place for her to break her neck diving off of. A perfect setup for a suicide verdict. Okay, we know that stinks because nobody would try to commit suicide by jumping off a ten-foot bridge into four feet of water – ice water to boot – but to Seward, in his upset state, it sounds swell. And,' said Ford sourly, 'he came a damn sight closer to making us believe it than he ever should have. The whole thing is full of holes!

'Anyway, that's his out and he loads Lowell's body in the trunk of his car, which is easy because the garage is part of the house, and leaves it there until late at night. Then he drives down to the flats and dumps it. After that, of course, it's a simple thing for him to drop Lowell's hair clip off the bridge in the next day or so and then sit back and relax.' Ford tilted his chair back and looked around.

'One thing, Chief,' said Lassiter. 'What would ever make him think we'd find that hair clip?'

Ford patted his sides as though he had just got up from Thanksgiving dinner. 'He didn't,' he said. 'At least he didn't think we'd find it before the body. It was just insurance. He doped it out that we'd find the body and decide she'd jumped off the bridge. We'd go examine the area around the bridge and maybe find the clip and, bang, we'd be convinced. We'd probably think so anyway even if we didn't find it, but if we did that would be the clincher. And of course if we didn't buy the suicide and things started getting hot for him, he knew it was there and, if he had to, he could "accidentally" manage to discover it himself. As I say, it was insurance, the added touch, and incidentally it damn near swung the deal in his favour.' He turned to Cameron. 'Can you tell it better?'

Cameron shook his head and grinned. 'Uh-uh. You just told it. If you watched it happen you wouldn't tell it any different.'

'Thanks. Now have you got a way of proving it?'

'Only through his car. She didn't bleed but we might pick up one of her hairs or thread from her clothes if we vacuum-cleaned his trunk.'

Lassiter said, 'We'd have better luck in his house.'

'It's got to be the car,' said Cameron. 'We've got to prove he had her in the trunk of the car.' He turned to Ford. 'And there's going to be a slight problem getting into it if he's got the keys.'

'We'll get into it,' said Ford. 'And we'll vac his house too. A little proof she was there is one more link in the chain. And there's something else I'm going to do. That's pull off two of the three men we've got tailing him.'

'He'll wise up. He's probably wise now.'

'Which is what I want him to do. Mildred's told him about Monday night and you can bet he's plenty worried. He's going to be on the lookout for men watching his house and following him. I want him to know he's being shadowed. Psychological effect, Burt. We aren't going to say anything to him, just keep watching. Pretty soon he'll get the jitters. I'm not saying he'll break down and confess, but it'll soften him up so if we ever get something solid to go on we might be able to drag him down here and open his mouth.'

'Or scare him out of town.'

'I don't think he'll dare leave town, Burt. He'll be afraid that's what we're trying to make him do. He'll be afraid it's some kind of admission of guilt. I think he'll stick it out right here and he won't make a single false move. I'll lay you ten to one he never buys another box of cough drops from Mildred.'

Monday, 3 April

At nine-thirty Monday morning Ford and Cameron descended upon the Seward place. Mrs Glover let them in and Cameron set the small vacuum cleaner he was carrying down in the middle of the living-room floor while Ford headed for the garage.

The car was a two-tone green Pontiac two-door sedan, polished and shiny, and the tyres showed little wear. Seward seldom used it, Mrs Glover said. He had bought it the preceding June, taken it to Virginia for the summer, and driven it to class when it rained. Outside of that, it spent most of the time in the garage, where he pampered it with a dustcloth every few days to keep it looking like a fugitive from a show window. The smell of it inside was new and the mileage indicator read only 3568.8, most of which had been put on down around Virginia six months before. There was an oil sticker from a Sunoco station against the doorframe saying the oil had last been changed at 3075, which meant it had probably been done before Christmas.

Ford tried the trunk and it was locked and the glove compartment was locked and the keys weren't in the ignition. He turned down the visors and felt under the dashboard and looked under the floor mat and under the seat but the keys weren't in the car. Cameron spread newspapers down on the kitchen floor and took the bag off Seward's vacuum cleaner and emptied it, turned the bag inside out, and picked it clean of dust. He found a large paper bag in the back hall behind the vegetable bin, poured the dust into it, folded it over, and wrote on it, *Seward's vacuum cleaner*.

Ford went upstairs and prowled around, looking through the linen closet and the drawers in the two guest rooms. He took the top off the toilet tanks of the two bathrooms and went into Seward's bedroom, which was at the rear of the house overlooking the wooded lot through which Mildred had come. There was a double bed against the wall in the corner, a small polished desk, a grey rug, two easy chairs, a floor lamp, a table with magazines and another lamp, a bureau with a mirror, and a closet. Ford tried the desk and it was locked tight. Then he went through the bureau with a heavy hand, turning over piles of shirts, underwear, slacks, and pyjamas. He rummaged around in the small top drawers through handkerchiefs, old chequebooks, insurance policies, a box of cuff links, and bank statements. He did not try to leave things as he found them. He went to the table and flipped through the magazines and then went into the closet and searched the pockets of the three suits, four sports jackets and pairs of pants there. He got the small chair from behind the desk and stood on it to peer over the shelf. He took down the two hats there and ran his fingers around the linings. Then he got down and thrust a stubby hand into the toe of each shoe on the floor. He closed the door, put the chair back, and went downstairs.

Cameron had cleaned up the kitchen and his bag of dust was lying in a corner of the couch. He had his own vacuum cleaner out and was running it over the rug, the walls, the furniture, underneath the bookcase in the corner, and over and under the window-seat cushion with a thoroughness that would put the most enterprising house-wife to shame.

Ford went out to the garage again, unscrewed the cap, and let half the air out of the right rear tyre with his finger. He rescrewed the cap, found Mrs Glover, and told her to leave a note for Seward saying he had a soft tyre. He went in to Cameron and said over the hum of the cleaner, 'No keys. I put Plan 4-G in operation.'

Cameron said, 'He might pump it up himself. Why don't I do a little job on his distributor and throw his timing off?'

'What do you know? A mechanical genius. You've been hiding your talents.'

'Me and cars. We understand each other.'

'Go talk to it then.' Ford took over the cleaning and Cameron went to the garage. When he came back Ford was through.

Cameron picked up the bag of dust while Ford took the vacuum cleaner. 'Next time he starts that thing,' he said, 'he's going to call the garage.'

They went out to the car and climbed in. Ford choked it into being and turned around in the driveway. They went left on Maple Street towards the outskirts of town for six blocks and drove into a Sunoco service station. Ford left the engine running and got out, intercepted the young, tousle-headed man in dark blue uniform who was approaching, took him inside for a few minutes' earnest conversation, and came back to the car. 'This is the place Seward takes his car to,' he said as he swung into the street again. 'He'll let us know as soon as his wrecker picks it up.'

'Okay, because if we don't get into his trunk we're stuck.

Lowell's shoes could be in that bag of dust we've got and it wouldn't prove any more than that they slept together.'

'We'll get in it, and we'll find something. If she was in that trunk, and she was, she'll leave a trademark if it's nothing but a smudge of lipstick or hair oil, and will he have himself a time explaining what a girl was doing there!'

They went down to the State Police lab and left their findings to be analysed and then came back to the station and Cameron said, 'I presume you told Mrs Glover not to mention our visit.'

'I did, but I left traces of it. Next time he goes for a clean shirt he's going to discover somebody's been rummaging around. That ought to scare him sky-high.'

'And right out of town.'

'We aren't close enough to make him do that and he knows it. What he doesn't know, and what's worrying him, is just how close we are. He's showing the strain, Burt. You read the reports of his tails. Ever since he had that talk with Mildred he's been walking with one eye behind him. Every time he steps out the door he looks all around trying to see who's watching him and where. He's nervous as hell, Burt. When he spots our man he's jumpy. When he doesn't spot him he's twice as jumpy.'

'And he's going to know that car didn't get that way by itself.'

'Which will make him sweat a little more. He's a worried man, Burt, and he's going to get worrieder and worrieder.'

The two of them checked in at headquarters and Ford gave Cameron the rest of the day off. Then he worked off his lunch pacing the floor waiting for the report from the service station. At three o'clock he called up McNarry for something to do and gave him the story. At four o'clock, when MacDonald relieved him, he went home. He called headquarters at six and again at seven and nothing had come in. At eight o'clock he called up Mrs Glover to make sure Seward had been notified about the soft tyre. She said she had left a note. He tried headquarters once more and then went down to the cellar and let off steam by sand-papering the old bureau his wife wanted refinished.

Nothing had come in by ten and he grumbled and cursed and got under a shower and into his pyjamas. He tried MacDonald once more and the sergeant told him the Sunoco station had called at nine to say they were closing and had heard nothing. Ford raised hell with the sergeant for not notifying him and told him he damn well wanted to be disturbed and if MacDonald didn't want to be back patrolling the streets he'd better damn well phone in all reports when ordered without taking it upon himself to decide whether they were important or not. Then he wanted to know why the reports of Seward's shadows hadn't come in and MacDonald said they had and Ford swore at him some more and told him to read them over the phone.

The report was encouraging. Seward, according to the man assigned to him, had returned home from classes a little after three and, twenty minutes later, opened the garage doors to get into the trunk of the car. He took out a pump and inflated a tyre, then backed the car into the drive, lifted the hood, and seemed bothered. He examined the tyre again, then the engine, then drove the car back into the garage and the engine was acting up. He shut the doors and that was the last time he had been out of the house.

Ford sounded a little less peeved. He told MacDonald to instruct all men tailing Seward to call in immediately should the car be taken anywhere other than the Sunoco station on Maple Street. Then he hung up, went into the living room and smoked a cigar slowly on the couch, put it out carefully, went back to the bedroom, climbed into bed, and fell asleep immediately.

Tuesday Through Sunday,
4–9 April

The call came in the next morning. Seward had phoned and a wrecker was being sent for the car. Cameron was taking the day off, so Ford went out Maple Street at forty miles an hour with Kennedy and the vacuum cleaner beside him. The tousle-haired lad who ran the station drove in a few minutes later, towing the car behind him, and took it into the garage. 'I listened to the engine,' he said, getting out of the truck, 'and told him I'd have it ready tomorrow.'

'Did you get the keys?'

'Right here.' He held them up.

Ford fairly snatched them. 'This is our baby,' he said, and unlocked the trunk.

'Just what *is* the deal?' the lad asked.

Ford edged him away. 'Police business. Just police business.' He fixed an extension cord to the vacuum cleaner and plugged it into an outlet under the work-bench.

The trunk looked as new as the rest of the car and just as clean but Ford paid no attention. He ran the cleaner over the lining as though he were weaving the cloth and it was fifteen minutes before he was satisfied. Then he had the lad come over and remove the spare from the trunk and went over the whole thing again. After that he gave the cleaner to Kennedy to put away and got a hundred-watt bulb in a wire protector on an extension and took that into the trunk with a magnifying glass and looked for spots or stains that the cleaner would not pick up. When he was satisfied on that score he slammed down the back, threw the keys to the lad, and walked out.

They took the contents of the cleaner bag to the lab for analysis and then Ford prepared himself for the wait. To pass the time he concentrated on keeping Seward under pressure. The history teacher was showing signs of the effects now. He knew that from the time he left the house in the morning until he got back his every move was under surveillance and the strain was telling. The Chief was keeping only one man on him but he kept shifting the man so that Seward was faced with the daily task of identifying his shadow and he was never more upset than before he made the discovery. In spite of all that, however, he made no move to elude the plain-clothes man. As Ford had predicted, he was trying to wait it out and discourage it by leading a most circumspect existence.

On Wednesday Ford worked a psychological twist. He called off all watchers and left Seward completely alone. On Thursday a man was reassigned and made the report that Seward had first discovered him at noon and promptly cut the rest of his classes to go to the Walston Tavern and drink beer all afternoon. 'It's getting him,' said Ford gleefully.

Friday morning the lab reported. Ford fell all over himself getting out to the main desk to tear the phone from Cameron without waiting for the call to be switched to his office. Lieutenant Dennison was the one who had done the work and he was a fifty-three-year-old man with a dry voice with a nasal twang in it. 'The dust you label as inside the house has a few odds and ends in it that might be of use to you,' he said. 'By odds and ends, I mean hair and pieces of hair. There are several kinds, grey, blonde, and dark, belonging to women, and black short hairs belonging to men, or a man. They all seem to have come from the head and have fallen from the scalp. The structure and the colour of the dark female hairs match the samples we have from the Mitchell girl although, due to lack of living roots, the identification can't be positive. Let us say the hair could have come from the Mitchell girl's scalp.'

'Let us, by all means, say so.'

'The dust you collected from the trunk of the car contains nothing at all that will be of any use to you.'

Ford spat his cigar halfway across the room. 'What?'

'Nothing. No hair, no lint, traces of wool, identifiable dust, or particles of skin. There were some microscopic traces of paper, newsprint, that is. That, I don't believe, will help you.'

'Why that – that—' Ford slammed down the phone and held his head. 'Newspapers,' he moaned. 'He used newspapers.'

Cameron said, 'For what?'

'On the floor of the trunk, before he put Lowell in.'

'You mean there's nothing?'

'Not a goddamned thing!'

Cameron whistled a couple of times and said, 'Well, it's been fun.'

Ford looked up. 'He killed her, damn it, and he knows it and you know it and I know it. But what the hell are we going to do about it?'

'Hound him is all I can think of. Maybe he'll crack.'

'On his deathbed – maybe. He won't jump at shadows. He'll crack when we can show him we got him but not before.'

'We can always pin a rap on him for contributing to the delinquency of a minor.'

Ford started pacing. 'The hell with that stuff. I want him for murder.' He picked his cigar up off the floor, looked at it, and threw it away. 'I want to get that guy. I want to hang him. So help me, I will hang him. There's got to be something. Somewhere there's *got* to be something!'

'It had better be something good,' said Cameron. 'It's going to have to be.'

Ford stooped and stuck his hands on his hips. 'What I need is a day off. I'm taking it as of right now. I may take two.' He went into his office and came out with everything he had that concerned the Lowell Mitchell case.

'Day off,' said Cameron. 'You're going to work harder than you ever did.'

'Shut up,' muttered the Chief. 'I'm going to catch up on my reading.'

'Good hunting. Any orders while you're gone?'

'Yes. Keep the watch on Seward. Don't let him out of your sight. I want the sweat sticking out on him like blood.'

That was the last anyone saw of Ford that day and all day the next. On Sunday he called in. It was Cameron he was after and he wanted him out at the house in a pretty damn fast hurry. It was hard to tell from his voice whether he was angry or excited.

The Chief was in his study when Cameron was admitted, seated at his small writing desk surrounded by the pile of documents that formed the Mitchell dossier. He told his wife to fetch the liquor and hitched his chair around. 'I think I've got a lead.'

'Yeah? What?'

Ford picked up a sheet and handed it over. It was a copy of the missing persons circular and his finger was pointed at the paragraph that read, 'Marilyn Lowell Mit-chell, 560 Evergreen Avenue, Philadelphia, Pa., a student at Parker College, Bristol, Mass., disappeared from college on the afternoon of 3 March 1950. Thought to be wearing a tan polo coat with plain brown buttons, yellow wool sweater, mother-of-pearl buttons, white blouse, grey wool skirt, ankle socks, brown and white saddle shoes, size 7, a gold hair clip with initials MLM inside, a small gold Elgin ladies' wristwatch with narrow gold band, and a brown leather purse with shoulder-strap, brass fastener, and initials MLM on the side. This girl likes dancing, tennis, dramatics, swimming, and playing the piano. She is interested in languages and is moderately fluent in French and Spanish. She has also done waitress work.'

Cameron read it through and said, 'What about it?'

'What was missing when we found her?'

'Her hair clip.'

'We found that. What was missing that we haven't found?'

'Her purse.'

'And where do you think it is?'

Cameron shrugged. 'Probably at the bottom of Long Island Sound by now.'

'Use your head, you dope. How far do you think a purse jammed with the junk a girl puts in a purse is going to float?'

'All right, it doesn't float. It sinks. So it's not in the water. It's in a garbage pail somewhere, or a junk heap.'

'Whose garbage pail? What junk heap?'

'Hell, who knows? What are you driving at?'

'If we can find that purse and trace it to Seward we can hang him.'

'It's the electric chair in this state. So what do we do,

call out the militia and the boy scouts to beat the bushes? And if you did find it, tell me how you're going to prove Seward put it there.'

Mrs Ford came in with two highballs on a tray and the Chief said to her, 'If Cameron is the next chief of police, crime is going to run riot in Bristol.'

She merely smiled, let them take a glass, and departed.

Cameron waited until she had gone and said, 'For a hard-headed, excuse me, thick-skulled, practical police officer, you're reaching pretty high into the stratosphere. What the hell is on your mind?'

'Just this. Let's go back to a scared Seward lurching around his living room wondering what he's going to do because he's got a corpse in the house. He gets the suicide brainstorm. He's going to dump the girl in the river and toss her hair clip off the bridge. That's fine, but there's one problem. That's the girl's purse. What's he going to do with it? He can't throw that in the river along with the hair clip because it's too noticeable. He can't have the girl jump Friday and her purse appear Saturday. And he can't leave it with the body because that doesn't look good. Suicides don't leap to their death carrying their purses with them. They get rid of all excess baggage and, when it's to be in water, a lot of them strip. If Lowell had a purse she would leave it at the railing and of course that's out. See? He's stuck with the goddamned purse.

'So now he gets thinking and it comes to him that unless the girl is going to leave a suicide note in the purse she probably wouldn't even take it with her. There's no note, so there's no reason for a purse. Nobody's seen her, so nobody can say she was carrying one.

'Now Lowell was apparently one of those girls who always had a purse with her. That's all to the good. The girl who always takes a purse is supposed on this particular day to have walked off without one. Why? Because she isn't going to need it. Why? Because she's going to kill herself. See? The lack of a purse is going to strengthen the suicide angle which he wants. Follow me?'

'I'm way ahead of you. I'm up to where he gets the idea we aren't going to know she had one.'

'He figures if we don't find one we'll guess she didn't have one. We aren't supposed to be thinking of murder. We're thinking of suicide and what's on her she took, what's not she didn't.'

'It wouldn't occur to him that we could inventory her things and figure what's missing she also took?'

'That's the chance he has to take. Hell, Burt, this isn't a planned murder he's committed. Out of a blue sky he's stuck with a body to get rid of. He's got to do the best he can with what he's got. Remember, he not only hasn't had time to work out a plan, he's also pretty goddamned upset. You try to think when you're in his position sometime and see how many details you can take care of. In fact try putting yourself in his spot right now with a clear mind. Take a week to think about it and see if you can come up with a better way out than he did.'

'Okay,' said Cameron. 'It is desirable to get rid of the purse. Go ahead.'

'You go ahead. Put yourself in his position. You've got to get rid of the purse. What are you going to do with it?'

'Throw it off in the woods somewhere.'

Ford said, 'God, I wish you had committed the murder. We would have sewn up this case long ago.'

'All right. What would you do with it, genius?'

'I wouldn't throw it in the woods somewhere.' Ford banged on his desk. 'Think, for Christ's sake. You're trying to put across the idea of suicide. You can't just toss the thing out of a car window somewhere because if it's found, blooey! The suicide idea goes up in smoke.'

'He tears the initials off the bag and throws it out bare. Then he scatters the initials, one by one, in other places.'

'Still too big a chance. We might identify it anyway.'

'Okay. Then what do you think he did with it, mail it to a fictitious address?'

'No. Again it might be opened or might be traced. It's got to disappear, not for a little while, but permanently.'

'He drives down to Springfield and throws it in the Connecticut River.'

'You mean about four o'clock in the morning?'

'He might.'

Ford shook his head. 'It's my guess he hid it somewhere around his home.'

'He wants to make it easy for us, huh?'

'No. Listen to me. If he threw it away somewhere we're sunk. We'll never be able to trace it to him. Our only chance is that he was afraid to do that and buried or burned it near by instead.'

'That's a pretty damn faint hope!'

'Not so faint. There's a good chance of it, Burt. Look at it this way. That purse, in his possession, is just as damning as Lowell's body. If anybody spots him carrying it after Lowell disappears he's in the soup. Therefore, he's going to want to get rid of it just as fast as he got rid of the body. When you've got something hot like that you're not going to want to take it very far. You're scared of getting caught with it. You might pass a red light or have an accident or do something that's going to call you to people's attention. I don't think he's going to drive out in the woods and dump it. I also don't think he's going to keep it any longer than absolutely necessary. In fact he probably got rid of it the same night he ditched the body. Now, working on that theory, where do you think he's put it?'

'No place where we'll ever find it.'

'Not by accident, no. But if we can think the way he thought we might come up with it. Any ideas?'

Cameron was starting to get interested. 'What about Parker Lake? It's only a couple of blocks and he could get to it at night easy enough without being seen.'

'Yeah, except we know it's not there. We went all over the lake bed after it was drained.'

'And he couldn't bury it, not with snow on the ground. He might have burned it.'

'We'll collect his ashes for analysis,' said Ford, and ground his palms together. 'There are four possibilities for getting rid of the purse as I see it. He could send it or throw it away, but I don't think he'd do that for fear it would turn up again. He could bury it except that that would require a pick, and the spot would be too obvious. He could burn it, which is possible, or he could hide it, which is likely. If he threw it away it wouldn't do us any good if we did find it, so we'll concentrate on the other possibilities. Map out the area, Burt. I want that property canvassed for all potential hiding places. Then we'll start in the order of probability and keep going until we've turned over everything, inside the house and out, as far as we can go and still be sure only Seward could have put it there. We'll use every man we've got if necessary, but this thing is going to be thorough and I mean thorough. Anything in that house of his that's locked, we're going to get into. Anything outside that doesn't look a year old, we're going to take apart.'

'And,' said Cameron, grinning wryly as he rose, 'if Seward's been worrying because he's being followed his hair's going to turn grey from here on out.'

Monday and Tuesday,
10 and 11 April

The police swung into action Monday morning as soon as Seward was safely at class. Eight men, including Ford, Cameron, and Lassiter, moved in at nine o'clock and worked till twelve, when they called a halt in view of the teacher's expected return. Ford and Cameron, aided by Mrs Glover, hunted inside the house. They did not get into Seward's desk or have time to cover the attic but they did make a thorough search of two floors and the cellar and they collected three cartons full of ashes. They cleaned out the fireplace, shovelled more than a boxful out of the disposal unit in the bottom of the chimney, and at least that much from the cement incinerator in the yard. The incinerator held an interesting assortment and that one was specially marked.

Lassiter and the other men handled the outside. They did not have time to probe the sewer just past the house at the street's end, nor did they rip up the flagstone walk, which had possibilities, and they did nothing about the suspiciously recent patch of cement in the drive. Other than that, however, they were thorough and not an inch of the soft wet ground within several hundred feet of the house was left unexplored. The purse was not found, but something else was. Trumbull was working beyond the end of Dorchester Street on the wooded hill that sloped down to Wheeler River when he found, deposited on the leaves and grass by the melted snow, a brass letter M. It was literally a stone's throw from the end of the street and it was identified later in the afternoon by the girls in Ann as belonging to Lowell's purse.

The search was intensified but no other letters came to light. Ford was jumping nevertheless. 'We're hot!' he kept exclaiming. 'We're getting close. That purse is around there somewhere!'

That night he had an idea where. Mrs Glover called up after dinner and there was anxiety in her voice. Mr Seward, she said, had telephoned her, very much upset by the disappearance of the ashes, and wanting an explanation. All she could think of to say was that some man in a refuse truck had come around and she had given them to him. It was an unconvincing lie but Seward had, strangely enough, accepted it without question and hung up abruptly.

Ford called headquarters immediately. 'Mac,' he said, 'get two more men out to Seward's fast! Keep the watch doubled and I want all men armed. There's something that belongs to Lowell in those ashes. Seward's cornered. He knows we've got them and I think he's going to make a run for it. Have the watches report every hour and, whatever you do, don't let him out of your sight.'

Ford hung up, but he couldn't stay away from the phone. He called in for reports at ten, eleven, and twelve. All they could tell him, though, was that Seward was in his house and the lights were blazing. At one o'clock only the light in his bedroom was on. At two it was still the only light in the house and at three, which was when Ford went to bed, it had not been turned out.

Harlan Seward did not run for it. He was still in town

the next morning. Stevenson called up at nine-fifteen to report. Seward had gone to his first class. All was not well with him, however. He looked as though he had not slept and he was exceptionally pale and more jittery than ever before. His condition was so apparent now that the faculty was talking about it, afraid he was overworking himself into a breakdown.

Since Seward had not fled, Ford gave up hope of the ashes producing anything and went out to the house with his men again to continue the hunt. He and Cameron handled the inside once more. They headed straight for the attic and started going through trunk after trunk and box after box.

They never finished. It wasn't ten minutes before Lassiter stopped them. He was screaming outside. They rushed down the stairs and out the front door and other men came running from all directions. Lassiter was standing by the open sewer with a rake in one hand. In the other was the purse.

They took it down to headquarters, slimy and dripping, and set it on newspapers on the main desk, where Ford clucked over it like a hen with a prize chick. 'See these holes? That's where the initials were. This M, it fits right here. Oh-brother-oh-brother-oh-brother.'

'Dumped it there that night,' said Cameron. 'Probably thought it would wash out to sea.'

The Chief was leaning close. 'It's been in the water five weeks,' he said, 'but there's just a chance we might pick up one of Seward's fingerprints on the compact or lipstick or mirror inside. It's a cinch he went through it for identifying items and I'll lay you ten to one he wasn't thinking about wearing gloves at the time. This should hang him as it is, but the fingerprints would be nice frosting.'

'We can check right now,' said Lassiter.

'The hell we will. That can wait. This thing is going to sit right here. Stinking and wet it's going to be the first thing Seward lays eyes on when we bring him in. If he doesn't crack wide open I haven't been in this business thirty-three years.' He rocked back and forth on his heels, his eyes never leaving the limp bag. 'Harlan P. Seward, the man the women can't stay away from,' he said. 'I've been wanting to meet him for a long, long time. For a while there I thought I never would but it looks like the day has come.' He turned to Cameron. 'Let's see Seward's schedule again!'

Cameron produced a folded slip from his notebook and Ford opened it, saying, 'It's an experience I don't want to miss.'

The electric clock on the wall by the steel door to the cell block said twenty minutes of eleven. Ford looked at it and at the paper. 'Burt,' he said, 'in ten minutes Mr Seward will be through with his class. I don't want any fuss or fireworks, but when he walks out of that classroom you'll be waiting.' The grin on his face grew into an expression of fierce satisfaction. He nodded at the detective.

'Go get him.'

THE PAN CLASSIC CRIME SERIES

Francis Iles

BEFORE THE FACT

With an introduction by **Colin Dexter**

Pan Classic Crime £5.99

Swept away by an admirer's inexhaustible charm, Lina McLaidlaw finds herself settled in a life she could never have imagined. Head of a fine household in a remote and exclusive part of Dorset – and guardian of both the morals and the finances of the man she has chosen to marry.

Feckless and irresponsible Johnnie Aysgarth may be. But despite a shaky start, she has finally got him under control. After all, Lina waited until she was thirty before accepting a marriage proposal. A further eight years after that before grudgingly accepting that her husband was – perhaps still could be – a murderer.

Eight years is a long time. And Johnnie still adores her. Doesn't he . . .?

With *Before the Fact*, and its equally sinister predecessor *Malice Aforethought*, Francis Iles brilliantly extended the horizons of crime fiction during the 1930s. The tense revelation of the villain's character also inspired Alfred Hitchcock to immortalize Lina and Johnnie in the movie *Suspicion*, starring Joan Fontaine and Cary Grant.

'One of the key texts in the history of crime fiction.'
H.R.F. Keating

THE PAN CLASSIC CRIME SERIES

Eric Ambler

EPITAPH FOR A SPY

With an introduction by **Robert Harris**

Pan Classic Crime £5.99

Josef Vadassy, a Hungarian language teacher, decides to break his journey from Nice to Paris at the windswept coastal town of St Gatien. And there his solitary nightmare begins . . .

Vadassy, a keen photographer, has made his first stop the village chemist, where he leaves a film to be developed. But instead of the expected picture of lizards, the film shows the locations of top secret military installations. The pictures cannot be released.

And, after a none too gentle arrest by two plainclothes policemen, neither can the man who calls himself Josef Vadassy . . .

In *Epitaph for a Spy*, published just a year before the outbreak of World War II, writer Eric Ambler echoed the confusions and changing views of a generation on the brink of world conflict. It remains a truly modern spy thriller.

'The foremost thriller writer of our time.'

Time Magazine

'Ambler is incapable of writing a dull paragraph.'

Sunday Times

THE PAN CLASSIC CRIME SERIES

Cyril Hare

TRAGEDY AT LAW

With an introduction by **Frances Fyfield**

Pan Classic Crime £5.99

In a well-conducted world – even in wartime – Judges of the High Court do not receive death threats in the course of their ordered circuit routine.

In the same world, to take the wheel of a motor car while inebriated, thereby injuring innocent pedestrians, would simply be the last thought to enter a judiciary's mind.

That both mishaps should befall the Honourable Sir William Hereward Barber on the very same day is proof – if proof is ever needed – that the world he inhabits is very disordered indeed.

After that first tiny fall from grace, Judge Barber is now a tragedy waiting to happen . . .

Cyril Hare's gently humorous legal mysteries kept the Golden Age tradition alive long after the war. *Tragedy at Law* is his finest and best-loved crime novel.

'On some rare occasions an author rises from the ruck with an original idea and towers above his fellows. Mr Cyril Hare now finds himself in this glorious situation.'
New Statesman

THE PAN CLASSIC CRIME SERIES

Eric Ambler

THE MASK OF DIMITRIOS

With an introduction by **Robert Harris**

Pan Books £5.99

'Ambler may well be the best writer of suspense stories . . . he is the master craftsman.'

Life

Much later, when he looked back, crime novelist Charles Latimer could see that it was in Istanbul where the true obsession began. It was there, from Colonel Haki, that he first heard the name Dimitrios Makropoulous.

There too that he first glimpsed a dead body, freshly retrieved from the Bosphorus. Stabbed, abandoned, left floating like scum. And with it, somehow, all the pictures of a tortured European past come reeling like a nightmare before his eyes – assassinations, insurgences, the extraordinary double-dealings of spies.

Unlike the police, Latimer couldn't abandon Dimitrios. But finding out who he really was might easily cost him his life . . .

'Not Le Carré, not Deighton, not Ludlum have surpassed the intelligence, authenticity or engrossing storytelling that established *The Mask of Dimitrios* as the best of its kind.'

The Times